Face-to-Face with the Dark Lord

LAY DOWN THE SWORD, MORTAL CREATURE!

Desperately, Shea fought against the urge to obey. Everything became hazy and he struggled to breathe. Far back in his mind, a familiar voice seemed to be calling his name. He tried to answer, screaming inside himself for help. Then the voice of the Warlock Lord ripped at him again.

LAY DOWN THE SWORD!

The blade dipped slightly. Shea felt his mind begin to grow numb, and the darkness moved closer to him. The Sword was of no use to him. Why not discard it and be done? He was nothing to this awesome being. He was only a frail, insignificant mortal. . . .

By Terry Brooks

THE MAGIC KINGDOM OF LANDOVER
Magic Kingdom for Sale—Sold!
The Black Unicorn
Wizard at Large
The Tangle Box
Witches' Brew

SHANNARA
First King of Shannara
The Sword of Shannara
The Elfstones of Shannara
The Wishsong of Shannara

THE HERITAGE OF SHANNARA
The Scions of Shannara
The Druid of Shannara
The Elf Queen of Shannara
The Talismans of Shannara

THE VOYAGE OF THE JERLE SHANNARA
Ilse Witch
Antrax
Morgawr

THE WORD AND THE VOID
Running With the Demon
Knight of the Word
Angel Fire East

Star Wars:® Episode I *The Phantom Menace*™
Hook
Sometimes the Magic Works

THE
SWORD OF SHANNARA

Part 3

THE SECRET OF THE SWORD

TERRY BROOKS

BALLANTINE BOOKS
NEW YORK

A Del Rey® Book
Published by The Random House Publishing Group

www.delreydigital.com

ISBN 0-345-46144-4

Manufactured in the United States of America

First Ballantine Digest Edition: July 2003

OPM 10 9 8 7 6 5 4 3 2 1

"Ｊ UNK, nothing but junk!" roared Panamon Creel in frustration, kicking once more the pile of worthless metal blades and jewelry that lay on the ground before him. "How could I have been such a fool? I should have seen it right away!"

Shea walked silently to the north end of the clearing, his eyes staring at the faint trail in the forest earth that the crafty Orl Fane had left in his flight northward. He had been so close. He had held the precious Sword in his own hands—only to lose it through an unforgivable failure to recognize the truth. The massive form of Keltset loomed silently beside him, the great bulk bending close to the damp, leaf-strewn ground, the inscrutable face almost next to his own as the strangely gentle eyes studied and searched. Shea turned quietly back to the raging Panamon.

"It wasn't your fault—you had no reason to suspect the truth," he muttered dejectedly. "I should have listened to his raving with a little more wisdom and a little less . . . whatever. I knew the signs to look for and I forgot to keep my eyes open when it counted."

Panamon nodded and shrugged, stroking the carefully trimmed mustache with the point of his piked hand. With a last kick at the discarded implements, he called once to

Keltset, and without further discussion the two began quickly to break camp, strapping together the gear and weapons that had been deposited for the night. Shea watched them for a moment, still unable to accept his failure to gain possession of the Sword. Panamon called gruffly to him to lend a hand, and he silently obeyed. He could not face the inevitable aftermath of this most recent setback. Panamon Creel had obviously been pushed as far as he would stand it, chaperoning a foolish and amazingly stupid little Valeman around in the dangerous borderlands of Paranor, searching for some people who might very well turn out to be enemies and for a Sword that only Shea knew anything about, but couldn't recognize when he had it in his own hands. The scarlet highwayman and his giant companion had nearly lost their lives once already over this mysterious Sword and undoubtedly once was more than enough. The Valeman had no choice now except to try to locate his friends. But when he did find them, he would have to confront Allanon and tell him how he had failed—failed them all. He shuddered at the prospect of facing the grim Druid, of feeling those remorseless eyes peer into his most carefully hidden thoughts for the whole truth. It was not going to be pleasant.

He recalled suddenly the strange prophecy related to them in the Valley of Shale on that dark, misted dawn over a week ago. It was the Shade of Bremen who had forewarned of the danger in the forbidding Dragon's Teeth—how one would not see Paranor, how one would not reach the other side of the mountain, yet would be first to lay hands on the Sword of Shannara. It had all been foretold, but Shea had forgotten it in the stress and excitement of the past few days.

The weary Valeman closed his eyes against the world for

a few moments and wondered how on earth he could possibly be a part of this incredible puzzle that centered around a war of power with the spirit world and a legendary Sword. He felt so small and helpless that it seemed that the easiest path for him to choose now was to bury himself and pray for a quick end to life. So much depended on him, if Allanon were to be believed, and from the beginning he had been completely inadequate to the task. He had been unable to do anything for himself, depending on the strength of other men to get him this far. How much had they all sacrificed for him so that he might lay hands on the magic Sword. Yet when he had it in his grasp . . .

"I've decided. We're going after him."

Panamon Creel's deep voice cut through the quiet of the little clearing like the sharp crack of an iron blade through dry wood. Shea stared at the broad, unsmiling face in astonishment.

"You mean . . . into the Northland?"

The scarlet thief shot him one of those angry looks that dismissed the Valeman as an idiot incapable of understanding sane men.

"He made a fool out of me. I'd rather cut my own throat than let the little rat get away from me now. When I get my hands on him this time, I'll leave him for the worms to chew on."

The handsome face was emotionless, but there was undisguisable hatred in the menacing tone of voice that cut through to the bone. This was the other side of Panamon—the cold professional who had ruthlessly destroyed an entire encampment of Gnomes and later stood in battle against the incomparable power of the Skull Bearer. He wasn't doing this for Shea or even to gain possession of the Sword of

Shannara. This was strictly a matter of his injured pride and desire for revenge on the unfortunate creature who had dared to bruise it. Shea glanced quickly at the motionless Keltset, but the giant Rock Troll gave no indication of either approval or disapproval; the barklike face was blank, the deep-set eyes expressionless. Panamon laughed sharply, taking a few quick strides toward the hesitant Valeman.

"Think on this, Shea. Our Gnome friend has made matters so much more simple by revealing the exact location of the Sword you have been searching so long to find. Now you don't have to search for it—we know where it is."

Shea nodded in silent agreement, still wary of the adventurer's true motives. "Do we have a chance of catching up with him?"

"That's more like it—that's the spirit we need." Panamon grinned at him, his face a mask of confidence. "Of course we can catch up with him—it's merely a matter of time. The difficulty will be if someone else catches up with him first. Keltset knows the Northland as well as anyone alive. The Gnome will not be able to hide from us. He will have to run, run, and keep running, because he has no one to turn to, not even his own people. It's impossible to know exactly how he stumbled onto the Sword, or even how he surmised its value, but I do know I was not mistaken about his being a deserter and a scavenger."

"He could have been a member of the band of Gnomes transporting the Sword to the Warlock Lord—or perhaps even a prisoner?" Shea suggested thoughtfully.

"More probably the latter," the other agreed, hesitating as if trying to recall something, staring northward into the gray mistiness of the forest morning. The sun had already cleared the horizon of the eastern edge of the world, its fresh light bright and warm, seeping slowly into the darkened corners of the forestland. But the mist of early morning had not yet cleared, leaving the three companions shrouded in a hazy mixture of sunlight and dying night. The sky to the north appeared unaccountably dark and forbidding even for early morning, causing the normally verbose Panamon to stare wordlessly at this curious blackness for several long minutes. Finally he turned back to them, his face clouded with doubt.

"Something strange is going on to the north. Keltset, let's move out now—find that Gnome before he has a chance to stumble onto a patrol of hunters. I don't want to share his final moments in this world with anyone!"

The giant Rock Troll moved into the lead in quick, easy strides, his head lowered slightly as he searched the ground before him, picking out the signs left by the fleeing Orl Fane. Panamon and Shea followed close behind in silent concentration. The trail of their quarry was readily apparent to the keen eyes of Keltset. He turned back to them and made a short signal with one hand, which Panamon translated for the curious Shea to mean that the Gnome was running hard and fast, not bothering to hide his footsteps, and had evidently decided on his eventual destination.

Shea began to speculate in his own mind where the wily little fellow would run. With the Sword in his possession, he might be able to redeem himself in the eyes of his own people by turning it over to them for presentation to the War-lock Lord. But Orl Fane had appeared highly irrational in his behavior while he was their prisoner, and Shea felt certain that the Gnome had not been faking. He had rambled on as if the victim of a madness he could only partially control, speaking in garbled sentences that had in a jumbled fashion revealed the truth concerning the whereabouts of the Sword.

If Shea had thought the matter through a little more carefully, he would have seen it—he would have known that Orl Fane had the coveted talisman with him. No, the Gnome had crossed the mental barrier between sanity and madness, and his actions would not be entirely predictable. He would run from them, but to whom would he run?

"I remember now." Panamon broke into his thoughts as they continued to make their way back toward the Plains of Streleheim. "That winged creature insisted that we had possession of the Sword when it confronted us yesterday. It kept telling us that it could sense the presence of the Sword—and so it could, because Orl Fane was concealed in the brush with the weapon hidden in his sack."

Shea nodded quietly, recalling the incident bitterly. The Skull Bearer had unwittingly tipped them off that the precious Sword was in the area, but they had failed to notice this important clue in the heat and fury of their battle to survive. Panamon continued to ramble on in barely concealed fury, threatening to dispose of Orl Fane when they caught up with him in a number of extremely unpleasant ways. Then abruptly the fringes of the forest broke away, opening into the vast expanse of the Plains of Streleheim.

In astonishment, the three halted together, their disbelieving eyes fixed on the awesome spectacle that loomed directly to the north—a huge, unbroken wall of blackness, towering skyward until it vanished into the infinity of space, stretching along the horizon to encircle the entire Northland. It was as if the Skull King had bound the ancient land in the shroud of darkness that lay upon the spirit world. It was more than the blackness of a clouded night. It was a heavy mistiness that rolled and swirled in deepening shades of gray as it ran northward toward the heart of the Skull

Kingdom. It was the most terrifying sight that Shea had ever witnessed. His initial fear was heightened twice over by a sudden, unexplainable certainty in his mind that this huge wall was crawling slowly southward, blanketing the entire world. It meant that the Warlock Lord was coming. . . .

"What in heaven's name is that . . . ?" Panamon trailed off into stunned silence.

Shea shook his head absently. There could be no answer to that question. This was something beyond the understanding of mortal man. The three stood looking at the massive wall for several long moments, as if waiting for something more to happen. Finally, Keltset stooped to peer carefully at the hard grassland before them, moving forward several yards at a time until he was some distance away. Then he rose and pointed directly into the center of the ominous black haze. Panamon started, his face frozen.

"The Gnome is running directly into that stuff," he muttered angrily. "If we do not catch him before he reaches it, the darkness will hide his trail completely. We will have lost him."

Several miles ahead, on the graying fringes of the blackened wall of mist and haze, the small, bent form of Orl Fane hesitated momentarily in its exhausting flight as the greenish eyes peered fearfully, uncomprehendingly into the swirling darkness. The Gnome had been moving northward since his escape from the three strangers during the early hours of the morning, running while his strength held out, then pushing forward in a shuffling trot, always with one eye straying back, waiting for the inevitable pursuit. His mind no longer functioned in a rational manner; for several weeks he had lived on instinct and luck, preying off the dead, avoiding the living. He could not force himself to think of anything beyond survival, a gut instinct to live another day among those who did not want him, would not accept him as one of their own. Even his own people had turned him away, scorning him as a creature lower than the insects that crawled the earth at their feet. It was a savage land that surrounded him—a land in which one could not survive alone for very long. Yet he was alone, and the mind that had once been sane had slowly turned inward on itself, shutting away the fears that were imbedded there until madness began to take hold and all reason began to die.

Yet the inevitable death did not come easily, as fate intervened with twisted humor and favored the outcast with a final glimmer of false hope, placing in his hands the means by which to regain the seemingly unattainable warmth of human companionship once more. While still a scavenger, still fighting a losing battle to stay alive, the desperate Gnome had learned of the presence of the legendary Sword of Shannara, its awesome secret gasped in faint warning from the rigid lips of one dying on the Streleheim Plains, the blinded eyes failing as the life thread snapped. Then the Sword was in his grasp—the key to power over mortal men in the hands of Orl Fane.

But the madness lingered, the fears and doubts wrenching ceaselessly at his failing reason as he pondered a course of action. This fatal hesitation resulted in the Gnome's capture and the loss of the coveted Sword—the lifeline back to his own kind. Reason gave way to despair and raving, and the already badly unbalanced mind collapsed. There was room now for only one burning, haunting thought—the Sword must be his or his life was over. He boasted irrationally to his unsuspecting captors that the Sword was his, that only he knew where it could be found, unwittingly betraying his last chance to keep possession. But the strangers failed to read between the lines, dismissing him too hastily as merely crazed. Then came the escape, the seizure of the Sword, and the flight northward.

He paused now, staring blankly at the mysterious wall of blackness that barred his way northward. Yes, northward, northward, he mused, smiling crookedly, the eyes widening madly. There lay safety and redemption for an outcast. Deep within, he could feel an almost uncanny desire to run back the way he had come. But the thought remained locked inescapably in his mind that his salvation lay in the Northland alone. It was there that he would find . . . the Master. The Warlock Lord. His gaze dropped momentarily to the ancient blade strapped tightly to his waist, its length dragging clumsily in the dirt behind him. The gnarled yellow hands strayed briefly down over the carved handle, touching the engraved hand raised high with burning torch, the gilt paint already flecking off in chips to reveal the burnished hilt beneath. He clutched the handle tightly, as if trying to draw his own strength from its sturdy grip. Fools! Fools all, that had not treated him with the respect he should command. For he was the bearer of the Sword, the keeper of the greatest legend their world had ever known, and it would be he who would . . . He shut out the thought hastily, fearful that even the void about him could read his mind, peer into his secret thoughts, and steal them away.

Ahead, the frightening darkness waited for him to enter. Orl Fane was afraid of this, as he was of everything else, but there was no other way to go. Dimly he recalled those who followed—the giant Troll, the man with one hand, whose hatred he instinctively sensed, and the youth who was half man, half Elf. There was something the Gnome could not explain about the latter, something that nagged with unshakable persistence at his already beleaguered mind.

Shaking his rounded head blankly, the little man moved forward into the graying fringes of the dark wall, the air about him dead and silent. He did not look back until the blackness was all about him and the silence had disappeared in a sudden rush of wind and chilling moisture. When he did glance back briefly, he saw to his horror that there was nothing there—nothing but the same blackness that lay all about in heavy, impenetrable layers. The wind began to rush violently as he moved on, and he became aware of other creatures in the darkness. They came first as a vague awareness in his mind, then as soft cries that seemed to seep through the haze and cling inquisitively about him. At last they appeared as living bodies, touching softly with cringing fingers the flesh of his person. He laughed in maddened frenzy, knowing somehow that he was no longer in a world of living creatures, but a world of death where soulless beings wandered in hopeless search of escape from their eternal prison. He stumbled on amidst them, laughing, talking, even singing gaily, his mind no longer a part of his mortal being. All about him, the creatures of the dark world followed in cringing companionship, knowing that the maddened mortal was almost one of them. It was all a matter of time. When the mortal life was gone, he would be as they were—lost forever. Orl Fane would be with his own kind at last.

Almost two hours passed, winding away with the slow, deliberate sweep of the morning sun, and the three pursuers stood on the fringes of the wall of mist into which their quarry had disappeared. They paused as he had done, silently studying the forbidding blackness that marked the threshold to the kingdom of the Warlock Lord. The haze seemed to lie upon the deadened earth in layers, each one a little darker as the eyes peered deeper into the unseen center, each one a little less friendly as the mind envisioned the heart's undetermined fears. Panamon Creel paced back and forth in measured steps, his eyes never leaving the darkness as he attempted to muster enough confidence to push on. The massive Keltset, after a cursory study of the ground and a short motion to indicate that the Gnome had indeed gone northward, lapsed into statuelike immobility, the great arms folded and the eyes faint slits of life beneath the heavy brow.

There was no choice, Shea reasoned, his mind already determined, his hopes not yet dampened by the thought of temporarily losing the trail in the darkness. He had regained something of the old faith in providence, certain since they had begun this pursuit that Orl Fane would be found and the Sword regained. There was something pulling at him, reassuring him, confiding in him that he would not fail—something deep within his heart that gave him fresh courage. He waited impatiently for Panamon to give the word to proceed.

"There is a madness in what we're doing," the scarlet thief muttered as he passed by Shea once more. "I can feel death in the very air of this wall . . ."

He trailed off sharply, halting at last, waiting for Shea to speak.

"We must go on," Shea responded quickly, tonelessly.

Panamon looked slowly at his giant friend, but the Rock Troll made no movement. The other waited a moment longer, clearly disturbed that Keltset had ventured no opinion since they had undertaken this journey into the Northland. Before, when it was just the two of them, the giant had always indicated agreement when Panamon had looked to him for support, but of late the Troll was strangely noncommittal.

At last the adventurer nodded affirmatively, and the three plunged resolutely into the graying haze. The plains were level and barren, and for a while they moved forward without difficulty. Then, as the mists gradually deepened about them, their vision began to fail badly until they appeared to one another as little more than vague shadows. Panamon quickly called a momentary halt, extracted a length of rope from his pack, and suggested they tie themselves together to avoid becoming separated. When this was accomplished, they continued on. There was no sound save the occasional faint scrape of their boots on the hardened earth. The mist was not damp, but nevertheless seemed to cling to their exposed skin in a most unpleasant manner, recalling to Shea the unhealthy, fetid air of the Mist Marsh. It appeared to be moving faster the deeper they proceeded, yet they could feel no wind propelling its widening gusts. Finally it closed in from all directions and the three were left in total darkness.

They walked for what must have been hours, but their sense of time became confused in the soundless black haze that encased their fragile mortal beings. The rope held them back from the loneliness of death which permeated the mist, its strands reaching not so much to one another as to the world of sunlight and vision they had left behind them. This place into which they had dared to venture was a limbo world of half-life, where the senses were stifled and fears grew in an unfettered imagination. One could feel the presence of death fragmenting the darkness, a touch here, a touch there, brushing softly the mortal creature it would one day claim. The unreal became almost acceptable in this strange darkness as all the restrictions of the human senses vanished into dreamlike remembrances, and the visions of the inner mind, the subconscious, pushed quickly to the fore, searching for recognition.

For a time it was almost pleasant to be able to lapse into this indulgence of the subconscious, and then it was neither enjoyable nor disagreeable, but simply deadening. For a long time this latter feeling persisted, soothing, caressing their minds into disinterest and vague boredom, leaving both bodies and minds with the sluggish drowsiness of the ancient lotus-eaters. Time disappeared entirely and the world of mist stretched on forever.

From out of the dim recesses of the world of life came the slow sensation of burning pain, coursing through Shea's deadened body with shocking abruptness. With a sudden wrenching, his mind was torn free of the listlessness which cloaked its thoughts and the searing sensation grew sharper in his breast. Still drowsy, his body strangely weightless, he groped tiredly at his tunic, his hand coming to rest at last on the source of the irritation—a small leather pouch. Then his mind snapped into alertness as he clutched tightly the precious Elfstones, and he was awake once more.

In sudden horror, he realized that he was stretched full length upon the earth, no longer walking, no longer even aware of where he had been going. Frantically he clutched the rope about his waist and pulled violently. He was rewarded by a sluggish groan from the other end; his companions were still with him. Struggling heavily, wearily to his feet once more, he realized what had happened. This frightening limbo world of eternal sleep had almost claimed them as its victims, lulling them, soothing them, dulling their senses until they had fallen and drifted closer and closer to quiet death. Only the power of the stones had saved them.

Shea felt incredibly weak but, summoning the little strength that remained, he tugged and pulled desperately on the length of rope, dragging Keltset and Panamon Creel back from the edge of the abyss of death, back to the world of the living. He shouted wildly as he yanked on the rope, then stumbled to them, kicking at the listless bodies until the pain brought them back to consciousness. Long minutes later they were roused sufficiently to be aware of what had happened; with the awakening, the spirit of life revived the will to survive, as both forced themselves to their feet. They hung on to one another with sleep-ridden limbs closely entangled, their minds fighting to remain conscious. Then they began to walk, stumbling blindly in the unbroken darkness, one foot before the other, each step an incredible struggle of mind and body. Shea was in the lead, uncertain of his direction, but relying on the instinct sparked by the powerful Elfstones to guide him.

For a long time they pushed ahead through the endless dark, fighting to remain awake and alert as the deadening mists swirled lazily about them. The strange, sleeplike sensation of death clung to them, trying to overpower their tired minds, silently urging their exhausted bodies to accept the welcome rest that waited. But the mortals resisted with iron determination, their strength a small fragment of courage and desperation that, when all else was gone, still would not quit.

At last the deep weariness began to draw back into the dark haze. Death had failed this time to stifle the will to survive. There would be other times for these three, but for the moment they would live on a little longer in the world of men. So the sluggishness passed away and the drowsiness faded—not in the normal manner of sleep, but with quiet warnings that it would come again. The three companions were suddenly the same as before, the muscles unfettered as if there had been no sleep, the mind released rather than awakened. There was no inner desire to stretch or to yawn, but only a lingering memory that the sleep of death was a slumber without sensation, without time.

For long minutes no one spoke, though all were fully revived, each still savoring in unspoken fear and quiet desperation the taste of dying they had experienced, knowing that one day its inevitable touch would claim them forever. For several brief seconds they had stood at the edge of life and gazed into the forbidden land beyond—something no mortal was permitted to do before the end of his natural life. To have been this close was numbing, frightening, even maddening. They should not have survived.

But then the memories were gone, all but the dim knowledge that the three had narrowly escaped dying. Regaining their composure, they continued to search for an end to the confining blackness. Panamon spoke once to Shea in low tones, asking whether he knew if they were proceeding in the right direction. The reluctant response was a curt nod. What difference did it make if he did not know, the little Valeman wondered to himself angrily. What other direction would they take? If his instincts were wrong, then there was nothing left that could help them anyway. The Elfstones had saved him once; he would trust them again.

He wondered how Orl Fane had fared in his attempt to pass through the strange wall of mist. Perhaps the maddened Gnome had found his own way to escape its deadening effects, but it seemed unlikely. And if the little fellow had fallen by the way, then the Sword was lost somewhere in the impenetrable blackness and they would never regain it in time. This unpleasant prospect caused the Valeman to pause mentally for several long moments, weighing the possibilities of the Sword lying about in this haze, perhaps only yards away from them, waiting for someone to discover it once again.

Then abruptly the darkness faded into dingy gray and the wall of mist was behind them. It happened so quickly that they were caught completely by surprise. One minute they were shrouded in blackness, barely able to distinguish one another, and the next they were standing in shocked silence beneath the leaden gray skies of the Northland.

They took a moment to study the country into which they had emerged. It was the most dismal land Shea had ever seen—even more forbidding than the dreary lowlands of Clete and the frightening Black Oaks in the distant Southland. The terrain was barren and desolate, a gray-brown earth totally devoid of sunlight and plant life. Not even the hardiest scrub brush had survived—a mute warning that this was indeed the kingdom of the Dark Lord. The earth stretched away to the north in low, uneven hills of hardened dirt, unbroken by even a wisp of grassland. Blunted, sprawling boulders thrust upright into the dim, gray horizon, and in places the lowlands were gutted by dusty gullies where rivers had long since dried away. There was no sound of life anywhere—not even the faint hum of insects to break the haunting stillness. Nothing remained in this once living land but death. Far to the north, jutting sharply into the vacant sky, rose a low series of treacherous-looking peaks. Without being told, Shea knew that this was the home of Brona, the Warlock Lord.

"What do you propose now?" Panamon Creel demanded. "We've lost the trail entirely. We don't even know if our Gnome friend got out of that stuff alive. In fact, I don't see how he could have managed it."

"We'll have to keep looking for him," Shea replied evenly.

"While those flying creatures keep looking for us," the other pointed out quickly. "The odds are becoming a little more than I bargained for, Shea. I don't mind telling you that I'm rapidly losing interest in this chase—especially when I don't know what it is I'm fighting. We almost died back there, and I couldn't even see what was killing us!"

Shea nodded understandingly, suddenly in command of the situation. For the first time in his life, Panamon Creel was worried about staying alive, even if it meant backing away with a severely wounded pride. It was up to Shea to make sure that the journey would continue now. Keltset stood apart from the two men, the soft brown eyes fixed on the Valeman as the heavy brows knitted in understanding. Again Shea was struck with the intelligence he saw, deep-rooted and unimposing in the gentle eyes of the massive creature. He still knew nothing about the giant Troll, but there was a great deal he wanted to learn. Keltset was the key to some strange, important secret that not even Panamon Creel knew, for all his boasting of their close friendship.

"The choices are limited," the little Valeman replied at last. "We can search for Orl Fane on this side of the mist and take our chances with the Skull creatures, or we can risk another journey back . . ."

He trailed off ominously, leaving the thought unspoken as he watched Panamon turn a shade paler.

"I'm not going back through that—at least not right away," the unnerved thief declared vehemently. He shook his head emphatically, the piked hand raising quickly to ward off the very air that carried such an insane suggestion. Then, almost sheepishly, the familiar broad smile returned as the old Panamon Creel reassumed command of his wits. He was too hardened an individual, too much a professional in the game of life, to allow anything to frighten him for very long. Grimly, he fought down the memories of what he had felt while stumbling blindly through the dead world within the darkness, calling on his long experience as an adventurer and border thief to rebuild his confidence. If he was destined to die in this venture, then he would meet it with the courage and determination that had carried him through so many hard years.

"Now let's think this situation through a minute," he mused, pacing away from them and back again. The old swagger and grit were returning. "If the Gnome did not make it out of the mist barrier, then the Sword will still be in there—we can get it anytime. But if he escaped, as we did, then where . . . ?"

He paused in midsentence, his eyes studying the surrounding countryside as he tried to narrow the possibilities. Keltset stepped quickly to his side and pointed directly north to the jagged peaks that marked the borders of the Skull Kingdom.

"Yes, of course, you're right again," Panamon agreed with a faint smile. "He must have been heading there all along. It's the only place he could go."

"The Warlock Lord?" Shea asked quietly. "Is he taking the Sword directly to the Warlock Lord?"

The other nodded briefly. Shea paled slightly at the prospect of tracking the elusive Gnome right up to the doorstep of the Spirit King without even the comparatively strong mystical prowess of Allanon to aid them. If they were discovered, they would be entirely defenseless except for the Elfstones. While the stones might have prevailed over the Skull Bearers, it seemed highly doubtful that they would have any chance against a creature as awesome as Brona.

The first question was whether or not Orl Fane had even managed to get through the treacherous mist. They decided to follow the fringes of the rolling wall westward in an effort to cut across any tracks the fleeing Gnome might have left once he broke through into this region. If they discovered no trail in that direction, they would try going eastward for the same distance. If there was still no trace of Orl Fane, then they must assume that he had fallen in the killing haze, and they would be forced to reenter it in an effort to find the Sword. No one favored the latter alternative, but Shea gave them some reassurance by promising to chance using the power of the Elfstones to locate the missing talisman. Using the precious stones would undoubtedly alert the spirit world of their presence, but it was a gamble they would have to take if they expected to find anything in that impenetrable blackness.

Quickly now, the three began to hike northward, Keltset's keen eyes studying the barren ground for traces of the Gnome's footsteps. Heavy cloud banks blocked out the entire sky, enfolding the Northland in an unfriendly gray haze. Shea tried to estimate how much time had lapsed since they had entered the wall of mist, but he was unsure. It could have been a few hours or even a few days. In any event, the grayness of the land was deepening steadily, signaling the approach of nightfall and a temporary end to their search for Orl Fane.

Overhead the massing gray clouds had begun to grow

darker and were rolling heavily across the hidden skies. The wind had picked up, gusting sharply through the barren hills and gullies, pushing angrily at the few clumps of boulders which barred its progress. The temperature was dropping quickly, turning so much colder that the three were forced to wrap themselves tightly in their hunting cloaks as they pushed ahead. Before long it became apparent that a storm was building, and they realized angrily that a heavy rain would wash away all traces of any footprints left by the fleeing Gnome. And if they were forced to guess whether or not he had escaped . . .

But in a rare stroke of good fortune, Keltset discovered footprints on the barren earth—footprints that came out of the wall of mist and continued northward. The Rock Troll showed Panamon Creel that the prints indicated a small person, probably a Gnome, and that whoever it was had been weaving and staggering badly, either from injury or exhaustion. Elated by this discovery and certain that they had found Orl Fane once again, they followed the faint trail northward, moving at a much faster pace than before. Forgotten was the ordeal of that morning. Forgotten was the threat of the omnipresent Warlock Lord, whose kingdom lay directly in their path. Forgotten was the exhaustion and despair they had felt since losing the precious Sword of Shannara. Orl Fane would not escape them again.

Overhead the skies continued to darken. Far to the west came the deep sound of thunder, an ominous rumble that was carried by the increasing force of the wind across the length and breadth of the Northland. It was going to be a terrific storm, almost as if nature had decided to breathe new life into this dying land by washing it clean so that it might again be fertile ground for living things. The air was bitingly cold, and although the temperature had ceased falling, the gusting wind knifed through the garments of the three travelers. Yet they scarcely felt it, their eyes scanning anxiously the northern horizon for any sign of their quarry. The trail was growing fresher; he was somewhere just ahead.

The face of the land had begun to change noticeably. The barren countryside had retained its basic feature, an ironhard ground studded with scattered rock and boulder clumps, but it had grown steadily more hilly and rutted, making travel increasingly difficult. The cracked, dry earth was particularly difficult to maneuver because it lacked the forms of vegetation that normally offered decent footing. As the hills and vales rose higher and dipped more sharply, the three pursuers found themselves slipping and clawing their way forward.

The rising west wind had grown in force to an earsplitting howl, at times nearly sweeping the unprotected men off their feet as it rushed across the desolate hilltops in frantic bursts. The loose topsoil flew in all directions at once in the merciless grip of the wind, striking at the skin, eyes, and mouths of the three men in stinging, choking thrusts. It soon became so bad that the entire countryside was swathed in wind and dirt, as if it were a sandstorm in a desert. It became difficult to breathe, much less to see, and eventually even the keen eyes of Keltset could no longer discern the faintest trace of the trail they were following. Quite probably there was nothing left to find, so completely had the wind cut into the unprotected earth, but the three pushed on.

The rumble of distant thunder had risen to a steady crashing, interspersed by jagged flickers of lightning directly to the west and almost on top of them. The sky above had turned black, though with the blinding effect of the wind and the dust, they scarcely noticed this added hindrance to their vision. Bit by bit, a heavy haze moved closer from the western horizon—a haze that was clearly formed by sheet upon sheet of driving rain blown by the shrieking wind. Finally it became so bad that Panamon yelled wildly above the rush of the wind for a halt.

"It's no use! We've got to find shelter before that storm hits us!"

"We can't give up now!" Shea cried angrily, his words almost entirely drowned out by a sudden crash of thunder.

"Don't be a fool!" The tall thief struggled to his side, dropping to one knee as he peered through the blowing dust, his hands shielding his eyes from the stinging, blinding particles. To the right, he spotted a large hill dotted with clusters of overhanging boulders that appeared to offer some shelter against the force of the wind. Signaling the other two, he abandoned all attempts to proceed north and turned toward the rocks. Heavy drops of rain were beginning to fall, striking with chilling effect against the warm skin of the sweating men; the crashing of thunder had risen to deafening proportions. Shea continued to peer northward into the darkness, unwilling to accept Panamon's decision to give up the chase when he knew they were so very close.

They had almost reached the shelter of the rocks when he saw something moving. A dazzling flash of lightning outlined a small form near the crest of a tall hill far, far ahead, struggling madly to gain the summit in the face of the driving wind. Yelling frantically, the little Valeman grabbed Panamon's arm and pointed toward the distant hill, now almost totally invisible in the darkness. For a second the three remained frozen in place, searching the blackness as the storm descended on them in blinding sheets of rain, completely drenching them in seconds. Then the lightning flashed with shattering brightness a second time to reveal again the distant hill with its tiny challenger, still clawing wildly for footing near the crest. Then the vision was gone and the rain fell again.

"It's him! It's him!" yelled Shea in frenzied recognition. "I'm going after him!"

Without waiting for the other two, the excited Valeman plunged down the side of the wet embankment, determined that the Sword should not escape him again.

"Shea. No, Shea!" Panamon called after him in vain. "Keltset, get him!"

Lunging quickly down the hill, the giant Troll overtook the little Valeman in several leaps, picking him up effortlessly with one huge arm and carrying him back toward the waiting Panamon. Shea was yelling and kicking furiously, but he had no chance of breaking the Troll's iron grip. The storm had reached its peak already, the rain cutting away the unprotected landscape in huge chunks of earth and rock that washed down into the gullies to form small, wild rivers. Panamon led them into the rocks, ignoring Shea's repeated threats and pleas as he searched for shelter on the east slope of the hill, away from the force of the wind and rain. After a quick study, he chose a point high on the crest which was protected on three sides by large clusters of boulders that would offer good protection from the force of the storm if not from its wetness and chill. Scrambling wearily, fighting with the little strength left them against the incredible thrust of the wind, the three at last reached the meager shelter, where they collapsed in exhaustion. Panamon quickly signaled Keltset to release the struggling Shea. Angrily the

Valeman confronted the tall adventurer, the rain running into his eyes and mouth in steady rivulets.

"Are you mad?" he exploded against the shriek of the wind and the deep, constant rumble of the storm. "I could have caught him! I could have had him. . . ."

"Shea, listen to me!" Panamon cut in quickly as he peered through the heavy grayness to meet the other's angry gaze. There was a sudden moment of stilled voices in the roar of the Northland storm as Shea hesitated. "He was too far ahead to be caught in this kind of a storm. We would have all been blown away or injured in mud slides. It's too treacherous in these hills to travel ten feet in a heavy rainstorm— much less several miles. Relax a bit and cool your temper. We can pick up the remains of the Gnome when this gale blows over."

For a second Shea felt compelled to argue the point, but again he paused and the anger quickly subsided as his good sense returned, and he realized that Panamon was right.

The full force of the storm was tearing away at the unprotected land, stripping away its barren face and reshaping its stark features. Slowly the hills were washing down into the water-logged gullies and the ancient Streleheim Plains began to widen gradually into the vast Northland. Huddled against the cold of the massive boulders, Shea stared out into the sheets of rain as they came and passed in endless torrents, masking out the desolation of this lifeless, dying land. It seemed as if there were no one else alive but the three of them. Perhaps if the storm continued long enough, they would all be washed away and life could begin anew, he thought disconsolately.

Although the rain did not fall directly on them within

the small refuge, they could not escape the chilling dampness of their waterlogged clothing, and so their discomfort persisted. At first they sat in expectant silence, as if waiting for the storm to abate and the pursuit of Orl Fane to begin again, but gradually they grew weary of the lonely vigil and settled back to other pastimes, convinced the rain and the wind would claim the entire day. They ate a little food, more from common sense than hunger, and then tried to sleep as best they could in the close quarters. Panamon had managed to salvage two blankets from his pack which had been sealed in watertight wrappings, and these he passed to Shea. The grateful Valeman refused, offering them to his friends, but the giant Keltset, who seemed seldom very distraught by anything, was already asleep. So Panamon and Shea wrapped themselves in the warmth of the blankets, huddled next to each other on one side of the enclosure, and stared quietly into the falling rain.

After a time they began to talk of things past, of quiet times and distant places which they felt compelled to share in this hour of vague despondency and loneliness. As usual, Panamon carried the conversation, but the stories of his travels were not the same as before. The element of improbability and wildness had been lifted, and for the first time, Shea knew the colorful thief was talking about the real Panamon Creel. It was idle, almost carefree talk that passed between the two men—a bit like the conversation of two old friends reunited after many years.

Panamon told of his youth and the hard times the people all around him had known and lived with while he grew into manhood. There were no excuses, no regrets offered, but only the simple narrative of years long past that lingered on in memories. The little Valeman told about his boyhood with his brother Flick, recalling their wild, exciting expeditions into the Duln forests. He spoke in smiles about the unpredictable Menion Leah, who in vague ways suggested Panamon Creel as a young man. Time drifted away as they talked, shutting out the storm and drawing the two strangely close to each other for the first time since they had met. As the hours passed and darkness came, Shea grew to understand the other man, to know him as he could not have known him otherwise. Perhaps the thief understood Shea a little better as well. The Valeman wanted to believe so.

At last, when night shrouded the entire land and even the pounding rain had disappeared from view, so that nothing remained but the sound of the wind and the splash of puddles and rivers, the conversation drew itself around to the sleeping Keltset. In quiet tones, the two men speculated about the giant Rock Troll's origin, trying to understand what had brought him to them, what had made him undertake this suicidal journey into the Northland. It was his home, they knew, and perhaps he planned to return to the distant Charnal Mountains. Yet had he not been driven from there—if not by his own people, then by something equally powerful and compelling? The Skull Bearer had known him on sight—but how? Even Panamon admitted that Keltset was more than a mere thief and adventurer. There was tremendous pride and courage in his bearing, a deep intelligence in his silent determination, and somewhere in his past, a terrible secret he had chosen to share with no one. Something unspeakable had happened to him, and both men could sense that it had something to do with the Warlock Lord, if only in an indirect way. There had been fear in the

Skull Bearer's eyes when he had recognized the massive Troll. The two men talked awhile longer until sleep came in the early-morning hours; then wrapped in the blankets for protection from the chill of the night and the rain, they drifted into slumber.

TWO

YOU THERE! Hold it a minute!"

The sharp command came out of the darkness behind Flick, cutting knifelike to the bone of his already waning courage. In slow shock, the terrified Valeman turned, lacking sufficient presence of mind even to attempt to run. He had been discovered at last. It was useless to draw the short hunting knife still grasped firmly beneath the hunting cloak, but his unresponding fingers remained locked in place as his eyes sought out the dim form of the approaching enemy. His comprehension of the Gnome language was poor, but the tone of voice alone was enough to enable him to understand that brief command. Rigidly, he watched a bulky, cursing form emerge from out of the darkness of the tents.

"Don't just stand there," the voice shrilled angrily as the roundish form waddled closer. "Lend a hand where it's needed!"

Astonished, the Valeman peered closely at the squat figure as his discoverer moved toward him, the thick arms laden with trays and platters and on the verge of dropping everything with each hesitant step of the stubby legs. Almost without thinking, Flick sprang to the fellow's assistance, removing the upper layer of trays and cradling them in his own arms, his nose catching the savory smell of freshly cooked meat and vegetables seeping from beneath the covers to the warm platters.

"There now, that's a whole sight better." The stocky Gnome breathed a sigh of relief. "I might have spilled the whole mess if I'd had to go another step on my own. A whole army encamped here, and can I get anyone to help carry the chieftains' own dinners? Not one Gnome so much as offers. I have to do it all. It's maddening—but you're a good fellow to lend a hand. I'll see you're properly repaid with a good meal. Hah?"

Flick didn't know what the verbose fellow was saying for the most part, and it didn't really matter. What did matter was that he had not been discovered after all. Breathing his silent gratitude, Flick adjusted his armload of food while his new companion continued to ramble on merrily about nothing, the heavy trays balanced precariously in the stubby arms. From beneath the concealing darkness of the hunting cloak's wide hood, the wary Valeman nodded in pretended understanding of the other's conversation, his eyes still fastened intently on the shadows moving within the great tent before them.

The thought remained indelibly fixed in his mind—he had to get inside that tent; he had to know what was going on in there. But then, almost as if he had read Flick's mind, the little Gnome began to move toward the canvas housing with measured steps, the trays before him, the little yellow face half turned so that his unending monologue might be better heard by his newfound companion. There was no question about it now. They were delivering dinner to the people in that tent, to the chieftains of the two nations comprising this giant army and to the dreaded Skull Bearer.

This is madness, Flick thought suddenly; *I'll be spotted the instant they lay eyes on me.* But he needed that one quick look inside . . .

Then they were at the entrance, standing quietly before the two giant Troll guards who towered over them like trees over stalks of grass. Flick could not bring himself to look anywhere but downward, though he was conscious of the fact that, had he drawn himself up to full height to face the enemy, he would have found himself staring directly into an armored, barklike chest.

Even though he was totally dwarfed in size, Flick's self-appointed friend barked a sharp command for admittance, apparently convinced that his presence was earnestly desired by those within—or at least the food he bore was. Quickly, one of the sentries stepped into the brightly lit interior of the canopy to speak briefly to someone, then reappeared a moment later, silently beckoning the two men to enter. With a quick nod over his shoulder to the trembling Flick, the little Gnome pushed past the guards into the tent and the Vale-man, scarcely daring to breathe, followed dutifully, praying for yet another miracle.

The interior of the large canvas structure was comparatively well lighted by slow-burning torches set on iron standards about a large, heavy wooden table that stood unoccupied at the center of the enclosure. There were Trolls of varying size moving busily within the great tent, some carrying rolled charts and maps from the table to a large, brass-bound chest while the others prepared to sit down to a long-awaited evening meal. All wore the military trappings and insignia of Maturens—Troll commanders.

The rear section of the canvas enclosure was screened off by a heavy tapestry which even the bright torchlight could not penetrate. The air in the army headquarters was smoky and fetid, so heavy in fact that Flick found it almost difficult to breathe. Weapons and armor lay piled neatly about the room, and battered shields hung on iron standards like crude attempts at decoration. Flick could still sense the undeniable presence of the terrifying Skull Bearer, and he quickly concluded that the dark monster was behind the bleak tapestry in the other section of the tent. Such a creature did not eat—its mortal self had long since passed into dust, and the spirit that remained needed only the fire of the Warlock Lord to nourish its hunger.

Then abruptly the Valeman saw something else. At the rear of the front portion of the enclosure, close to the tapestry and half hidden by the torch smoke and moving Trolls, was a dim form seated in a tall wooden chair. Flick started involuntarily, certain for an instant that the man was the missing Shea. The eager Trolls were moving up to him now, removing the platters of food and placing them on the heavy table, and for a moment they blocked the Valeman's view of the figure. The Trolls conversed quietly among themselves as they stood over the two servers, their strange tongue completely unintelligible to Flick, who was attempting to shrink farther down into the shadowed folds of his hunting cloak in the revealing torchlight. He should have been discovered, but the unsuspecting Troll commanders were tired and hungry and much too concerned with the invasion plans to notice the unusual features of the rather large Gnome who had waited on them.

The last of the trays was removed and set upon the table as the Maturens gathered wearily about it to begin the meal. The little Gnome who had brought Flick into the quarters turned to leave, but the eager Valeman paused a moment longer to study quickly the form at the rear.

It was not Shea. The prisoner was Elven, a man of about thirty-five, with strong, intelligent features. More it was impossible to tell at this distance. But Flick felt certain it was Eventine, the young Elven King who Allanon had declared could mean the difference between victory or defeat for the Southland. It was the Westland, the great, secluded kingdom of the Elven people, that housed the mightiest army of the free world. If the Sword of Shannara were lost, then this man alone commanded the power to stop the awesome might of the Warlock Lord—this man, a prisoner, whose life could be snuffed out at a single command.

Flick felt a hand on his shoulder, and he started violently at the sudden touch.

"C'mon now, c'mon, we must leave," the hushed voice of the little Gnome cajoled him earnestly. "You can stare at him some other time. He'll still be here."

Flick hesitated again, a sudden, daring plan forming as he stood there. If he had taken time to dwell on it, the idea would have terrified him, but there was no time and he had long since passed the point of rational deliberation. It was already too late to escape the encampment and return to Allanon before daylight, and he had come to this dreadful place to do an important task—one which remained uncompleted. He would not leave yet.

"C'mon, I said, we have to . . . Hey, what're you doing . . . ?" The little Gnome yelled involuntarily as Flick grasped him harshly by one arm and propelled him forward toward the Troll commanders, who had paused momentarily in their eating at the sharp cry and were staring curiously at the two small figures. Quickly Flick raised one hand and pointed questioningly at the bound prisoner. The Trolls followed his gaze mechanically. Flick waited breathlessly as one of them gave a curt command and the others shrugged and nodded.

"You're mad, you're out of your head!" the little Gnome gasped in amazement, trying vainly to hold his voice down to a whisper. "What do you care whether or not the Elf gets something to eat? What does it matter if he shrivels up and dies . . . ?"

His comments were cut short. A Troll called over to them, one gnarled hand extending a plate of food. Flick hesitated momentarily, glancing quickly at his astonished companion, who was shaking his head and grumbling inaudibly at the whole proposition.

"Don't look at me!" he exclaimed shortly. "This was your idea. You feed him!"

Flick failed to pick up everything the Gnome said, but he got the gist of the exclamation, and moved quickly to take possession of the plate. At no time did he glance into anyone's face for more than an instant, and even then the shadows of the wide cowl masked his identity. He kept his cloak wrapped tightly about him as he moved cautiously toward the prisoner on the other side of the tent, inwardly cheering madly that his gamble had paid off. If he could get close enough to the bound figure of Eventine, he could let him know that Allanon was close and that some sort of attempt to rescue him would be made. Still wary, he glanced back once at the other occupants of the enclosure, but the Troll commanders had returned to their dinner and only the little Gnome chef was still staring after him. If he had tried this kind of foolish stunt anywhere but in the very teeth of the enemy forces, Flick was well aware that he would have been discovered immediately. But here, in the commanders' own headquarters, with the awesome Skull Bearer just yards away and the entire area surrounded by thousands of Northlanders, the idea of anyone even sneaking into camp, let alone into this guarded tent, was preposterous.

Quietly, Flick approached the waiting captive, his face still concealed within the dark recesses of the hood, the plate of food extended before him. Eventine was of normal height and stature for a man, although for an Elf he was big. He wore woodland garb covered by the remnants of a chain mail vest, the worn insignia of the house of Elessedil still faintly visible in the dim torchlight. His strong face was battered and cut, apparently from the battle that had ended with his capture. At first glance there appeared to be nothing distinctive about him; he was not the kind of man who would be singled out in a group. His expression was set and impassive as Flick came to a halt directly in front of him, his thoughts apparently concentrated elsewhere. Then his head moved slightly as if aware he was being studied, and the deep green eyes fastened on the small figure facing him.

When Flick saw those eyes, he froze in sudden shock. They reflected a fierce determination, a fiery strength of character and inner conviction that reminded the Valeman, rather strangely, of Allanon. They reached into him, seized his own mind in a manner of speaking, demanding his attention, his obedience. He had seen this look in no other man, not even Balinor, whom they had all felt drawn to as a natural leader. Like those of the dark Druid, the eyes of the Elven King frightened him. Looking down quickly at the plate of food in his hands, Flick paused to consider what he should do next. Mechanically, he fitted a piece of the still-warm meat to the tip of the fork. His corner of the large tent was dimly lit, and the haze of smoke aided in concealing his movements from the enemy. Only the little Gnome was watching him closely, he was certain, but a single mistake would bring them all down on him.

Slowly he raised his face until the light from the torches had fully revealed his features to the watchful captive. As their eyes met, a flicker of curiosity crossed the otherwise impassive Elven face and one eyebrow lifted sharply. Quickly Flick pursed his lips, warning silence, and looked down again at the food. Eventine was unable to feed himself, so the Valeman began to hand-feed him slowly and carefully as he planned his next step. Now the captive Elven King knew he was not a Gnome, but Flick was terrified that if he spoke to the Elf, even in a faint whisper, he would be overheard. He abruptly recalled that the Skull Bearer was just on the other side of the heavy tapestry, perhaps only inches away, and if he should possess unusual hearing powers . . . But there was no other alternative; he had to communicate somehow with the prisoner before he left. There might not be another chance. Mustering the little courage he had reserved, the Valeman leaned forward a few inches farther as he lifted the fork, carefully putting himself between Eventine and the Trolls.

"Allanon."

The word was spoken in a barely audible whisper. Eventine took the proffered bite of food and responded with a faint nod, his face stony and impassive. Flick had had enough. It was time to get out of there before his luck ran out. Taking the plate of half-finished food, he slowly turned and walked back across the enclosure to the waiting Gnome chef, whose face mirrored mingled disgust and edginess. The Troll commanders were still eating as he passed them, their conversation low and earnest. They didn't even look up. Flick handed the plate to the little Gnome as he passed him, mumbling something incoherent, then quickly hastened from the tent, exiting between the two giant Troll guards before his astonished companion could think to act. As he strolled unconcernedly away from the tent, the Gnome appeared suddenly in the open entrance, yelling and grumbling in garbled phrases that the Valeman could not begin to comprehend. Turning, the Valeman waved quickly to the little figure, a faint smile of satisfaction on his broad face, and disappeared into the darkness.

At dawn, the Northland army began its march southward toward Callahorn. Flick had been unable to work his way clear of the encampment before then; so, as a bitter and gravely concerned Allanon watched from the seclusion of the Dragon's Teeth, the subject of his misgivings was forced to continue his disguise another day. The heavy morning rains had almost persuaded the Valeman to make a dash for safety, so convinced was he that the downpour would wash out the coloring Allanon had applied to his skin to give it a yellow hue. But escape in daylight was impossible, so he wrapped himself tightly in the hunting cloak and tried to remain inconspicuous. Before long, he was thoroughly drenched. To his happy astonishment, the yellow coloring on his skin did not appear to be washing out after all. There was a certain amount of fading, but in the excitement of moving the camp, no one had time to take notice of anyone else. It was the terrible weather, in fact, that saved Flick from being unmasked. Had it been a warm, dry summer day filled with sunshine and good spirits, the army would have been more concerned with exchanging pleasantries. If the sun had been shining, there would have been no need for the heavy hunting cloaks, and Flick would have attracted the attention of everyone around him by continuing to wear his. Once it had been removed, the Northlanders would have seen through his thin disguise immediately. The bright sunlight would have revealed to anyone casting so much as a passing glance in his direction that the Valeman did not even remotely resemble a Gnome in his facial bone structure and individual features. The heavy rains and wind saved Flick from all of this and permitted him to remain isolated and concealed as the huge invasion force trudged steadily across the grasslands into the Southland kingdom of Callahorn.

The bad weather persisted throughout the remainder of that day and, as it turned out, for several days thereafter. The storm clouds sullenly locked in place between the sun and the earth in great gray and black masses that churned and rolled with ferocious discontent. The rains fell unchecked, sometimes in pounding sheets driven by the unrelenting force of the west winds, sometimes in a steady melancholy drizzle that gave false hope to the belief that the storm's end was near. The air was chill and at times almost bitter, leaving an already water-drenched army shivering and disconsolate.

Flick remained on the move throughout the day's tiring, unpleasant march, soaked through by the blowing rains, but relieved that he could move about without calling attention to himself. He made it a point to avoid walking with any particular group for very long, always staying apart, always avoiding a situation which might force him to engage in conversation with anyone. The Northland invasion force was so vast that it was an easy matter to avoid ever being with the same men twice, and his deception was further facilitated by the fact that there appeared to be no overt attempts to exercise marching discipline over the great army. Either discipline was extremely lax or so thoroughly ingrained in

the individual soldier that superior officers were not needed
to maintain order. Flick could not conceive of the latter and
concluded that fear of the omnipresent Skull Bearers and
their mysterious Master kept the individual Troll or Gnome
from doing anything foolish. In any event, the little Valeman
remained just another member of the Northland army, bid-
ing his time until nightfall, when he planned to make his escape back to Allanon.

By midafternoon, the army had reached the swollen
banks of the upper Mermidon, directly across from the island city of Kern. Again the invasion force encamped. Its
commanders realized immediately that, due to the heavy
rain, the Mermidon could not be crossed without tremendous hazard; even so, it would require large rafts capable of
transporting vast numbers of men in order to secure the far
bank. They had no rafts, so those would have to be built.
That would require several days, and by that time the storms
should have diminished and the waters of the Mermidon retreated sufficiently to permit an easy crossing. Across the
river in the city of Kern, the Northland force had been
sighted while Menion Leah still slept in the house of Shirl
Ravenlock, and the people were beginning to panic as they
realized the extent of their danger. The enemy invasion force
could not afford to bypass Kern and proceed to Tyrsis, the
main objective. Kern would have to be taken; considering the
size of the city and the extent of the reduced army defending
it, this would not be difficult. Only the rising river and the
fortuitous storm delayed its fall.

Flick knew nothing of these matters, his own mind preoccupied with thoughts of escape. The storm could abate in
a matter of hours, leaving him defenseless in the very heart
of the enemy camp. Worse still, the actual invasion of

the Southland was under way, and a battle with the Border Legion of Callahorn could come at any time. Suppose he was forced into battle as a Gnome hunter against his own friends?

Flick had changed considerably since his first meeting with Allanon weeks earlier in Shady Vale, developing an inner strength and maturity and a confidence in himself he had never believed himself capable of sustaining. But the past twenty-four hours had proved a supreme test of raw courage and perseverance that even a seasoned border fighter like Hendel would have found frightening. The little Valeman, unseasoned and vulnerable, could sense that he was on the verge of cracking under the extreme pressures, of giving way completely to the terrible sense of fear and doubt gripping him with every move he made.

Shea had been the reason behind his decision to make the hazardous journey to Paranor in the beginning, but more than that, he had been the one steadying influence on a pessimistic, distrustful Flick. Now Shea had been lost to them all for many days with little indication as to whether he was dead or alive, and his faithful brother, while refusing to give up hope that they would eventually find him, had never felt more alone. Not only was he in a strange land, embroiled in a mad venture against a mysterious creature not even of the mortal world, but now he was isolated in the midst of thousands of Northlanders who would kill him without a second thought the moment they discovered who he really was. The entire situation was impossible, and he was beginning to doubt that there was any real point to anything he had done.

While the vast army encamped on the banks of the Mermidon in the shadows of the late afternoon and the gray of twilight, a disconsolate, frightened Valeman moved uneasily through the camp, trying desperately to maintain a firm grip on his fading resolve. The rain continued to fall steadily, masking faces and bodies until they were merely moving shadows, drenching men and earth alike in a cold, cheerless haze. Fires were out of the question in such weather, so the evening remained dark and impenetrable and the men remained faceless. As he moved silently about the encampment, Flick mentally noted the arrangement of the commanders' quarters, the deployment of the Gnome and Troll forces, and the setting of the sentry lines, thinking that this knowledge might be of some value to Allanon in planning a rescue of the Elven King.

He relocated without difficulty the large tent that housed the Troll Maturens and their valuable prisoner, but, like the rest of the enemy camp, it was dark and cold, shrouded in mist and rain. There was no way even to be sure that Eventine was still there; he could have been moved to another tent or removed from the camp entirely during the march southward. The two giant Troll sentries remained posted at the entrance, but there was no sign of movement within. Flick studied the silent structure for several long minutes and then slipped quietly away.

As night descended, and Troll and Gnome alike retired to a chill, water-drenched slumber that more closely resembled an uneasy doze, the Valeman decided to make his escape. He had no idea where he might find Allanon; he could only presume the giant Druid had followed the invasion force as it moved southward to Callahorn. In the rain and darkness, it would be nearly impossible to locate him, and the best he could hope to do would be to hide out somewhere until daylight and then attempt to find him. He moved silently toward the eastern fringes of the encampment, treading carefully over the huddled forms of the half-sleeping men, winding his way through the baggage and armor, still wrapped protectively in the water-soaked hunting cloak.

He could very likely have walked through the camp without any disguise on this night. In addition to the darkness and the persistent drizzle, which had finally begun to taper off, a low rolling mist had moved across the grasslands, blanketing everything so completely that a man could see no more than a few feet in front of his nose. Without wanting to, Flick found himself thinking about Shea. Finding his brother had been the major reason behind his decision to slip into this camp disguised as a Gnome. He had learned nothing of Shea, though he had scarcely expected to. He had been fully prepared to be discovered and captured within minutes after he entered the vast encampment. Yet he was still free. If he could escape now and find Allanon, then they could find a way to help the imprisoned Elven King and . . .

Flick paused, his progress abruptly halted as he sank down into a crouch beside a canvas-covered pile of heavy baggage. Even if he did eventually find his way back to the Druid, what could they hope to do for Eventine? It would take time to reach Balinor in the walled city of Tyrsis, and they had little time remaining. What would become of Shea while they were trying to find a way to rescue Eventine— who was unquestionably more valuable to the Southland, since the loss of the Sword of Shannara, than Flick's brother? Suppose that Eventine knew something about Shea? Suppose he knew where Shea was—perhaps even where the powerful Sword had been carried?

Flick's tired mind began to rush quickly over the possibilities. He had to find Shea; nothing else was really important to him at this point. There was no one left to help him since Menion had gone ahead to warn the cities of Callahorn. Even Allanon seemed to have exhausted his vast resources without result. But Eventine might know Shea's whereabouts, and Flick alone was in a position to do something about that possibility.

Shivering in the chill night air, he brushed the rain from his eyes and peered in numbed disbelief into the mist. How could he even consider going back? He was virtually on the edge of panic and exhaustion now without taking any further risks. Yet the night was perfect—dark, misty, impenetrable. Such an opportunity might not come again in the short time left, and there was no one to take advantage of it but himself. Madness—madness! he thought desperately. If he went back there, if he tried to free Eventine alone . . . he would be killed.

Yet he decided suddenly that that was exactly what he was going to do. Shea was the only one he really cared about and the imprisoned Elven King appeared to be the only man who might have any idea what had happened to his missing brother. He had come this far alone, spending twenty-four torturous hours trying to stay hidden, trying to stay alive in a camp of enemies that had somehow overlooked him. He had even managed to get inside the Troll commanders' tent, to get close enough to the great King of the Elven people to pass him that brief message. Perhaps it had all been the result of blind chance, miraculous and fleeting, yet, could he flee now, with so little accomplished? He smiled faintly at his own dim sense of the heroic, an irresistible challenge he had always successfully ignored before, but which now ensnared him and would undoubtedly prove his undoing. Cold, exhausted, close to mental and physical collapse, he would nevertheless take this final gamble simply because circumstances had placed him here at this time and this place. He alone. How Menion Leah would smile to see this, he thought grimly, wishing at the same time that the wild highlander were here to lend a little of his reckless courage. But Menion was not here, and time was slipping quickly away. . . .

Then, almost before he realized it, he had retraced his steps through the sleeping men and the rolling fog, and was crouching breathlessly within yards of the long Maturen tent. The mist and his own sweat ran in small rivulets down his heated face and into his soaked garments as he stared in motionless silence at his objective. Doubts crowded remorselessly into his tired mind. The terrible creature that served the Warlock Lord had been there earlier, a black, soulless instrument of death that would destroy Flick without thinking. It was probably still within, waiting in sleepless watch for exactly this sort of foolish attempt to free Eventine. Worse still, the Elven King might have been removed, taken anywhere . . .

Flick forced the doubts aside and breathed deeply. Slowly he mustered his courage as he finished his study of the canvas enclosure, which was no more than a misty shadow in the unbroken darkness before him. He could not even make out the forms of the giant Troll guards. One hand reached into the damp tunic beneath his cloak and withdrew the short hunting knife, his only weapon. Mentally he pinpointed the position on the canvas of the silent tent where he imagined Eventine had been bound at the time he had fed him that previous night. Then slowly he crept forward.

Flick crouched next to the wet canvas of the great tent, the chill imprint of the weave rough against his cheek as he listened for the sounds of human life that stirred uneasily within. He must have paused for fifteen long minutes, motionless in the fog and the dark as he listened intently to the muffled sound of heavy breathing and intermittent snores emitted by the sleeping Northlanders. Briefly he contemplated attempting to sneak through the front entrance of the structure, but quickly discarded that idea as he realized that once he was inside, he would have to navigate his way in the darkness over a number of sleeping Trolls in order to reach Eventine. Instead he selected the section of the tent where he imagined the heavy tapestry formed a divider—the corner in which the Elven King had been bound to the chair. Then, with agonizing slowness, he inserted the tip of his hunting knife into the rain-soaked canvas and began to cut downward, one strand at a time, just a fraction of an inch with each pressured stroke.

He would never remember how long it took him to make the three-foot incision—only the endless sawing in the silence of the night, afraid that the slightest sound of tearing would arouse the entire tent. As the long minutes passed, he began to feel as if he were entirely alone in the giant encampment, deserted by all human life in the black shroud of the mist and the rain. No one came near him, or at least he did not see anyone pass, and the sound of human voices did not reach his straining ears. He might indeed have been alone in the world for those brief, desperate minutes. . . .

Then a long, vertical slit in the glistening canvas stared back at him in slack anticipation, inviting him to enter. Cautiously he advanced, feeling his way carefully with his hands just inside the opening. There was nothing except the canvas floor, dry, but as cold as the damp earth that braced his knees and feet. Carefully he inserted his head, peering fearfully into the deep blackness of the interior that was filled with the sounds of sleeping men. He waited for his eyes to adjust to this new darkness, trying desperately to hold his breathing to a steady, noiseless whisper, feeling horribly exposed from the rear, the bulk of his body outside the tent and vulnerable to anyone who happened to pass.

It was taking his eyes much too long to adjust and he could not risk being discovered by a chance passerby at this stage, so he risked moving a few feet farther, slipping his stocky frame through the opening and into the dark shelter of the tent. The labored breathing and the snores continued undisturbed, and there was the occasional sound of a heavy body shifting position somewhere in the darkness beyond him. But no one awoke. Flick remained crouched just inside the long slit for more endless minutes, his eyes working madly to distinguish the faint shapes of men, tables, and baggage against the blackness of the night.

It seemed to take forever, but at last he was able to discern the huddled forms of sleeping men scattered about the floor of the tent, their bodies rolled tightly in the warmth of their blankets. To his astonishment, he realized that one motionless form lay slumbering only inches in front of his balanced body. Had he attempted to crawl any farther before his eyes had adjusted to this darkness, he would have stumbled onto and undoubtedly awakened the sleeper. The old sensation of fear returned sharply, and for a moment he fought back against a rising sense of panic that commanded him to turn and run. He could feel the sweat sliding down his crouched body beneath the water-soaked clothing, tracing thin, searching paths over the heated skin as his labored breathing became more ragged. At that moment, he was aware of his every feeling, his mind pushed right to the brink of collapse—yet later, he would recall nothing of these feelings. Mercifully, they would be blocked from his memory, and all that would remain would be one sharp picture etched indelibly in his brain of the sleeping Troll Maturens and the object of his search—Eventine. Flick spotted him quickly, the lean form no longer seated upright in the wooden chair at the corner of the heavy tapestry, but lying on the canvas floor only a few feet from the poised Valeman, the dark eyes open and watching. Flick had judged his point of entry correctly, and now he moved catlike to the King's side, the hunting knife severing quickly the taut ropes that bound hands and feet.

In an instant the Elf was free, and the two shadowy figures were moving quickly to reach the vertical opening in the side of the tent. Eventine paused momentarily to pick something up from the side of one of the sleeping Trolls. Flick did not wait to see what the Elf had seized, but hastened through the slit into the misty darkness beyond. Once outside, he crouched silently next to the tent, glancing anxiously about for any sign of movement. But there was only the persistent drizzle of the rain breaking the night's deep silence. Seconds later, the canvas parted again, and the Elven King passed through and hunched down beside his rescuer. He was carrying an all-weather poncho and a broadsword. As he wrapped himself in the cloak, he paused momentarily and smiled grimly at a frightened, but elated Flick, then gripped his hand in warm, unspoken gratitude. The Valeman grinned back in satisfaction and nodded.

So Eventine Elessedil was rescued, snatched from the very teeth of the sleeping enemy. It was Flick Ohmsford's finest moment. He felt now that the worst was over, that once clear of the great Maturen tent with Eventine a free man, escape from the camp could never be denied them. He had not even thought to look beyond his entry into the Troll commanders' quarters. Now the moment to look ahead was there, but as the two paused in the shadows, the moment passed and was lost.

From out of nowhere strolled three fully armed Troll sentries, who instantly spotted the two figures crouching at the side of the Maturen tent. For an instant everyone froze; then slowly Eventine rose, standing directly in front of the tear in the canvas. To Flick's astonishment, the quick-thinking Elven King waved the three over to them, speaking fluently in their own language. Hesitantly, the sentries approached, their long pikes lowered carelessly as they heard the familiar sound of their own tongue. Eventine stepped aside to reveal the gaping slit, nodding warningly to Flick as the unsuspecting Trolls now rushed forward. The terrified Valeman stepped away, his hand gripping the short hunting knife beneath his cloak. As the Trolls reached them, their eyes still momentarily fastened on the torn canvas, the Elven King struck out with the broadsword.

Two of the Trolls were silenced before they had a chance to defend themselves, their throats cut away. The final sentry got off a quick cry for help and slashed wildly at Eventine, cutting into the exposed flesh of the Elf's shoulder; then he, too, fell lifeless into the muddied earth. For a moment there was silence once more. Flick stood white-faced against the tent wall, staring in fright at the dead Trolls as the wounded Elven King tried vainly to stem the blood flow from his slashed shoulder. Then they heard the sharp sound of voices from close by.

"Which way?" Eventine whispered harshly, the bloodied sword still tightly clenched in his good hand.

In mute silence the little Valeman rushed to the Elf's side and pointed into the darkness behind him. The voices grew louder now, coming from more than one direction, and swiftly, wordlessly, the two fugitives fled from the Troll sleeping quarters. Stumbling between the fog-shrouded tents and baggage, unable to find their footing on the water-soaked grasslands and blinded by the darkness and the rolling mist, the two struggled to outdistance their pursuers. The voices faded to either side of them and then fell behind, only to rise sharply in alarm within seconds as the bodies of the sentries were discovered. The two dashed on as the deep, haunting sound of a Troll battle horn shattered the night sleep of the Northland army, and everywhere men awoke to the call to arms and battle.

Flick was in the lead, frantically trying to remember the quickest way back to the camp perimeter. He was running blindly now, terrified beyond reason, his one thought to gain the safety of the silent darkness beyond this hateful camp. Struggling painfully to keep up with the Valeman, his shoulder bleeding freely from the pike wound, Eventine realized what had happened to his young rescuer and called vainly after him, trying to warn him to be careful.

Too late. The words had just left his mouth when they ran headlong into a band of still-groggy Northlanders who had been abruptly awakened by the battle horn's blast. Everyone went down in a tangle of arms and legs, both parties completely caught by surprise and unable to avoid the collision. Flick felt the hunting cloak ripped from his body as he was kicked and buffeted by unseen hands and feet, and in maddened terror he fought back, slashing wildly with the hunting knife at anything that came within reach. Howls of pain and fury went up from his attackers, and for an instant the arms and legs drew back and he was free again. He leaped to his feet, only to be borne back a moment later by a renewed assault. He caught the dull flash of a sweeping sword blade as it whisked past his unprotected head and his own knife came up to ward off the blow. For several minutes, everything became chaotic as the Valeman rolled and thrashed his way through the clinging hands and heavy bodies, the fogbound night a maze of wild cries and scuffling figures. He was cut and battered unmercifully as he sought to fight his way clear, sometimes forced back to the earth, but always rebounding within seconds and struggling onward, calling sharply for Eventine.

What he did not realize was that he had stumbled into a band of unarmed Northlanders who were caught completely by surprise when he charged madly into them, wielding the hunting knife. For several minutes they sought to pin him down and disarm him, but the terrified Valeman struggled so violently they were unable to contain him. Eventine rushed quickly to his aid, battling his way through the mass of attackers to reach the youth and at last they gave way entirely, scattering for the safety of the darkness. Quickly downing the last persistent Northlander, a rather large Gnome who had fastened himself bodily to the struggling Flick, the Elven King grabbed his rescuer by the tunic collar and hauled him to his feet. The Valeman continued to struggle violently for a moment more; then realizing who held him, he abruptly relaxed, his heart beating wildly. All around him the sounds of the Northland battle horns blasted in deafening tones through the camp, mingling with the rising cries of the aroused army. Vainly he tried to listen to what the other was saying, his battered head still ringing from the blows struck.

". . . find the quickest way out. Don't run—walk steadily,

but unhurriedly. Running will just call attention to us. Now go!"

Eventine's words died into the darkness as his strong hand gripped Flick's shoulder and turned him about. Their eyes locked momentarily, but the Valeman could only meet the Elven King's piercing stare for an instant, feeling it burn right through to his frightened heart. Then they were moving toward the perimeter of the awakened encampment, side by side, their weapons held ready. Flick was thinking rapidly but clearly now, recalling vague landmarks within the Northland camp that indicated he was proceeding in the right direction. The fear was momentarily buried as a cold sense of determination gripped him, fostered in part by the strong presence striding quietly at his side. It might have been Allanon himself, so unshakable was the confidence that the Elven King radiated.

Dozens of the enemy rushed past them, some coming within several feet, but no one stopped them or spoke to them. Unmolested, the two men passed quietly through the chaos that had engulfed the Northlanders at the unexpected call to battle, moving steadily toward the sentry lines surrounding the encampment. The cries continued from within, although they were dropping behind the fugitives little by little. The rains had momentarily ceased altogether, but the heavy mist continued unbroken, shrouding the entire grasslands from the Streleheim to the Mermidon. Flick glanced once at his silent companion, noticing with concern that the lean figure was bent slightly in pain, the left arm hanging limp and bleeding freely. The valiant Elf was tiring rapidly, growing steadily weaker from loss of blood, his face pale and drawn from the effort to stay on his feet.

Unconsciously, Flick slowed the pace, walking closer to his companion in case he should stumble.

They reached the camp perimeter within a very short time—so quickly, in fact, that the word of what had taken place at the Maturen headquarters had not yet reached the sentries. But the battle horn had put them on the alert, and they stood close to the encampment in small groups, their weapons ready. Ironically, they believed that the danger lay from an enemy outside the camp. Their eyes were fastened dutifully away from the camp, permitting Eventine and Flick to approach undetected to the very edge of their lines. The Elven King did not hesitate, moving forward between the outposts at a steady walk, trusting to the darkness, the mist, and the confusion to prevent their discovery.

Time was running out. Within a matter of minutes the entire army would be mobilized and ready for battle, and once it was discovered that he had managed to escape, trackers would be out searching for him. He would find safety if he could reach the borders of Kern, just to the south, or alternatively, if he could reach the concealment of the Dragon's Teeth and surrounding forests to the east. It would take several hours in either case and his strength was fading. He could not pause now, even if it meant risking almost certain discovery by passing into the open unprotected.

Boldly the two strolled directly between two of the sentry parties, looking neither left nor right as they moved into the emptiness of the open grasslands beyond. They succeeded in not calling attention to themselves until they were past the perimeter of the guard lines. Suddenly several of the sentries caught sight of them at the same moment and called out. Eventine turned slightly and waved with his good arm, calling back in the Troll language, all the while maintaining a steady pace as he moved farther into the darkness. Flick followed warily, waiting expectantly as the sentries stared after them, still undecided. Then abruptly one of them called sharply and began to move after them, waving them back in excited motions. Eventine yelled to Flick to run for it, and the chase was on. As the two men raced for safety, close to twenty guards took up the pursuit, brandishing their pikes and yelling wildly.

It was an uneven contest from the beginning. Both Eventine and Flick were of lighter build and under normal circumstances could have outdistanced their pursuers. But the Elf was wounded badly and weakened from loss of blood, while the little Valeman was physically exhausted from the ordeal of the last two days. The pursuers were fresh and strong, well rested and fed. Flick knew that their only hope was to find concealment in the mist and darkness, hoping their enemies would be unable to find them. Breathing harshly, stumbling with labored strides, they pushed their failing bodies to the limits of physical endurance. Everything became a large black blur made up of rolling mist all about them and the slickness of the grasslands beneath their racing feet. They ran until they thought they could run no farther, and still there were no mountains, no forests, no place to hide.

Abruptly, from out of the darkness ahead of them, there flashed an iron-tipped pike, piercing Eventine's cloak and pinning him to the damp earth. The outer perimeter of sentries, Flick thought in horror—he had forgotten about them! A dim form shot out of the mist, hurtling itself on the fallen Elf. With the last of his waning strength, the wounded King twisted sharply to one side to avoid the sword blade that buried itself in the earth next to his head, at the same instant bringing his own weapon around and up. The rushing figure fell forward with a quick gasp, impaled on the blade.

Flick stood rooted in place, staring wildly about for other attackers. But there had only been the lone sentry. Quickly he rushed to his companion's side, wrenching the pike free and pulling the exhausted Elf to his feet with almost super-human effort. Eventine took a few steps before collapsing to the ground once more. Fearfully, the Valeman dropped to his knees beside him, trying to shake the man awake.

"No—no, I'm finished," the hoarse reply came at last. "I can go no farther. . . ."

Behind them, the cries of the Northlanders shot out of the darkness. Their pursuers were drawing closer! Again Flick tried in vain to pull the limp form to its feet, but this time there was no response at all. Helplessly the Valeman stared into the darkness about him, the short hunting knife held ready. This was the end. In final desperation, he called wildly into the darkness and the mist.

"Allanon! Allanon!"

The call died quickly into the night. The rain had begun once more, falling in a slow drizzle onto an already oversat-urated earth to form still larger puddles and mires on the quiet grasslands. Dawn was no more than an hour away, al-though it was impossible to tell time in such weather as this. Flick crouched silently next to the unconscious Elven King and listened to the sounds of the men closing in about him. He could tell by their voices that they were drawing nearer, though they still had not seen him. As if to further mock the futility of the situation, he realized that after risking every-thing to free Eventine, he had still failed to learn what had befallen the missing Shea. Sudden shouts from his left brought him about to face dim figures approaching from out of the fog. They had found him! Grimly, he rose to meet them.

An instant later the hazy darkness between them exploded in a blinding flash of fire that seemed to erupt from out of the earth, the terrific force throwing Flick to the ground, leaving him dazed and blinded. Showers of sparks and burning grass fell all about him and the thunder of a long series of explosions shook the ground violently. One instant the Northlanders were shadowy figures caught in the dazzling light and the next they disappeared altogether. Columns of crackling flame shot upward into the night like giant pillars, thrusting through the darkness and fog to reach the heavens. Squinting into the maelstrom of destruction, Flick thought it was the end of the world. For several endless minutes the wall of fire blazed skyward in unabated fury, tearing the earth into blackened chunks, scorching the night air until the heat began to burn Flick's skin. Then with a final flash of surging energy, it flared up brightly and disappeared into a hush of mingled smoke and steam, blending quickly into the mist and rain until all that remained was the intense heat of the night air, drifting slowly to rest.

Flick rose cautiously to one knee and peered into the emptiness before him, then turned sharply as he sensed rather than heard the approach of someone behind him. From out of the rolling mist and steam emerged a giant black form, cloaked in flowing robes and reaching outward as if it were the angel of death come to claim her own. Flick stared in numbed terror and then started in recognition as the awesome form passed before him. It was the dark wanderer come at last. It was Allanon.

THREE

Dawn had just broken with dazzling brightness against a cloudless, deep blue sky as the last band of refugees from the island city of Kern passed through the gates of the great Outer Wall and entered Tyrsis. Gone was the damp, impenetrable mist and the vast dark ceiling of storm clouds that had blanketed the land of Callahorn for so many days. The grasslands remained soggy and sprinkled with small ponds the saturated earth could not yet manage to absorb, but the persistent rains had moved on to be replaced by a fresh sky and sun that brought a new cheerfulness to the morning. The people of Kern had been arriving in scattered groups for several hours, all weary, horrified by what had happened and frightened of what lay ahead. Their home had been completely destroyed, though some did not yet realize the Northlanders had put everything to the torch following the unexpected attack on their encampment.

The evacuation of the doomed city had been a miraculous success, and, although their homes were gone, they were still alive and, for the moment, secure. The Northlanders had failed to detect the mass escape, their attention completely occupied by the courageous band of Legion soldiers that had assaulted the central camp and drawn them away from even the most distant outposts in the mistaken belief that a full-scale attack was under way. By the time they realized the strike was only a feint designed to confuse them, the island had been evacuated and its people were far down the swift Mermidon and beyond the reach of the maddened enemy.

Menion Leah was one of the last to enter the walled city, his lean frame battered and exhausted. The wounds on his feet had been reopened during the ten-mile march from the Mermidon to Tyrsis, but he had refused to be carried. It was with the last of his strength that he struggled up the wide ramp leading to the gates of the Outer Wall, supported on one side by the faithful Shirl, who had refused to leave his side even to sleep, and gripped firmly on the other by an equally weary Janus Senpre.

The youthful Legion commander had survived the fighting of that terrible night battle, escaping the besieged island on the same small raft that had carried Menion and Shirl. The ordeal they had been through had brought them closer together, and on the trip southward they had spoken frankly, though in hushed tones, about the disbanding of the Border Legion. They were in complete accord that if the city of Tyrsis were to withstand an assault by a force the size of the Northland army, the Legion would be needed. Moreover, only the missing Balinor possessed the battle knowledge and skill necessary to lead them. The Prince must be found quickly and placed in command, even though his brother would undoubtedly oppose such a move, just as he was certain to oppose the re-forming of the legendary fighting force he had so foolishly demobilized.

Neither the highlander nor the Legion commander realized at this moment how difficult their task would be, though they suspected that Balinor had been seized by his brother upon entering Tyrsis some days earlier. Nevertheless, they were resolved that Tyrsis would not be destroyed as easily as Kern. This time they would stand and fight.

A squad of black-clad palace guards met the little group just inside the gates of the city, extending warm greetings from the King and insisting that they come to him at once. When Janus Senpre remarked that he had heard the King was deathly ill and confined to his bed, the squad captain quickly, though somewhat belatedly, added that his son Palance extended the offer in his father's place. Nothing could have pleased Menion more—he was anxious to get inside the palace walls for a look around. Forgotten was the fatigue and pain, though his companions still stood close to offer their support. The squad captain signaled to the guards near the Inner Wall, and an ornate carriage was quickly brought up to convey the privileged party to the palace. Menion and Shirl climbed into the carriage, but Janus Senpre declined to accompany them, explaining that he wished first to see to the welfare of his soldiers in the vacant Legion barracks. With disarming warmth, he promised he would join them later.

As the carriage drew away to the Inner Wall, the youthful commander waved once in sharp salute to Menion, his face impassive. Then accompanied by the grizzled Fandrez and several select officers, he strode purposefully toward the Legion barracks. In the coach, Menion smiled faintly to himself and gripped Shirl's hand.

The carriage passed through the gates of the Inner Wall and moved slowly onto the crowded Tyrsian Way. The people of the walled city had risen early that day, anxious to welcome the unfortunate fugitives from their sister city, eager to offer both food and shelter to friends and strangers alike. Everyone wanted to know more about the massive invasion force that was now advancing on their own homes. Throngs of worried and frightened people lingered uncertainly in the busy streets, talking anxiously among themselves, pausing to stare curiously as the carriage escorted by the palace guards rolled slowly past them. A few pointed or waved in astonishment as they recognized the slim girl who rode within, the dark, rust-colored hair shadowing her worn and drawn face. Menion sat close to her, suddenly aware once more of the pain stabbing in quick twinges from his battered feet. He was grateful now that it was not necessary to walk any farther.

The great city seemed to rush past him in short flashes of buildings and overpasses, all crowded with men, women, and children of all ages and descriptions, all rushing somewhere in noisy waves. The highlander breathed deeply and settled back in the cushioned seat, his hand still holding Shirl's, his eyes closing momentarily as he allowed his tired mind to drift into the gray haze that clouded his thoughts. The city and its multitudes faded quickly into a faint drone of sound that soothed him, lulled him quietly toward the comfort of sleep.

He was on the verge of slipping away entirely when a gentle shaking of his shoulder brought him quickly around, and his eyes opened to view the distant palace grounds as the carriage mounted the wide avenue of the Sendic Bridge. The youth gazed appreciatively down on the sunlit parks and gardens beneath the bridge, their tree-shaded lawns dotted with color from seemingly countless carefully tended flower beds. Everything lay in peace and warmth, as if this sector of the city were somehow an unrelated part of the turbulent human existence that had created it.

At the other end of the bridge the gates to the palace swung open in reception. Menion peered ahead in disbelief.

The entire entryway was lined with soldiers of the palace guard, all immaculately dressed in their black uniforms crested by the emblem of the falcon, all standing stiffly at attention. From within the enclosure, trumpets announced the arrival of the coach and its passengers. The highlander was astonished. They were being accorded the formal welcome normally reserved for only the greatest leaders of the four lands, a policy strictly observed by the few monarchies remaining in the vast Southland. The pomp and display of a full military salute clearly indicated that Palance Buckhannah was determined to ignore not only the circumstances under which they had arrived, but the inviolate tradition of centuries.

"He must be mad—absolutely mad!" the angered Southlander stormed. "What does he think this is? We're besieged by an invading army, and he turns out the troops for a dress parade!"

"Menion, be careful what you say to him. We must be patient if we are to be of any use to Balinor." Shirl gripped his shoulder and faced him for a moment, smiling quickly in warning. "Remember as well that he loves me, misguided though he may be. He was a good man once, and he is Balinor's brother still."

Impatient and impulsive as always, Menion nevertheless realized that she was right. There was nothing to be gained by showing he was angered with the foolish pageant, and he was well advised to go along with the Prince's whims until Balinor was located and freed. He sat quietly back in the coach as it entered the palace gates, passing in slow review before the rows of expressionless soldiers that formed the elite of the King's personal guard. The fanfares continued to roll from all sides, and a small squad of cavalry wheeled in precise formation about the courtyard for the benefit of the new arrivals. Then the carriage came to a gentle halt, and the big figure of the new ruler of Callahorn appeared at the coach door, the broad face smiling in nervous delight.

"Shirl—Shirl, I thought I would never see you again!" He reached into the coach and helped the slim girl from the small enclosure, holding her close to him for a moment and stepping away to view her once more. "I . . . I really thought I had lost you."

Burning quietly, an impassive Menion helped himself from the carriage, stepping down beside them, smiling faintly as Palance turned to greet him.

"Prince of Leah, you are indeed welcome in my kingdom," the big man greeted the lean highlander, reaching warmly for his hand. "You have done me . . . a very great service. Anything I have is yours—anything. We shall be great friends, you and I! Great friends! It has been . . . so long since . . ."

He trailed off sharply, looking intensely at the highlander, suddenly lost in thought. His speech was stilted and nervous, almost as if he weren't quite sure of what he was saying at any one point. If he weren't completely mad already, Menion thought quickly, he was certainly very ill.

"I'm very pleased to be in Tyrsis," he responded, "although I wish the circumstances could have been more pleasant for all concerned."

"You mean my brother, of course?" The question shot out as the other snapped awake again, his face flushed. Menion started momentarily in surprise.

"Palance, he means the invasion of the Northlanders, the burning of Kern," Shirl interposed quickly.

"Yes . . . Kern . . ." Again he trailed off, this time looking anxiously about as if someone were missing. Menion glanced about uneasily, realizing that the mystic Stenmin was strangely absent. According to Shirl and Janus Senpre, the Prince never went anywhere without his adviser. Quickly he caught Shirl's watchful eye.

"Is there something wrong, my Lord?" Menion used the formal address to catch the other's instant attention, smiling quickly in reassurance that he was a concerned friend prepared to help. The deception brought unexpected results.

"You can help me . . . and this kingdom, Menion Leah," Palance responded quickly. "My brother seeks to be King in my place. He would have me killed. My adviser Stenmin has saved me from this—but there are other enemies . . . all around! You and I must be friends. We must stand together against those who seek to take my throne—to bring harm to this lovely woman whom you have returned to me. I . . . I cannot talk with Stenmin . . . the way I would talk with a friend. But you, I could talk with you!"

Like a small child, he gazed eagerly at the amazed Menion Leah, awaiting his reply. A sudden feeling of pity for this son of Ruhl Buckhannah swept over the highlander, and he truly wished there was something he could do to help the unfortunate man. Smiling sadly, he nodded his agreement.

"I knew you would stand with me!" the other exclaimed excitedly, laughing in delight. "We are both men of royal blood, and that . . . binds us closely. You and I shall be great friends, Menion. But now . . . you must rest."

He seemed to recall suddenly that his palace corps were still standing stiffly at parade attention, waiting patiently for the Prince to give the order for dismissal. With a sharp wave of his hand, the new ruler of Callahorn led his two guests toward the Buckhannah home, nodding to the commander of his personal guard as they passed to signal that his soldiers could be dispersed for regular duty. The trio passed into the entryway of the ancient home, where a number of servants stood waiting to escort the guests to their rooms. Pausing briefly once more, the host turned to his guests, bending close to whisper.

"My brother is locked in the dungeons beneath us. You need not be afraid." He stared meaningfully at them for a moment, glancing quickly at the curious servants who waited respectfully in the background. "He has friends everywhere, you know."

Both Menion and Shirl nodded, because it was expected of them.

"He won't escape from the dungeons then?" Menion pursued the matter a bit further.

"He tried last night . . . with his friends." Palance smiled with satisfaction. "But we caught them and trapped them . . . trapped them in the dungeon forever. Stenmin is there now . . . you must meet him . . ."

Again he straightened up with the thought left unspoken, his attention given over to the servants, several of whom he beckoned to his side. He crisply directed them to escort his friends to their quarters where they could bathe themselves and don fresh clothing before joining him for breakfast. It was still only about an hour after dawn and the refugees from Kern had not eaten since the previous night. Menion needed medical treatment for his hastily bandaged wounds, and the house physician stood ready to change the dressings and apply fresh medicines. He needed rest, too, but that could wait. The small party started down one long hallway when suddenly a distracted voice called after Shirl, and the new ruler of Callahorn came after them, approaching the wondering girl with hesitant steps, finally stopping before her and quickly embracing her. Menion kept his face averted, but their words were clear.

"You must not go away from me again, Shirl." It was a command, not a request, though the words were softly spoken. "Your new home must be in Tyrsis—as my wife."

There was a long moment of silence.

"Palance, I think we . . ." Shirl's voice shook as she tried to interpose a quiet explanation.

"No—say nothing. No discussion is necessary now . . . not now," Palance interrupted quickly. "Later . . . when we are alone, when you are rested . . . there will be time. You know I love you . . . I always have. And you have loved me, I know."

Again the long moment of silence, and then Shirl was walking quickly past Menion, forcing the servants to dash ahead in order to lead the way to the guest quarters. The highlander quickly came up beside the beautiful girl, not daring to reach for her while his host stood silently watching them move down the hallway. Shirl's face was lowered, shaded by the long red hair, the slim, bronzed hands clasped tightly before her. Neither spoke as the servants led them down the wide corridor to their rooms in the west wing of the ancient home. They separated briefly while Menion allowed the persistent physician to treat his wounds and wrap them in fresh bandages. Clean clothing lay on the huge, four-poster bed, and a hot bath stood waiting, but a distraught Menion ignored them both. Quickly he slipped from his room into the empty hallway; he knocked softly, pushed open the door to Shirl's room, and entered. She rose slowly from the bed as he closed the heavy wooden door, then ran quickly to him, her arms encircling and holding him tightly to her.

They stood in silence for several minutes, just holding each other, feeling the warm life flow quickly through their bodies, knotting and winding in unbreakable ties. Softly Menion stroked the dark red tresses, gently pressing the beautiful face close against his chest. She depended on him; the thought flashed with relief through his numbed mind. When her own strength, her own courage had faltered, she had turned to him, and Menion realized that he loved her desperately.

It was very strange that it should happen now, when their world seemed destined to crumble about them and death stood waiting in the shadows. Yet Menion's turbulent life of the past several weeks had drawn him from one frightening struggle to the next, each a battle for survival that seemed senseless in mortal terms and found its logic solely in the strange legend of the mystic Sword of Shannara and the Warlock Lord. In those terrible days since Culhaven, life had raged around him like a battle, and he had surged directionless through its center. His deep friendship and love for Shea, and his now broken companionship with the members of the company that had journeyed to Paranor and beyond, had provided a faint sense of stability, an indication that something constant would remain while the rest of the world rushed away. Then unexpectedly, he had found Shirl Ravenlock, and the fast pace of events and dangers shared in those past few days, combined with a totally predictable meshing of personal needs, had drawn and bound them inextricably to one another. Menion closed his eyes and pressed her closer.

Palance had been helpful in at least one respect—he had

told them that Balinor and probably the others with him were imprisoned in the dungeons somewhere beneath the palace. Evidently one escape had already failed, and Menion was determined that he would not make any mistakes. Quietly he conversed with Shirl, trying to decide what their next step should be. If Palance insisted on keeping Shirl close to him in order to assure her protection, her movement would be severely restricted. A worse threat was the Prince's obsession with marrying her in the false belief that she truly loved him. Palance Buckhannah seemed poised on the brink of total madness, his sanity precariously balanced. It could be tipped at any moment, and if that should happen while Balinor was his prisoner . . .

Menion paused mentally, aware that time did not permit speculation of what might happen tomorrow. By then it would make little difference because the Northland invasion force would be at the gates and it would be too late for anyone to do anything. Balinor had to be freed now. Menion had a strong ally in Janus Senpre, but the palace was secured by the special black-garbed soldiers who served only the ruler, and at the moment it appeared they served Palance Buckhannah. No one seemed to know what had become of the old King; he had not been seen for weeks. Evidently he was unable to move from his sickbed, yet there was only his son's word for that—and his son relied on the word of the strange mystic Stenmin.

Shirl had once remarked that she had never seen Palance alone for more than a few moments without his adviser close at hand, yet when they arrived from Kern, Stenmin had been nowhere in sight. This was peculiar, especially since it was common knowledge that Stenmin had made himself the real power behind the unstable Prince. Shirl's father had stated in the council chambers of Kern that the evil mystic seemed to possess some strange hold over the younger son of Ruhl Buckhannah. If only Menion could discover what that power was—for he was sure that the mystic was the key to the Prince's unbalanced behavior. But there was no time left. He would have to do the best he could with what little he knew now.

When he left Shirl and returned to his own room, ready now for that hot bath and a clean change of clothing, a plan for freeing Balinor was already forming in his mind. He was still filling in the details when the bath was finished and there was a knock on the door. Slipping into a robe his host had furnished, he crossed the room and opened the door. One of the palace servants had brought him the sword of Leah. Smiling gratefully, he thanked the man and dropped the precious weapon on the bed, recalling that he had deposited it on the seat in the carriage during his ride to the palace and forgotten to remove it. His mind wandered briefly as he dressed, remembering proudly the service that battle-worn implement had seen. He had been through so much since Shea had appeared in Leah those many weeks ago—it might have been a lifetime for any man.

Pausing momentarily, he reflected sadly on his missing friend and wondered for the thousandth time if the little Valeman were still alive. He should not be in Tyrsis, he chided himself in bitter recrimination. Shea had depended on him for protection, but it appeared that his trust had been badly misplaced. Menion had repeatedly allowed himself to be governed by the wishes of Allanon, and each time his conscience had warned him that he was somehow failing his companion by following the Druid's counsel. He felt deeply angered at the thought that he had ignored his clear responsibility to the Valeman, and yet the choices that had brought him to Tyrsis had been his own. There were others besides Shea who desperately needed him. . . .

Crossing the spacious bedroom in measured steps, still lost in thought, he dropped heavily to the welcome softness of the large bed, his outstretched hand coming to rest on the cool metal of his sword. He fingered it lightly as he lay back wearily and pondered the problems facing him. Shirl's frightened face lingered in his mind, her eyes searching Menion's own. She was very important to him; he could not leave her now in order to resume the search for Shea, no matter what the consequences might be. It was a bitter choice to make, if indeed there was any real choice at all, for his duty ran beyond those two single lives to those of Balinor and his imprisoned comrades and ultimately to those of the people of Callahorn. It would be for Allanon and Flick to find and rescue the missing Valeman if he were still alive. So much depended on them all, he thought absently, his tired mind and body already drifting toward a much-needed sleep. They could only pray for success . . . pray and wait. He hovered on the brink of slumber and then softly dropped off.

A moment later his sleeping mind jerked sharply and he was instantly awake. There may have been a slight noise or perhaps only a highly keyed sixth sense, but whatever it was snapped him back from a sleep that would have ended in his death. He lay motionless on the great bed as his listening ears caught a faint scraping sound from the far wall, and through the slits of his eyelids he saw a portion of a tapestry ripple with movement. A part of the heavy stone behind the tapestry seemed to push outward and a bent, scarlet-cloaked figure slid noiselessly into view.

Menion forced himself to continue breathing in measured intervals, although his heart was beating wildly, urging him to leap from the bed and seize the mysterious intruder. The cloaked figure moved silently across the bedroom floor, the unfamiliar face glancing quickly about the room and then turning back to the highlander's sprawled form. The intruder was only several feet from the bed when a lean hand slipped beneath the scarlet cloak and emerged, gripping a long, wicked dagger.

Menion's outstretched hand rested loosely on the sword of Leah, but still he did not move. He waited a moment longer until the attacker was within about a yard of the bed, the dagger held at waist level; then with the lightning speed of a cat, he struck. The lean body whipped upward and toward the startled intruder, one hand clenching the sword still sheathed in its leather scabbard as the flat of the blade snapped sharply around at the man's unprotected face, striking it in a stinging slap. The mysterious figure reeled backward, the dagger raised defensively. The sword struck a second time, and the weapon clattered to the floor as the numbed fingers of the attacker clenched suddenly in pain. Menion did not pause, but threw himself at the scarlet figure, his own weight dragging the struggling man to the floor where he quickly pinned him, twisting one arm sharply as his fingers closed tightly about the windpipe.

"Speak up, assassin!" Menion growled menacingly.

"No, no wait, you've made a mistake . . . I'm not an enemy . . . please, I can't breathe. . . ."

The voice choked sharply and the man's breath rasped in ragged gulps as the highlander's grip remained unaltered and the cold dark eyes surveyed the face of his captive. To his knowledge, Menion had never seen the man. The face was pinched and sharp, framed by a small black beard and lined with pain. Even as he studied the teeth clenched in anger and the eyes burning with hatred, the highlander instinctively knew there had been no mistake made. Stepping quickly to one side, he jerked the intruder to his feet, one hand still firmly fastened on the scrawny neck.

"Tell me about my mistake, then. You have about a minute before I cut your tongue out and turn you over to the guards!"

He released his grip on the man's throat, his hand dropping to seize the front of the scarlet tunic. Tossing his sword on the bed, he quickly picked up the fallen dagger, holding it ready should his attacker attempt anything further.

"This was a gift, Prince of Leah . . . merely a gift from the King." The voice broke slightly as the fellow struggled to regain his composure. "The King wanted to show his gratitude, and I . . . I came through another door so as not to disturb your sleep."

He paused as if waiting for something, the sharp eyes riveted on the highlander's own. He wasn't waiting to see if his story would be believed—it was something else, almost as if he were expecting Menion to see something more. . . . The Prince of Leah jerked him sharply, snapping the lean face close to his own.

"That is unquestionably the weakest tale I have ever heard! Who are you, assassin?"

The eyes burned into his own with intense hatred.

"I am Stenmin, the King's personal adviser." He seemed to have suddenly regained his senses now. "I did not lie to you. The dagger was a present from Palance Buckhannah which I was asked to bring to you. I meant you no harm. If you do not believe me, go to the King. Ask him!"

There was a hint of confidence in the man's voice that convinced Menion that Palance would affirm his adviser's story whether it was true or not. He had in his grasp the most dangerous man in Callahorn, the evil mystic who had become the power behind the monarchy—the one man he had to eliminate if Balinor were to be rescued. Why the man had chosen to attack him when they had never met was something he did not understand, but it was clear that if he released him now or even took him before Palance in an effort to discredit him, the highlander would lose the initiative and place his own life in danger again. Roughly he threw the mystic into a nearby chair and ordered him to remain motionless. The man sat quietly, his eyes drifting aimlessly about the room, the hands moving nervously to stroke the small pointed beard. Menion eyed him absently, his mind carefully pondering the choices open to him. It took him only a moment to decide. He could no longer bide his time, waiting for the right moment to free his friends; the decision had been taken out of his hands.

"On your feet, mystic, or whatever you prefer to call yourself!" The evil face stared menacingly at him, and in fury Menion yanked the man violently up from the chair. "I ought to dispose of you without further consideration; the people of Callahorn would be much the better for it. But for the time being, I need your services. Take me to the dungeons where Balinor and the others are imprisoned now!"

Stenmin's eyes went wide in sudden shock at the mention of Balinor.

"How could you know of him . . . a traitor to this kingdom?" the mystic exclaimed in astonishment. "The King himself has ordered his brother imprisoned until his natural death, Prince of Leah, and even I . . ."

His sentence ended in a strangled gasp as Menion grabbed him roughly by the throat and began to squeeze. Stenmin's face turned slowly purple.

"I didn't ask for excuses or explanations. Just take me to him!"

Once more he tightened his iron grip and finally the gasping captive violently nodded his acquiescence. Menion released him with a snap of his wrist and the nearly throttled man fell dizzily to one knee. Quickly the highlander slipped out of his robe and into his clothing, strapping on the sword and shoving the dagger into his belt. For an instant he thought about arousing Shirl in the next room, but quickly discarded that idea. His plan was dangerous enough; there was no reason to risk her life as well. If he succeeded in freeing his friends, there would be time enough to come back for her. He turned to his captive, drawing the dagger from his belt and holding it up for the other to see.

"The present that you were so kind to bring me will be returned to you, assassin, if you attempt to trick or betray me in any way," he warned in his most menacing tone of voice. "So don't try to be clever. When we leave this room, you will take me down the back corridors and stairs to the prison where Balinor and his companions are held. Don't try to alarm the guards—you won't be fast enough. If you doubt anything I've told you, then understand this. I was sent to this city by Allanon!"

Stenmin seemed to go suddenly white at the mention of the giant Druid and undisguised fear shot into his widening eyes. Apparently cowed into obeying his captor, the scarlet mystic moved silently toward the bedroom door and Menion fell into step directly behind him, the dagger back in his belt with one hand gripping the hilt. Time was the

all-important factor now. He had to act quickly, freeing Balinor and the other imprisoned members of the company of
friends and seizing the deranged Palance before the members of the palace guard were alerted. Then a quick message
to Janus Senpre would bring to their aid those still loyal to
Balinor, and the power of the monarchy would be restored
without a battle.

Already the massive Northland army would be mobiliz-
ing on the grasslands above the island of Kern, preparing to
move on Tyrsis. If the Border Legion could be reassembled
and deployed quickly enough that day, there was a chance
the invader might be stopped on the north shore of the Mermidon. It would be a nearly impossible task to cross that
flooded river with a defensive force holding the opposite
bank, and it would take the enemy several days to manage a
flanking maneuver—more than enough time for the armies
of Eventine to reach them. Menion knew it would all depend
on the next few minutes.

The two men stepped cautiously into the hallway beyond
the room. Menion quickly glanced in both directions for any
sign of the black-garbed sentries, but the hall was deserted,
and the highlander motioned Stenmin ahead. The mystic reluctantly led his captor toward the inner rooms of the central palace, winding his way along the corridors that ran to
the rear of the ancient building, carefully avoiding the occupied rooms. Twice they passed members of the palace guard,
but each time Stenmin withheld any comment or greeting,
his dark face lowered in grim determination.

Through the latticework of the castle windows, Menion
could see the gardens that decorated the grounds of the Buckhannah home, the sunlight falling warmly on the brightly
colored flowers. It was already midmorning, and before much

longer the normal gathering of visitors and business person-
ages would begin. There had been no sign of Palance Buckhannah, and Menion was hopeful that the Prince was
preoccupied with other matters.

As the two walked slowly down the hallways, the sound
of voices was distinctly audible in all directions. Servants
began to appear in increasing numbers, moving busily about
their assigned tasks. When they passed, they pointedly ignored Stenmin and his apparent companion, a good indication that they neither liked nor trusted the mystic. None
questioned their presence and at last they approached the
massive doorway that led to the castle cellars. Two armed
sentries were stationed before the door, and a huge metal bar
now held the latches firmly in place.

"Be careful what you say," Menion cautioned in a sharp
whisper as they neared the guards.

They came to a slow halt before the massive cellar door,
the watchful highlander placing one hand in a leisurely manner on the hilt of the dagger as he stood close behind Stenmin. The guards glanced curiously at him for a moment,
then turned their attention to the King's adviser, who had
begun to address them.

"Open the door, guards. The Prince of Leah and I will in-
spect the wine cellar and the dungeons."

"All persons are forbidden to enter this area by order of
the King, my Lord," the guard to the right stated pointedly.

"I am here by order of the King!" Stenmin shouted angrily, causing Menion to give him a warning nudge.

"Sentry, this is the King's personal counselor—not an
enemy of the Kingdom," the highlander pointed out with a
deceiving smile. "We are on a tour of the palace, and since it
was I who rescued the King's betrothed, it was his belief that

I might recognize the lady's abductors. Now if necessary, I shall disturb the King and bring him down here . . ."

He trailed off meaningfully, praying that the guards would be sufficiently forewarned of Palance's irrational behavior to think twice about calling him down. The guards hesitated momentarily, then nodded quietly, released the latches on the door and stepped aside, swinging the massive portal open to reveal the stone stairway leading downward. Stenmin again led the way without comment. Apparently he had decided to follow Menion's instructions to the letter, but the cautious highlander knew that the mystic was no fool. If Balinor were successfully freed and restored to command of the Border Legion, then his own power over the throne of Callahorn would be finished. He would undoubtedly attempt something, but the time and the place had not yet come. The heavy door closed quietly behind them and they began their descent into the torchlit cellar.

Menion saw the trapdoor in the center of the cellar floor almost immediately. The guards had not bothered to conceal it a second time with the wine barrels, but had fastened a series of iron bars and latches across the stone slab, effectively preventing anyone imprisoned below from breaking free. Although Menion could not have known, the prisoners had not been returned to their cells following the aborted escape attempt earlier that same morning. Instead, they had been left to roam in the darkness of the dungeon corridors. Two guards were stationed next to the sealed opening, their attention now focused on the two men who had just been admitted from the palace. Menion saw a plate of cheese and bread resting half eaten on one of the wine barrels and two cups of wine placed next to a half-drained flask. They had been drinking. The highlander smiled slightly.

As the two reached the stone flooring, Menion pretended to glance about the wine cellar in great interest, beginning a jovial conversation with the silent Stenmin. The guards rose slowly and came to attention at the sight of the King's adviser, who was looking decidedly grim about something. The highlander knew they had been caught off balance by this unexpected visit and he decided to make the most of it.

"I see what you mean, my Lord." He glowered fiercely at the mystic as they drew near to the sentries. "These men have been drinking while on duty! Suppose the prisoners should have escaped while these men lay in a drunken stupor? The King must be told of this as soon as we have finished our business here."

The guards turned pale with fear at mention of the King.

"My Lord, you are mistaken," the one pleaded hastily. "We were only taking a little wine with our breakfast. We have not been lax . . ."

"The King should decide that." Menion cut him off with a wave of his hand.

"But . . . the King will not listen . . ."

Stenmin glowered in fury at the deception, but the guards misunderstood and quickly assumed he meant to have them punished. The mystic tried to say something, but Menion moved quickly in front of him, as if in an effort to restrain his advance toward the unfortunate guards, drawing the dagger and holding it close to the man's unprotected chest.

"Yes, of course they are probably lying," Menion continued without changing his tone of voice. "Still the King is a busy man and I hate to bother him with little problems. Perhaps a word of warning to them . . . ?"

He glanced back at the guards who nodded dumbly, grasping at any chance to avoid Stenmin's wrath. Like everyone else in the Kingdom, they were frightened of the power the strange mystic possessed over Palance and were more than eager to avoid angering him.

"Very good, then, you have had your warning." Menion sheathed the dagger and turned back to the still-shaken sentries. "Now open the dungeon door and bring up the prisoners."

He stood close to Stenmin, glancing at him quickly in warning. The dark face did not seem to see him anymore, the eyes staring vacantly at the stone slab that barred their entry to the dungeons beneath. The sentries had not moved, but were glancing at each other in new desperation.

"My Lord, the King has forbidden anyone to see the prisoners . . . for any reason," the one guard gulped at last. "I cannot bring them out of the dungeon."

"So you would bar the King's adviser and his personal guest." Menion did not hesitate. He had expected this. "Then we have no choice but to call the King down here . . ."

That was all it took. There was no further deliberation as the sentries raced to the stone slab, quickly sliding back the latches and bolts. Bracing themselves, the guards pulled back on the iron ring and the trapdoor swung ponderously upward and fell back heavily against the stone flooring, leaving a gaping black hole. Holding their swords ready, the sentries called down into the darkness, commanding the prisoners to come out. There were footsteps on the ancient stone stairway as Menion waited expectantly at Stenmin's side, his own sword now drawn. His free hand held the mystic's arm tightly, and in a sharp whisper he warned the lean adviser not to speak or move. Then Balinor's broad form appeared from out of the pit, closely followed by the Elven brothers and the durable Hendel, his own attempt to rescue his friends thwarted only hours earlier. They did not see Menion · at first. Quickly the highlander stepped forward, still holding the silent Stenmin.

"That's it, keep them moving, keep them together. Such men must be watched carefully. They are always dangerous."

The wearied prisoners glanced over abruptly, only thinly masking their astonishment on seeing the Prince of Leah. Menion winked quickly behind the guards' backs, and the four captives turned away, only the slow smile on Dayel's young face betraying the sudden joy they were experiencing at the sight of their old friend. They were out of the pit now and standing quietly a few feet from the guards, who stood with their backs to the highlander. But before Menion could act, the heretofore passive Stenmin wrested his whiplike form free from his captor's iron grip and sprang aside to shout a quick warning to the unsuspecting sentries.

"Traitor! Guards, it's a trick . . ."

He was never able to finish. As the distracted sentries whirled about, Menion leaped catlike at the fleeing mystic, throwing him violently to the stone floor. The soldiers realized their mistake too late. The four prisoners sprang into action, closing the short space of ground separating them from their jailers and disarming them before they could recover. Within seconds the guards were subdued, quickly bound and gagged, and dragged into a corner of the cellar where they were hidden from sight. A thoroughly beaten Stenmin was yanked unceremoniously to his feet to face his new captors. Menion glanced anxiously at the closed door at the top of the cellar stairway, but no one appeared. Apparently the shout had gone unheeded. Balinor and the others came over to him with smiles of gratitude on their tired faces, clapping him on the back and shaking his hand once again.

"Menion Leah, we owe you more than we can ever hope to give back." The giant borderman gripped his hand tightly. "I did not think we would ever see you again. Where is Allanon?"

Quickly Menion explained how he had left Allanon and Flick concealed above the camp of the Northland army and come to Callahorn to warn of the impending advance against Tyrsis. Pausing momentarily to gag Stenmin in the event the evil adviser should attempt to call out another warning to the guards posted outside the cellar door, the highlander told of rescuing Shirl Ravenlock, fleeing to Kern and subsequently to the walls of Tyrsis after the island city was besieged and destroyed. His friends listened grimly until he had finished.

"Whatever else may come out of this, highlander," Hendel declared quietly, "you have proved yourself this day and we shall never forget it."

"The Border Legion must be re-formed and sent to hold the Mermidon immediately," Balinor cut in quickly. "We must get word to the lower city. Then we must find my father . . . and my brother. But I want to secure the palace and the army without a battle. Menion, can we trust Janus Senpre to come to our aid if we call for him?"

"He is loyal to you and to the King." Menion nodded affirmatively.

"You must get a message to him while we remain here," the Prince of Callahorn continued, pacing over toward the captive Stenmin. "Once he arrives with help, we should have no trouble—my brother will be left without support. But what of my father . . . ?"

Towering over the dark form of the mystic, he removed the gag from the captive's mouth and stared coldly down at him. Stenmin met his gaze briefly, his own eyes furtive and filled with hate. The mystic knew he was beaten if Palance was captured and removed as monarch of Callahorn, and he was becoming increasingly desperate as the end drew near and his plans began to break apart. Standing with the Elven brothers and Hendel as Balinor confronted the mysterious captive, Menion found himself wondering what the man had hoped to gain by encouraging Palance to take the steps he had. Certainly it was no mystery why he had supported the distraught and unstable Prince as the new King of Callahorn. His own position was assured with Balinor's brother ruling. But why had he encouraged the disbanding of the Border Legion when he knew that an invading army was threatening to overrun the little Southland kingdom and put an end to its enlightened monarchy? Why had he gone to such pains to imprison Balinor and to secrete his father in a distant wing of the palace when they could have been quietly disposed of? And why had he tried to kill Menion Leah, a man he had never met before?

"Stenmin, your rule over this land and its people and your domination of my brother are over," Balinor declared with cold determination. "Whether or not you will ever see the light of another day depends on what you do from now until the time I am again in command of the city. What have you done with my father?"

There was a long moment of silence as the mystic looked desperately around, the dark face ashen with fear.

"He ... he is in the north wing ... in the tower," the answer was a whisper.

"If he has been harmed, mystic ..."

Balinor turned away sharply, leaving the terrified man momentarily forgotten. Stenmin shrank away against one wall, gazing after the tall figure of the borderman. One hand came up nervously to stroke the small pointed beard. Menion watched him, almost in pity, and then suddenly something clicked in his mind. An image flashed sharply—a memory of a scene he had witnessed several days earlier on the banks of the Mermidon north of the island of Kern as he had lain concealed on a small hillock overlooking a windy beachhead. That same mannerism—the stroking of a small pointed beard! Now he knew exactly what Stenmin was attempting to do! His face turned to a mask of rage and he started forward, brushing past Balinor as if he wasn't even there.

"You were the man on the beach—the kidnapper!" he accused in undisguised fury. "You tried to kill me because you thought I would recognize you as the man who kidnapped Shirl—the man who turned her over to the Northlanders. You traitor! You intended to betray us all—to turn the city over to the Warlock Lord!"

Heedless of the cries of his companions, he rushed toward the now hysterical mystic, who somehow managed to evade his initial lunge and break away toward the cellar stairway. Menion was after him with a bound, the gleaming sword of his father raised to strike. Halfway up the stone steps he caught him, one hand jerking the dark form about as the man shrieked in terror. Yet the end did not come, for as the sword drew back and Menion held the maddened

Stenmin tightly against the stone wall, the massive door to the ancient cellar suddenly swung open, the thrust of the pull slamming the ironbound wood back against the wall with a jarring crash. Framed in the entryway stood the broad figure of Palance Buckhannah.

FOUR

OR A MOMENT no one moved. Even the terrified Stenmin had gone limp against the cellar wall, his dark face staring blankly at the silent form that waited statuelike at the top of the ancient stairway. The lined face of the Prince was drained of color, and the eyes reflected a curious mixture of anger and confusion. Resolutely, Menion Leah met those searching eyes, his sword arm lowering slowly, his own hatred fading with the sudden turn of events. Their lives might all be forfeited if he didn't act fast. Roughly he yanked Stenmin to his feet and threw him disdainfully toward the Prince.

"Here is your traitor, Palance—the real enemy of Callahorn. This is the man who gave Shirl Ravenlock to the Northlanders. This is the man who would give Tyrsis to the Warlock Lord. . . ."

"My Lord, you've come just in time." The mystic had recovered his wits enough to cut Menion off before any more damage could be done. He stumbled fearfully to his feet and rushed up the stairs, throwing himself at Palance's feet and pointing down at the company of friends. "I discovered them escaping—I was running to warn you! The highlander is a friend of Balinor—he came to kill you!" The words were tumbling out of the man's mouth in undisguised hatred as

he groped at his benefactor's tunic and raised himself slowly to his side. "They would have killed me—and then you, my Lord. Can't you see what is happening?"

Menion fought down the urge to rush up the steps and cut the evil mystic's lying tongue out, forcing himself to remain outwardly calm, his gaze riveted on that of the stunned Palance Buckhannah.

"You have been betrayed by this man, Palance," he continued evenly. "He has poisoned your heart and your mind. He has sapped you of your will to think for yourself. He cares nothing for you; he cares nothing for this land, which he has so cheaply sold to the enemy that has already destroyed Kern." Stenmin roared in fury, but Menion continued in stony disregard. "You once said we would be friends, and friends must have trust for each other. Do not be deceived now, or your kingdom will surely be lost."

At the bottom of the stairway, Balinor and his friends watched silently, afraid that any distraction might break the strange spell Menion Leah was weaving, for Palance was still listening, his clouded mind struggling to break the wall of confusion surrounding it. Slowly he stepped forward on the landing, closing the door quietly behind him and brushing past Stenmin as if he hadn't seen him. His adviser hesitated in confusion, glancing uncertainly at the cellar door as if debating the wisdom of attempting to flee. But he was not yet prepared to accept defeat, and he whirled quickly, catching Palance by the arm and thrusting his lean face next to the man's ear.

"Are you mad? Are you as insane as some say, my King?" he whispered venomously. "Will you throw everything away now—give it all back to your brother? Was he meant to be

King—or you? This is all a lie! The Prince of Leah is a friend to Allanon."

Palance turned toward him slightly, his eyes widening.

"Yes, Allanon!" Stenmin knew he had struck a nerve and was determined to pursue it. "Who do you think seized your betrothed from her home in Kern? This man who speaks of friendship was part of the kidnapping—it was all a ruse to get inside the palace and then assassinate you. You were to be killed!"

Below the stairway, Hendel took a step forward, but Balinor put out a restraining hand. Menion stood quietly, knowing that any sudden move now would only confirm Stenmin's charges. He directed a withering glance at the wily mystic, turning quickly back to Palance and shaking his head.

"He is a traitor. He belongs to the Warlock Lord."

Palance took several steps down the stairway, glancing briefly at Menion and then staring fixedly at his brother who waited patiently at the foot of the stairs. A faint smile crossed his lips as he paused confusedly.

"What do you think, brother? Am I really . . . mad? If not me, then . . . why, it must be everyone else, and I alone am . . . sane. Say something, Balinor. We should have that talk now . . . Before . . . I did want to say something . . ."

But the sentence was left unfinished as he straightened his tall frame and looked back once again at Stenmin, who had taken on the appearance of a dangerously cornered animal, crouched and waiting to attack.

"You are pathetic, Stenmin. Stand up!" The sharp command cut through the stillness and the bent figure of the mystic snapped upright. "Advise me what I should do,"

Palance ordered sharply. "Do I have everyone killed—will that protect me?"

In an instant Stenmin was back at his side, the sharp eyes cold with fury.

"Call your guard, my Lord. Dispose of these assassins now!"

Suddenly Palance seemed to waver, his tall frame drooping, his eyes glancing at the walls of the cellar in studied concentration of the stonework. Menion sensed that the Prince of Callahorn was again losing his grip on reality and falling back into the clouded world of madness that had impaired his once sound reason. Stenmin recognized it as well, a grim smile creeping over his dark face, his hand coming up to stroke the small pointed beard. Then abruptly, Palance spoke once more.

"No, there will be no soldiers . . . no killing. A King must be a man of judgment . . . Balinor is my brother though he wishes to be King in my place. He and I must talk now . . . he is not to be harmed . . . not harmed." His voice trailed off and he smiled unexpectedly at Menion. "You brought Shirl back to me . . . I thought I had lost her, you know. Why . . . would you do that . . . if you were an enemy . . . ?"

Stenmin screamed in fury, grasping furiously at the other's tunic, but the Prince did not seem to realize he was even there.

"It is difficult for me . . . to think clearly, Balinor," Palance continued in a low whisper, shaking his head slowly. "Nothing is clear anymore . . . I don't even feel angry toward you for wanting to be King. I have always . . . wanted to be King. I have, you know. But I have to have . . . friends . . . someone to talk to . . ."

He turned dispassionately toward Stenmin, his eyes blank

and expressionless. Something his adviser saw there caused the mystic to release his grip on the other's arm and shrink limply back against the stone wall, his jaw sagging in fear. Only Menion was close enough to realize what had happened. Whatever hold the evil mystic had managed to secure over Palance Buckhannah was gone. The man's already muddled thought processes had been pushed beyond the brink of even basic comprehension of identities, and Stenmin was now no more than another face in a sea of indistinguishable beings that haunted the nightmare world of the maddened Prince of Callahorn.

"Palance, listen to me," Menion called softly to him, reaching through the web of darkness to the man beneath for just an instant. The broad figure turned slightly. "Call Shirl down from her room. Call Shirl and she will help you."

The Prince hesitated for a moment as if trying to remember, then a small smile crossed his haggard face and a deep calm seemed to settle through his whole body. He remembered her soft voice, her gentle manner, her fragile beauty— memories that recalled peace and serenity, moments of deep affection that he had never found with any other human being. If he could just be with her for a while . . .

"Shirl," he spoke her name softly and turned back to the closed cellar door, one hand outstretched. As he brushed past Stenmin, the crouched mystic seemed suddenly to go berserk. Shrieking with rage and frustration, he threw himself at the other man, grappling wildly at his tunic front. Responding instantly, Menion Leah bounded quickly toward the high landing to part the struggling men. But he was still several steps away when Stenmin's lean hand drew back momentarily, holding high a long dagger seized from beneath his robes. The weapon raised and for one terrible second hung poised above the men, as Balinor cried out in helpless shock. Then it fell. Palance Buckhannah rose sharply to his full height, the dagger buried to the hilt in his broad chest, a terrible whiteness flooding his young face.

"I give you back your brother, fool!" shrieked the maddened Stenmin, shoving the rigid form down the stone stairway.

The stricken Prince fell heavily into Menion's outstretched arms, knocking him back roughly against the wall, causing him momentarily to lose his balance and the opportunity to reach the hated enemy. Stenmin had already turned to flee, pulling frantically on the massive cellar door. Balinor bounded up the stairway, desperately trying to stop the mystic's escape, the Elven brothers immediately behind him, yelling for the guards. The scarlet figure had pulled the door partially open and was just slipping to freedom when Hendel, still standing at the foot of the stairs, seized a discarded mace and hurled it wildly at the fleeing man. It struck the mystic's exposed shoulder with bone-crunching force, and a scream of pain echoed off the dank walls. Yet it wasn't enough to stop him completely, and a moment later he had disappeared through the doorway. From the hallway beyond they could hear his shrill cry that the prisoners had assassinated the King.

Balinor paused only an instant in his pursuit to glance down on the still form resting quietly in the strong arms of Menion Leah, then raced for the open cellar door. Two black-clad palace guards appeared suddenly from the hallway beyond, swords drawn, to confront the unarmed borderman. They could have been statues for all the difference their unexpected appearance made to Balinor, who bowled them over with a lightning assault, seizing a fallen sword as he disappeared from view. Durin and Dayel were only steps behind. Menion knelt alone on the stairway, gazing after them and holding the stricken Palance, cradling gently the body of the self-proclaimed King of Callahorn. Silently, Hendel climbed the stone steps to stand beside him, shaking his grizzled head sadly. The Prince was still alive, the shallow breathing harsh and the eyelids twitching sporadically. Grimly the Dwarf reached down as Menion held the limp form and slowly withdrew the deadly blade, casting the weapon away with disgust. The Dwarf bent to help the high-lander raise the wounded man, and abruptly the eyes opened for an instant. Palance spoke softly, a barely perceptible mur-mur, and then drifted into unconsciousness once more.

"He's calling for Shirl," Menion whispered, tears in his eyes as he glanced briefly at the other. "He still loves her. He still loves her."

In the hallway beyond, Balinor and the Elven brothers were struggling to catch the fleeing Stenmin. Everything was in a state of utter confusion as guards, household servants, and visitors milled through the panic-stricken palace. Shouts of terror echoed off the ancient walls, decrying the death of the King and warning of assassins bent on killing everyone. The sounds of still another battle rose from the palace gates to add to the growing chaos. Balinor and his two compan-ions fought their way through the knots of frightened peo-ple, who seemed to go into a state of complete hysteria at the sight of drawn weapons. A few scattered guards even at-tempted to bar their passage, but each time the giant bor-derman merely flung the unfortunate men aside without pausing and raced in pursuit of the red-cloaked figure stum-bling ahead. Stenmin was still in sight when the three pur-suers reached the central hallway, but he had broken through the hindering throngs and was beginning to draw away. With unbelievable fury Balinor pushed ahead, heedlessly knocking everyone in his path aside, his face grim and terrible.

Then suddenly the palace doors shuddered under the weight of dozens of battling men and burst open with a crash, directly in front of the giant borderman and his Elven friends. The confusion was complete as a huge knot of fighting men rushed wildly into the entryway and the halls beyond, shouting for Balinor and waving their drawn weapons with grand flourishes. For a moment, the Prince was uncertain who they were; then he saw that they were wearing the leopard insignia of the Border Legion. The few palace guards who remained either fled or threw down their weapons and were seized. The Legion soldiers immediately spotted Balinor and rushed over to him, grasping him and raising him to their shoulders with cheers of victory. Durin and Dayel were cut off from him, and the cheering mass of men barred their pursuit of the rapidly disappearing Stenmin. Balinor shouted and struggled furiously, desperately trying to break away, but the sheer weight of numbers prevented him from resisting the tide that suddenly surged forward, carrying him back toward the cellar.

The frustrated Elves finally broke through the mass of bodies, racing after their quarry, who had turned down a different hallway and was momentarily lost from sight. The lean Elves were very fast, however, and closed the gap between themselves and Stenmin in a matter of seconds. Rounding the corner of the hallway, they caught sight of him once again, the dark face flushed with terror, the right arm hanging limp and useless. Silently Durin cursed himself for having failed to pick up a longbow. Abruptly, the fleeing man halted and vainly tried to wrest open one of the several doors lining the left side of the passage. The latch held despite the mystic's repeated efforts to force it, and at last he turned once more and raced to open the next door down the hall. Durin and Dayel were only yards away as Stenmin succeeded in opening this one and disappeared inside, closing it with a resounding crash. The Elves were there in seconds. Finding the door secured from within, they proceeded to force the iron latch with their swords. The clasp was sturdy and it took them several endless minutes to break through. By the time they pried open the door and burst into the room with swords held ready, it was deserted.

Menion Leah stood quietly at the front gates of the Buck-hannah home as Balinor conversed in low tones with the commanders of the Border Legion. Shirl was next to him, one slim arm locked in his, her young face lined with worry in the noon sunlight. Menion glanced down at her momentarily and smiled reassuringly, holding her closer to him. Beyond the great Outer Wall of the city of Tyrsis, two divisions of the reassembled Border Legion waited patiently for the command that would take them into battle against the awesome Northland army. The huge invasion force had reached the northern banks of the swollen Mermidon River, and even now was beginning to make its crossing. If the Legion could hold the southern bank, even for a few days, it might give the Elven armies a chance to mobilize and march to their aid. Time, Menion thought bitterly—all they needed was just a little more time, and so far they hadn't gotten it. The Border Legion had been reassembled as quickly as possible once the city was secured and Balinor was reinstated as commander, but by that time the advancing Northlanders had already reached the Mermidon and begun preparations for the crossing.

Balinor was now King of Callahorn, though it was anything but a cause for celebration. His brother lay in a coma, weakened and extremely close to death. The best physicians in Tyrsis had examined him with labored patience in an effort to determine the cause of his irrational behavior and after some time had concluded that he had been given a powerful drug over a long period of time to break down his resistance and reduce him, for all practical purposes, to a mindless puppet. Finally, the dosage had been increased to the point where his mind and body had been pushed beyond the point of physical and mental endurance. In the end, his madness was real.

Balinor had listened to their conclusions without comment. An hour earlier, he had found his father in a deserted room in the north tower of the Buckhannah home. The aged King had been dead for several days and a physician's report revealed that he had been systematically poisoned. Stenmin had kept everyone from that room except himself and the already unbalanced Palance, so the secret of Ruhl Buckhannah's death had been easily kept. Had the mystic succeeded in having Balinor killed, it would have been a simple matter to persuade Palance to open the gates to the armies of the Warlock Lord, and in so doing, assure the destruction of Tyrsis. He had nearly succeeded once, and he might still do so. Stenmin had managed to elude the Elven brothers and was hidden somewhere within the city.

In a very real sense, the future of the Southland rested in the hands of the Prince of Callahorn. The people of Tyrsis looked to the Buckhannah family for dependable government and strong leadership. The Border Legion functioned best as a fighting unit when Balinor was in command. Now the giant borderman was the last of his family and the man to whom everyone turned for leadership, whether openly or subconsciously. If anything were to happen to him, the Legion would lose its finest commander and the heart of its fighting strength, while the city would lose the last Buckhannah. The few who fully understood the gravity of the situation realized that Tyrsis must be held against the advancing Northland army, or the Southland would be lost and a wedge driven between the armies of the Elves and the Dwarfs. Allanon had warned them that if this should happen, the Warlock Lord had won. Tyrsis was the key to success or failure, and Balinor was the key to Tyrsis.

Janus Senpre had carried out his part in securing the city earlier that morning. After Menion left him at the gates, he sought out the Legion commanders Fandwick and Ginnisson. Secretly, they reassembled key members of the disbanded Legion and, striking quickly and quietly, seized the gates and the army barracks. Moving rapidly toward the palace, they gained strength almost without opposition until finally the entire city surrounding the Buckhannah family home and gardens was resecured. Waiting just outside the palace grounds for a signal from Menion, the three commanders and their followers heard the cries within of assassination; fearing the worst, they rushed the gates, forcing their way inside just in time to prevent Balinor from catching the fleeing Stenmin. There was almost no loss of life in the brief uprising, and the followers of Palance were either imprisoned or freed to rejoin their old units in the Legion. Already two of the five Legion divisions were reassembled, and the other three would be formed up and properly armed by sunset. But scouts from the city had reported to Balinor the progress of the Northlanders in reaching the Mermidon, and concluded that he must act immediately to prevent the crossing.

Hendel and the Elven brothers lounged restlessly off to the right on the steps of the palace, their faces reflecting mixed emotions. The Dwarf appeared as resolute as ever, his aging countenance implacable as he glanced casually over at the highlander and his beautiful charge. Durin seemed somehow older, his lean Elven features clouded by the knowledge of what lay ahead, while Dayel, though shadowed by the same uncertainty, managed a cheerful smile. Menion shifted his gaze back to Balinor and the Legion commanders. Ginnisson was heavyset with shocking red hair and powerful arms; Fandwick was aged and grizzled with a drooping white mustache and a scowl to match; Acton was a man of medium height and regular appearance, whose horsemanship was said to be matchless; Messaline was tall and broad shouldered, almost arrogant-looking as he rocked carelessly back on his heels while Balinor spoke to them; and last came Janus Senpre, recently promoted to full commander in recognition of his courageous stand at Kern and his vital role in the recapture of Tyrsis. Menion studied them carefully for long minutes as if somehow his visual appraisal could ascertain their worth. Then Balinor turned and walked over to him, motioning for Hendel and the Elves to join them.

"I'm leaving at once for the Mermidon," he informed them quietly when they were all together. Menion started to speak, but Balinor quickly cut him off. "No, Menion, I know what you are going to ask, and the answer is no. You will all remain here in the city. I would trust any one of you with my life, and since my life is of secondary importance in comparison with Tyrsis, I ask you to guard the city instead. If anything should happen to me, you will know best how to continue the battle. Janus remains with you in command of the city defenses, and I have instructed him to confer with you on all matters."

"Eventine will come," Dayel spoke quickly, trying hard to sound cheerful.

Balinor smiled and nodded in agreement.

"Allanon has never failed. He won't fail us now."

"Don't expose yourself unnecessarily," Hendel warned grimly. "This city and its people depend on you. They need you alive."

"Good-bye, old friend." Balinor gripped the Dwarf's hand tightly. "I depend on you most of all. Your experience is twice mine, and you are twice the strategist. Take care."

He turned quickly, motioning for his commanders, and entered the waiting carriage that would convey them to the city gates. Janus Senpre waved reassuringly to Menion as the palace coach drew away, the mounted escort falling into sharp formation to the rear, and the gallant procession galloped with a clashing of iron-shod hooves toward the Sendic Bridge. The four companions and Shirl Ravenlock watched until they were lost from sight and the thunder of the horses had drifted into silence. Then Hendel muttered absently about checking the palace once more for some sign of the missing Stenmin and, without waiting for a response, reentered the Buckhannah home. Durin and Dayel trailed after him, feeling strangely disconsolate. It was the first time they had been separated from Balinor for more than several hours since the long journey from Culhaven had begun many weeks earlier, and it was a disquieting experience to allow him to go on alone to the Mermidon.

Menion knew exactly how they felt, his own restless nature inwardly urging him to go after the borderman, to

join him in the crucial battle against the hordes of the Warlock Lord. But he was nearly exhausted—he had not slept for
almost two days. The strain of the battle above the island of
Kern, the long flight down the Mermidon, and the rapid series of events which had led to the freeing of Balinor and the
others had sapped even his great stamina. Almost drunkenly,
he steered Shirl into the gardens at the side of the palace,
dropping heavily onto a wide stone bench. The girl sat quietly next to him, watching his face as he closed his eyes and
forced his mind to relax.

"I know what you must be thinking, Menion." Her soft
voice drifted gently through his weariness. "You want to be
with him."

The highlander smiled and nodded slowly, his thoughts
hazy and jumbled.

"You must get some sleep, you know."

Again he nodded, and suddenly he thought of Shea.
Where was Shea? Where had the Valeman wandered in his
futile search for the elusive Sword of Shannara? Quickly he
raised himself, snapping awake and turning to Shirl, almost
as if he thought she might not be there. He was exhausted,
but he wanted to talk—he needed to talk, because there
might never be another chance. In low, somber tones he
began to speak to her, telling her about himself and Shea,
unfolding in bits and pieces the friendship that had so
closely bound them in the years they had known each other.
He spoke of the times they had spent in the highlands of
Leah, drifting gradually into the full story behind the journey to Paranor and the search for the Sword. At times he
rambled in vain attempts to explore in depth the rationale
behind feelings they had shared and philosophies they could
not. As the highlander continued, Shirl began to realize that

it was not really Shea that Menion was trying to describe—
it was himself. Finally she stopped him, reaching without
thinking to place a slim hand over his lips.

"He was the only person you ever really got to know,
wasn't he?" she asked quietly. "He was like a brother, and you
feel responsible for what happened to him?"

Menion shrugged disconsolately. "I couldn't have done
anything but what I did. Keeping him in Leah in the first
place would have only prolonged the inevitable. But knowing all that doesn't help. I still feel a sort of . . . guilt . . ."

"If he feels as deeply for you as you do for him, then he
knows in his heart the truth of what you have done, wher-
ever he is now," she responded quickly. "No man can fault
you for the courage you have shown these past five days—
and I love you, Menion Leah."

Menion stared at her stupidly, the sudden declaration
catching him off balance. Laughing at his confusion, the slim
girl wrapped her arms around him, the reddish locks falling
like a soft veil about his face as she clung to him. Menion
held her close for a moment, then gripped her shoulders
gently and pushed her back to study her face and eyes. She
met his gaze squarely.

"I wanted to say it out loud. I wanted you to hear it, Menion. If we are going to die . . ."

She choked suddenly on the words and looked away, and
the wondering Southlander saw tears slowly roll down her
cheeks. He reached up and quickly brushed them away, smiling in the old way as he raised himself to his feet, drawing
her up with him.

"I came a long, long way," he murmured gently. "I could
have been dead a hundred times, but I survived. I've seen the
evil there is in this world and in worlds that mortals only

dream exist. There is nothing that can hurt us. Love supplies a kind of strength that can withstand even death. But you need a little faith. Just believe, Shirl. Believe in us."

She smiled in spite of herself.

"I believe in you, Menion Leah. Now you remember to believe in yourself."

The weary highlander smiled back at her, gripping her hands tightly. She was the most beautiful woman he had ever seen, and he loved her as much as his own life. He leaned down and kissed her warmly.

"It will be all right," he assured her quietly. "It will all work out."

They remained a few minutes longer in the solitude of the gardens, talking quietly and absently following the little paths that wound through the warm, fragrant summer flowers. But Menion was fighting to remain awake, and Shirl was quick to demand that he get some sleep while he had the opportunity. Still smiling to himself, he retired to his bedchamber in the palace, where he collapsed, still fully clothed, onto one of the wide, soft beds and immediately fell into a deep, dreamless slumber. While he slept, the hours of the afternoon drifted slowly away, the sun slipping into the western sky and finally sinking in a brilliant scarlet blaze beneath the horizon. At the coming of complete darkness, the highlander awoke, fully rested but strangely disturbed. He hastened to find Shirl, and together they walked the almost deserted corridors of the Buckhannah home, searching for Hendel and the Elven brothers. The long hallways echoed the low tapping of their boots as they hastened past statuelike sentries and darkened rooms, pausing only momentarily to observe the still, deathlike form of Palance Buckhannah, as his physicians watched over him with expressionless faces.

His condition remained unchanged, his wounded body and shattered spirit struggling to survive the crushing weight of a death that was slowly, inevitably pushing down against him. When the two silent forms moved at last from his bedside, there were tears again in Shirl's dark eyes.

Convinced that his friends had gone to the city gates to await the return of the Prince of Callahorn, Menion saddled two horses and the couple rode toward the Tyrsian Way. It was a cool, cloudless night lighted by the silver shimmer of the moon and stars, and the towers of the city stood clearly outlined against the sky. As the horses swung onto the Bridge of Sendic, Menion felt the welcome coolness of a friendly night breeze blowing in soothing waves over his flushed face. It was unusually quiet along the Tyrsian Way, the streets deserted and the houses that lined the Way lighted but empty of laughter and friendly conversation. An audible hush had settled over the besieged city, a grim whispering solitude that hovered and waited for the death that came with battle. The riders rode anxiously through this eerie silence, trying to find some comfort in the beauty of the starlit sky that seemed to promise a thousand tomorrows for the races. The towering heights of the Outer Wall loomed blackly in the distance, and on the parapets burned hundreds of torches, lighting the way home to the soldiers of Tyrsis. They had been gone a long time, Menion thought to himself. But perhaps they had been more successful than anyone had dared to hope. Perhaps they had held the Mermidon against the Northland hordes. . . .

Moments later the riders were dismounting at the mammoth gates of the giant wall. The Legion barracks were alive with activity as the restless garrison worked feverishly in preparation for the battle to come. There were knots of soldiers at every turn, and it was with considerable difficulty that Menion and Shirl finally managed to reach the ramparts at the top of the broad walls, where they were greeted warmly by Janus Senpre. The youthful commander had maintained his vigilant lookout without rest since Balinor had departed, and the slim face was lined with weariness and anxiety. After a few moments, Durin and Hendel appeared out of the darkness to join them, followed somewhat later by a wandering Dayel. The little group stood in silence and stared into the darkness that ran northward to the Mermidon and the Border Legion. From far away they could hear the muffled shouts and cries of men fighting, the sounds carried tauntingly by the fresh night wind to the straining ears of those who waited.

Janus remarked absently that he had sent out half a dozen scouts in an effort to discover what was happening at the river, but none had returned—an ominous sign. He had decided several times to go himself, but a gruff Hendel had reminded him each time that he had been placed in charge of the defense of Tyrsis, and each time he had reluctantly discarded the idea. Durin had resolved in his own mind that if Balinor did not return by midnight, he was going out to search for his friend. An Elf could travel undetected through almost any opposition. But for the time being, he waited like the others in growing apprehension. Shirl spoke briefly of the unchanged condition of Palance Buckhannah, but she received only a disinterested response and quickly gave up the impossible task of trying to take their minds off the battle at the river. The little group waited one hour, then two. The sounds had grown slowly louder and more desperate, and it seemed that the fighting had moved closer to the city.

Then suddenly a vast formation of horsemen and foot

soldiers appeared out of the darkness almost directly in front of the bluff, winding in staggered columns onto the wide stone rampway leading into the city. Their approach had been almost imperceptible, and their unexpected appearance from out of nowhere caused everyone atop the Outer Wall to gasp audibly. Janus Senpre sprang in alarm toward the mechanism that secured the iron fastenings to the giant gates, fearful that somehow the enemy had managed to outflank Balinor. But Hendel quietly called him back. He recognized what was happening even before the others suspected. Leaning out over the rim of the wall, the Dwarf called down sharply in his own language, and received an almost instant response. Nodding grimly to the others, Hendel pointed to the tall rider who had moved to the point of the long column. In the soft moonlight, the dust-covered face of Balinor peered upward, the grim visage confirming what they all had suspected the moment they recognized him. The Border Legion had failed to hold the Mermidon, and the army of the Warlock Lord was moving against Tyrsis.

It was nearly midnight when the five who remained together of the little band from Culhaven gathered in a small, secluded dining room in the Buckhannah family home for a brief evening meal. The long afternoon and evening battle to hold the Mermidon against the Northland army had been lost, although the cost in lives to the enemy had been terrible. For a while it appeared that the veteran soldiers of the Border Legion would succeed in preventing the floundering Northlanders from gaining the southern bank of the swift river. But there were thousands of the enemy, and where hundreds failed, thousands ultimately succeeded. Acton's horsemen had swept lightninglike along the fringes of the

Legion line, shattering every attempt by the enemy to outflank the entrenched foot soldiers. Advances into the heart of
the Southland ranks had resulted in the death of hundreds of
Trolls and Gnomes. It was the most dreadful slaughter Balinor had ever witnessed, and eventually the Mermidon began
to change color with the blood of the wounded and dying.
And still they kept trying—trying as if they were mindless
creatures without feeling, without understanding, without
human fear. The power of the Warlock Lord had so enslaved
the collective mortal mind of the giant army that even
death had no meaning. Finally a large band of ferocious
Rock Trolls breached the far right tip of the Legion's line
of defense; although they were slain almost to a man, the
diversionary tactic forced the Tyrsians to shorten their left
flank. In the end, the Northlanders were across.

By this time it was almost sunset, and Balinor quickly
realized that even the finest soldiers in the world would be
unable to retake and hold the southern bank once darkness
set in. The Legion had suffered only mild losses during the
afternoon's fighting, and so he ordered the two divisions to
fall back to a small rise several hundred yards south of the
Mermidon and reassemble in battle formation. He kept the
cavalry busy on the left and right flanks, making short rushes
at the enemy to keep them off balance and to prevent an
organized counterthrust. Then he waited for darkness. The
hordes of the Northland army began to cross in force as twilight fell; in mingled astonishment and fear, the men of the
Border Legion watched as the hundreds that had first
crossed turned to thousands and still they kept coming. It
was a frightening spectacle the bordermen beheld—an army
of such incredible size that it completely covered the land on
both sides of the Mermidon as far as the eye could see.

But its size hampered its maneuverability, and the chain of command seemed disorganized and confused. There was no concentrated effort made to dislodge the entrenched Tyrsians from the small rise. Instead the bulk of the army milled about on the banks of the southern shore after crossing, as if waiting for someone to tell them what to do next. Several squads of heavily armed Trolls made a series of rushes at the Legion command, but they were equally matched in numbers and the veteran soldiers quickly repelled them. When darkness came at last, the enemy army suddenly began to organize into columns five deep, and Balinor knew that the first sustained rush would break the Legion to pieces.

With the skill and daring that had made him the spirit behind the fabled Border Legion and the finest field commander in the Southland, the Prince of Callahorn began to execute a most difficult tactical maneuver. Without waiting for the enemy to strike, he suddenly divided his army and attacked far to the right and left of the Northland columns. Striking sharply in short feints, and taking full advantage of the darkness, in terrain every borderman knew well, the soldiers of the Legion drew in the flanks of the enemy to form a ragged half circle. Each time the circle grew tighter and each time the Tyrsians retreated a little farther. Balinor and Fandwick held the left flank while Acton and Messaline commanded the right.

The enraged enemy began to charge madly, stumbling awkwardly over the unfamiliar ground in the growing darkness, the retreating soldiers of the Legion always just a few steps out of reach. Slowly Balinor drew his flanks in and narrowed his lines, pulling the searching Northlanders in with him. Then, when the foot soldiers had completely fallen back in retreat, covered by the darkness and the battle behind them, the skilled cavalry drew their lines together in a final feint and slipped from between the jaws of the closing enemy trap and was gone. Suddenly the right and left flanks of the harried Northland army met, each believing that the other was the hated enemy that had eluded it for several hours. Without hesitating, they attacked.

How many Trolls and Gnomes were slain by their own people would never be known, but the fighting was still raging when Balinor and the two divisions of the Border Legion arrived safely at the gates of Tyrsis. The horses' hooves and soldiers' feet had been muffled to cover their retreat. With the exception of a squad of horsemen who had strayed too far west and been cut off and decimated, the Legion had escaped intact. Yet the damage done to the mammoth Northland army had not stopped its advance, and the Mermidon, the first line of defense to the city of Tyrsis, had been lost.

Now the vast encampment of the enemy sprawled on the grasslands below the city, the night fires burning as far as the eye could see through the moonlit darkness. At dawn the assault on Tyrsis would begin as the combined strength of thousands of Trolls and Gnomes, obedient to the will of the Warlock Lord, hurled itself against the towering band of stone and iron that formed the Outer Wall. One would eventually shatter.

Hendel, sitting thoughtfully across from Balinor at the small dining table, recalled again the ominous sensation he had felt earlier that day while inspecting with Janus Senpre the fortifications of the great city. Unquestionably, the Outer Wall was a formidable barrier, but there was something wrong. He had been unable to put his finger on exactly what was causing his uneasiness; but even now, in the solitude of the dining room and the warm companionship of his friends, he could not shake the nagging suspicion that something vital had been overlooked in preparing for the long siege that lay ahead.

Mentally, he retraced the lines of defense protecting the sprawling city. At the edge of the bluff, the men of Tyrsis had erected a low bulwark to prevent the enemy from gaining a foothold on the plateau. If the Northlanders could not be contained on the grasslands below the bluff, then the Border Legion would fall back into the city proper and rely on the mammoth Outer Wall to halt the enemy advance. The rear approach to Tyrsis was cut off by the sheer cliffs that rose hundreds of feet into the air directly behind the palace grounds. Balinor had assured him that the cliffs could not be scaled; they were like smooth sheets of rock, completely without the normal nooks and crannies that would permit a foothold. The defenses surrounding Tyrsis should be impenetrable, and yet Hendel remained dissatisfied.

For a moment his thoughts drifted back to his homeland—to Culhaven and to his family, whom he hadn't seen in weeks. He had never spent much time with them, his whole life expended in the ceaseless border wars in the Anar. He missed the woodlands and the green shading that came with the spring and summer months, and he suddenly wondered how he had let so much time pass without a visit home. Perhaps he would never get back. The thought swept through his mind and vanished; he had no time for regrets.

Durin and Dayel conversed soberly with Balinor, their own thoughts centered on the Westland. Dayel, like Hendel, was thinking of his home. He was frightened of the battle that lay ahead, but he accepted his fear, encouraged by the presence of the others and determined that he would do no less than they in standing firm against the army that had come to destroy them. He thought quietly of Lynliss, her shy, warm face a permanent fixture in his mind. He would be fighting for her safety as well as his own. Durin studied his brother, noting the sudden smile, and he knew without asking that the youth was thinking of the Elven girl he was to marry. Nothing was more important to Durin than the safety of Dayel; from the beginning he had made a point of staying close to his brother to protect him. Several times during the long journey to Paranor, they had nearly lost their lives. Tomorrow would bring still greater danger, and once again, Durin would be watching over his brother.

Briefly he thought of Eventine and the mighty Elven armies, wondering if they would reach Tyrsis in time. Without their great strength to supplement the Border Legion, the hordes of the Warlock Lord would eventually break through the city's defenses. He picked up his wineglass and drank deeply, the liquid warm in his throat. His sharp eyes surveyed the faces of the others and came to rest momentarily on the troubled face of Menion Leah.

The lean highlander had devoured his dinner ravenously, having eaten nothing for almost twenty-four hours. Finishing long before his companions, he had contented himself with a fresh glass of wine, directing continual questions to Balinor about the afternoon's battle. Now, in the quiet hours of early morning, with dinner completed and the wine seeping through him like a slow drowsiness, it suddenly occurred to him that the key to everything that had happened since Culhaven, and everything that would happen in the days remaining, was Allanon. He could not bring himself to think any more of Shea and the Sword, nor even of Shirl. He could only see in the forefront of his mind the dark, forbidding figure of the mysterious Druid. Allanon held the answers to every question. He alone knew the secret of the talisman men called the Sword of Shannara. He alone knew the purpose behind the strange appearance of the shrouded wraith in the Valley of Shale—the Druid Bremen, a man over five hundred years dead. He alone, in every instance, along every step of the dangerous journey to Paranor, had known what to expect and how to deal with it. Yet the man himself had remained an enigma.

Now he was gone from them, and only Flick, if he were still alive, could ask him what was going to happen to them. They all depended on Allanon for survival—but what would the giant Druid do? What was left to him when the Sword of Shannara was lost? What was left when the young heir of Jerle Shannara was missing and probably dead? Menion bit his lip in anger as the hated thought slipped quickly through his mind and was banished. Shea had to be alive!

Menion cursed everything that had brought them all to this sorry end. They had allowed themselves to be backed into a corner. There was only one path still open to them. In the holocaust of tomorrow's battle, human beings would die, and few, if any, would know the reason. It was an unavoidable part of war, that men should die for unknown reasons—it had been happening for centuries. But this war was something beyond human comprehension, this war between a substanceless spirit being and mortals. How could evil such as the Warlock Lord be destroyed when it could not even be understood? Only Allanon seemed to fully appreciate the nature of the creature. But where was the Druid when they needed him most?

The candles burned low on the table before them, and the darkness of the secluded room deepened. On the wood and tapestry-decorated walls, torches sputtered slowly in

their iron racks, and the five voices dropped to low mur-
murs, hushed as if the night were a child in danger of being
unexpectedly awakened. The city of Tyrsis slept now, and in
the grasslands beyond, the Northland army. In the peace and
solitude of the moonlit night, it seemed that all forms of life
were at rest, and that war, with its promise of death and pain,
was merely a vague, nearly forgotten memory of years past.
But the five who spoke in quiet tones of better days and the
friendship shared could not, even for a few moments, completely stifle the lingering realization that the horror of war
was no more distant than the sunrise and as inevitable as the
darkness of the Warlock Lord, reaching slowly, inexorably
from out of the north to snuff out their frail lives.

O N THE MORNING of the third day of the search for Orl
Fane, the torrential rains that had swept through the vastness of the barren Northland subsided, and the sun reappeared as a dim, fuzzy ball of white fire, burning through the
misty darkness left with the passing of the Warlock Lord's
black wall to the mud and rock-strewn terrain with the fury
of an oven. The storm had left the topography of the land
completely altered, the rains sweeping away almost every
distinguishable landmark and leaving only four identical
horizons of rocky hillocks and muddied valleys.

At first the appearance of the sun was a welcome sight.
The heat from its rays penetrated the hateful gloom that had
become permanently affixed to the barren surface of the
earth to warm away the chill left by the now-vanished storm
as the temperature rose steadily, and the character of the
land began to alter once more. But in an hour's time, the
temperature had risen thirty degrees and was continuing to
rise unchecked. The rivers that washed through the winding
gullies carved out by the force of the rain began to steam and
mist in the heat, and the humidity soared, drenching everything in a new, even more uncomfortable wetness.

The little plant life born in the aftermath of the devastating storm withered and died in suffocation, cut off from the sun's life–giving brightness and choked by the stifling heat that permeated the graying mist. The muddied earth lay unprotected from the heat and soon baked into a cracked, hardened clay that would support no life. The rivers and lakes and puddles began to dry up quickly, and in almost no time had disappeared altogether. The exposed surface of the huge boulders that dotted the parched land quickly absorbed the burning heat like iron settled in live coals. Slowly, inexorably the land became what it had been before the rains had swept its surface—a dry, barren slab of earth, devoid of life, silent and forbidding beneath a vast, cloudless sky. The only movement came from the slow, unchanging arc of an ageless, disinterested sun as it followed its ceaseless path from east to west, turning days into years and years into centuries.

Three bent figures stepped gingerly from beneath the shelter of a rocky alcove cut in the side of one of the countless, nondescript hillocks, their cramped bodies straightening slowly, their eyes peering grimly into the unbroken wall of mist. They stood for long moments in the lifeless gloom, staring into the dying land that seemed to stretch on forever, a dismal graveyard of rocky mounds that covered the mortal remains of those who had ventured into this forbidden kingdom. There was absolute silence filtering evilly through the misty grayness, hanging its unspoken warning of death in the minds of the three living creatures. They stood in apprehensive watchfulness, staring at the wasteland surrounding them.

Shea turned to his companions. Panamon Creel was arching his back and rubbing his limbs in an effort to awaken the benumbed muscles. His dark hair was shaggy and unkempt, his broad face shaded by a three-day beard.

He had a haggard look about him, but the keen eyes burned warily as he met Shea's inquisitive stare. The massive Keltset had moved noiselessly to the summit of the hill and was surveying the northern horizon.

They had huddled in the sparse shelter of their rocky alcove for almost three days while the fierce Northland storm had raged unchecked through the empty lands about them. Three days lost in the pursuit of Orl Fane and the Sword of Shannara—three days during which all traces of the elusive Gnome had been thoroughly obliterated. They had crouched restlessly amid the boulders, eating because it was necessary, sleeping because there was nothing else to do. Talking had given Shea and Panamon a greater understanding of each other, though Keltset still remained a complete enigma. Shea persisted in his belief that they should have ignored the storm and pursued their quarry, but Panamon had refused to discuss the idea. No one could travel far in such a storm, and Orl Fane would be forced to seek shelter or risk being caught in a mud slide or drowned in the swift gully rivers. In any event, the thief had calmly reasoned, the Gnome would have made little progress. Keltset descended from the crest of the hill, making a quick sweeping gesture with one hand. The horizon was clear.

There was no further discussion of what should be done. It was already decided. Picking up their meager possessions, they trudged briskly down the side of the steep embankment, angling northward. For once Shea and Panamon were in complete agreement. The search for the Sword of Shannara had become more than a matter of injured pride, more than a mission to seek out a mysterious talisman. It had become a dangerous, frantic hunt for the one means, however questionable, by which they might stay alive in this savage land.

The fortress of the Warlock Lord lay amid the tall, black peaks directly north. Behind them lay the deadly wall of mist that marked the outer boundaries of the Skull Kingdom. To escape this hated land, they would have to pass one way or the other. The obvious choice was to go back through the misty darkness, but while the Elfstones might show them a passage to the Southland, using them would also reveal their presence to the spirit world. Allanon had told Shea so at Culhaven, and he in turn had told Panamon. The Sword of Shannara was the one weapon that could protect them from the Warlock Lord, and if they had it in their possession, they could be assured of at least a fighting chance. The basic plan was to regain possession of the talisman and escape back through the wall of darkness as quickly as possible. It was hardly a brilliant strategy, but under the circumstances it would have to do.

Traveling was as difficult as it had been prior to the storm. The ground was hard and coated with rubble and loose topsoil that made the footing treacherous. Scrambling and clawing their way over the rough terrain, the three were quickly covered with dirt and bruised by continual falls. Because of the unevenness of the topography, it was difficult to keep their bearings and nearly impossible to calculate their progress. Landmarks were nonexistent and the country looked almost exactly the same in every direction. The minutes wore away with agonizing slowness, and still they discovered nothing. The humidity continued to rise and the garments worn by the three men were quickly soaked through with sweat. They removed their cloaks and tied them on their backs; it would be cold again when night descended.

"This is the place we last saw him."

Panamon stood motionlessly at the summit of the broad hill they had just scaled, breathing heavily. Shea reached his side and glanced about in disbelief. All the surrounding hills looked exactly the same as this one, save for small variations in size and shape. He stared dubiously at the horizon. He wasn't even sure where they had come from.

"Keltset, what do you see?" the other man demanded.

The Rock Troll strode slowly about the hilltop, scanning the ground for any trace left by the passage of the little Gnome, but the storm appeared to have erased any signs. He moved about noiselessly for several minutes more, then turned to them and shook his head negatively. Panamon's dirt-stained face burned red in sudden anger.

"He was here. We'll walk on a bit farther."

They moved ahead in silence, scrambling unceremoniously down one hill and up the next. There was no further discussion. There was nothing further to be said. If Panamon were mistaken, nobody had any better idea, except to keep looking. An hour crawled by as they labored northward. Still there was nothing. Shea began to realize the hopelessness of their task. It would be impossible to search all of the land stretching east and west; if the wily Gnome had traveled just fifty yards to either side of them, they would probably never know he had gone that way. Perhaps he had been buried in a mud slide during the storm along with the Sword and they would never find him.

Shea's muscles ached from the strenuous climbing, and he considered calling a brief halt to reassess their decision to proceed in this direction. Perhaps they should try to cut across the elusive trail. Yet a glance at Panamon's dark face quickly dissuaded the Valeman from even suggesting such an action. The tall adventurer had the same look in his face Shea had seen just before he had destroyed the Gnomes days ago. He was the hunter once more. If Panamon found him, Orl Fane was a dead man. Shea shuddered involuntarily and looked away.

Several hills later, they found a piece of what they were searching for. Keltset spotted it from atop a small hillock, his sharp eyes picking out the foreign object as it lay half buried in dust at the bottom of a small ravine. Directing the other two, he slid quickly down the rock-strewn hill and rushed eagerly over to the discarded object, snatching it up and holding it out to them. It was a large strip of cloth—cloth that had once been the major portion of a tunic sleeve. They stared at it quietly for a moment, and then Shea looked at Keltset for confirmation that it was indeed Orl Fane's. The giant Troll nodded solemnly. Panamon Creel impaled the piece of cloth on the end of his pike, smiling grimly.

"So we've found him again. This time he won't get away!"

But they didn't find him that day, nor did they discover any further signs of his passing. In the heavy dust, the Gnome's footprints would have clearly shown, yet there were none. Despite Panamon's earlier opinion, Orl Fane had somehow wandered on during the storm, escaping both mud slides and drowning. The rain had washed away his tracks but, with freakish perversity, had left uncovered the torn sleeve. It could have been washed down from anywhere, so there was no way to tell which direction the Gnome had come from or gone. By nightfall, the blackness shrouding the land was so heavy that it was impossible to see more than several feet, and the search was reluctantly abandoned for the night. With Keltset standing the first watch, Panamon and Shea collapsed in near exhaustion and fell asleep almost instantly. The night air was cool, though the humidity of the day lingered on, and all three wrapped themselves once again in the half-dry hunting cloaks.

The morning returned all too swiftly in the familiar graying haze. This day was not as humid as the previous one, but it was no more cheerful; the sun was still nearly blotted out by the leaden mist that hung immovably overhead. The same eerie silence persisted and the three men stared about with a feeling of complete isolation from the living world. The vast emptiness was beginning to have a noticeable effect on both Shea and Panamon Creel. Shea had grown edgy and nervous in these past several days and the normally cheerful and talkative Panamon had lapsed into almost total silence. Keltset alone retained his usual demeanor, his face as bland and implacable as ever.

A short breakfast was consumed without interest, and the search began again. They resumed the hunt almost with distaste; their common desire was to end this wearing trek quickly. They went ahead partly out of a sense of self-preservation and partly because they had nowhere else to go. Although neither realized it, both Panamon and Shea were beginning to wonder why Keltset continued the pursuit. He was in his own country and could probably have survived alone, had he chosen to go his own way. The two men had tried unsuccessfully to decipher Keltset's reasons for continuing on with them during the three-day rain, and now, too worn to reason the matter further, they had fallen back on suspicious acceptance of his presence and a growing determination that they would know who and what he was before this journey ended. They plodded on through the dust and the haze as the morning drifted dully into noonday.

It was totally unexpected when Panamon suddenly drew up short.

"Tracks!"

The tall thief let out a wild yell of delight and charged madly into the small draw to their left, leaving both Keltset and Shea staring after him in amazement. Moments later the trio knelt eagerly over a set of clearly defined footprints outlined in the heavy dust. There was no mistaking their origin; even Shea recognized that they were made by Gnome boots, worn and cracked about the heels. The trail they left was undisguised, leading generally northward, but weaving badly as if the destination of the man passing were no longer certain. It almost appeared as if Orl Fane were wandering aimlessly. They paused a moment longer and then rose hurriedly at Panamon's urgent command. The tracks were only hours old and, judging from their meandering nature, the elusive Orl Fane could be overtaken easily. Panamon could only thinly disguise the almost vicious glee that surged through his revitalized body as he saw the end of the long hunt in sight. Without speaking further, the three hitched up their cumbersome gear and moved northward in grim resolution. This was the day they would catch Orl Fane.

The trail left by the little Gnome wound in erratically confusing fashion through the dusty hills of the lower Northland. At times the three found themselves traveling almost directly eastward, and once they were turned about entirely. The afternoon wore on with tedious precision, and while Keltset indicated that the footprints were growing fresher, it appeared that they were still not gaining rapidly. If nightfall set in before they had caught up with their quarry, they might very well lose him once again. Twice before they had been on the verge of catching him, and each time an unexpected occurrence had forced them temporarily to abandon the search. They were not in the mood to have this happen a third time, and Shea had inwardly vowed that, if need be, he would track Orl Fane even in total darkness.

The giant peaks of the forbidding Skull Kingdom loomed menacingly in the distance, their black, razor tips jutting knifelike into the horizon. There was a sense of fear in the mind of the Valeman that he could not shake, a fear that had grown steadily stronger as the three men had pushed deeper into the Northland. He had begun to feel that he was undertaking much more than he had originally imagined, that somehow the search for Orl Fane and the Sword of Shannara was only a small part of a much larger scheme of events. He was not yet panicked by what he felt, but he was prodded by an urgent need to finish this insane chase and turn back to his own land.

It was midafternoon when the hilly terrain began to level off into a rolling plainland that enabled the three men to see for greater distances and to walk upright in an almost relaxed manner for the first time since they had passed through the black wall. The country ahead spread out before them with breathtaking starkness, a bleak, empty plain of brown earth and gray rock that rolled unevenly northward toward the tall peaks that bordered the Skull Kingdom and the home of the Warlock Lord. These vast flatlands diminished the farther north the eye traveled, breaking around masses of rock and mountainous ridgeland that led in stepping-stone manner to the awesome peaks beyond. The entire expanse, naked, hot, and desolate, lay masked in the same eerie, deathly silence. Nothing moved, no creature stirred, no insect hummed, no bird flew, not even the wind brushed against the layered dust. Everywhere there was the same blasted emptiness, unmarked by life, shrouded with death. The winding tracks of Orl Fane led into this vastness and disappeared far in the distance. It was as if the land had swallowed him up.

The hunters paused for several long minutes, their faces mirroring their obvious reluctance to proceed into this unfriendly land. But there was little time for weighing the merits of the matter, and they moved ahead. The twisting path was visible for a greater distance in this rolling plainland, and the three pursuers were able to track on a more direct course. They began to make up time quickly. Less than two hours later Keltset indicated that they were no more than an hour behind their quarry. Dusk was rapidly approaching, the sun dipping behind a broken horizon far to the west. The dim twilight was masked further still by the ever-present gray haze, and the terrain was beginning to take on a peculiarly fuzzy appearance.

The trio had followed the Gnome's trail into a deep draw that was formed by a series of high ridges cropped by sharp overhangs and great, jutting rock formations. The fading sunlight was lost almost entirely in the shadows of the darkened valley, and Panamon Creel, who had eagerly taken the lead sometime earlier, was forced to squint sharply to find the outline of the footprints in the heavy dust. They slowed to a halting walk as the thief bent closer to the earth. So intent was Panamon Creel on studying the tracks immediately before him that it came as a shock when the prints abruptly ended. Shea and Keltset were at his side instantly, and it was only after a careful study of the ground ahead of them that they were able to discover that someone had methodically brushed away all further traces of the little Gnome's passing.

It was in that same instant that the huge, dark forms

began to detach themselves from the shadows of the draw, lumbering ponderously forward in the deepening twilight. Shea saw them first, but believed his eyes were playing tricks on him. Panamon was quicker to realize what was happening. Springing upright, the thief drew out the great broadsword and raised his pike. He might have made a rush to break through the tightening ring, but the normally predictable Keltset did a surprising thing. Springing quickly forward, he pulled the astonished thief back. Panamon stared incredulously at his silent companion, then reluctantly lowered his weapons. There were at least a dozen forms standing guardedly all around the three men, and even in the hazy twilight a terrified Shea realized that they had been discovered by a band of giant Trolls.

The company of weary Elven riders reined in their sweating mounts and gazed absently down the valley slopes into the broad length of the Rhenn. Two miles of empty valley stretched eastward before them, the high slopes to either side cresting in sharp ridges lined with thinning stretches of trees and scrub brush. The legendary pass had served for over a thousand years as the gateway from the lower Streleheim Plains to the great forests of the Westland, a natural door to the homeland of the Elves. It was in this famous pass that the awesome might of the armies of the Warlock Lord had been broken in defeat by the Elven legions and Jerle Shannara. It was here that Brona had faced and run from the aged Bremen and the mysterious power of the Sword of Shannara—run with his great armies back into the plainlands, only to be halted by advancing Dwarf armies, trapped, and destroyed. The Pass of Rhenn had seen the beginning of the downfall of the greatest threat the world had encoun-

tered since the devastating Great Wars, and the people of all
the races looked upon this peaceful valley as a historic landmark. It was a natural monument of mankind's history that
some had journeyed halfway around the world to see just so
that they, too, might feel somehow a part of that terrible
event.

Jon Lin Sandor gave the order to dismount, and the
Elven riders climbed down gratefully. His concern was not
with the history of the past but with the immediate future.
Worriedly, he stared at the heavy black wall descending from
the Northland across the Plains of Streleheim, its hazy
shadow drawing daily nearer to the borders of the Westland
and the home of the Elves. His sharp eyes peered far into the
eastern horizon where the darkness had already permeated
into the forests surrounding the ancient fortress of Paranor.
He shook his head bitterly and cursed the day he had permitted himself to leave the side of his King and oldest friend.
He had grown to manhood with Eventine, and when his
friend became King he had stayed with him as his personal
counselor and self-appointed watchdog. Together they had
prepared for the invasion of the armies of Brona, the Spirit
Lord they had once believed destroyed in the Second War of
the Races. The mysterious wanderer Allanon had warned the
Elven people, and while some had scoffed in misconceived
disdain, Eventine had known better. Allanon had never been
wrong; his ability to see into the future was uncanny, but un-
erringly accurate.

The Elven people had followed Eventine's advice and
they had prepared for war, but the invasion did not come as
expected. Then Paranor had fallen and with it the Sword of
Shannara. Again Allanon had come to them, asking that they
patrol the Plains of Streleheim above Paranor to guard

against any attempt by the Gnomes holding the Druid fortress to move the Sword northward to the castle of the Warlock Lord. Again they had obeyed without question.

But the unexpected had happened, and it had happened while Jon Lin Sandor was away from the King. The Gnomes entrenched at Paranor had unexpectedly decided to break for the safety of the deep Northland, and three heavy patrols made a rush at the Elven lines. Eventine and Jon Lin had led separate commands to intercept two of these forces and would have destroyed the Gnomes easily had it not been for the planned intervention of a combined army of Gnomes and Trolls detached from the now advancing Northland army of the Warlock Lord. Jon Lin's command was nearly annihilated, and he barely escaped with his life. He had been unable to reach Eventine, and the Elven King had disappeared with his entire patrol. Jon Lin Sandor had been searching for him for nearly three days.

"We will find him, Jon Lin. He is not an easy one to kill. He will find a way to survive."

The grim Elf nodded with a barely perceptible shake of his close-cropped head, his darting eyes glancing quickly at the young face of the man standing next to him.

"It's a strange thing, but I know he's alive," the other continued soberly. "I can't really explain how I know—it's just something I can sense."

Breen Elessedil was Eventine's younger brother; he was also the next King of the Westland Elves if his brother were dead. It was a position he was not yet ready for and quite honestly did not want. Since Eventine's disappearance he had done nothing to assume command of the languishing Elven armies or of the dismayed King's Council, but had joined immediately in the search for his brother. As a result, the Elven government was in a state of near chaos, and what had only two weeks earlier been a people united against the imminent threat of invasion from the north was now an unsure, divided cluster of separated groups, badly frightened because there was no one prepared to assume leadership of the government.

The Elven people would not panic altogether; they were far too disciplined to allow matters to fall apart totally. But Eventine had been an undeniably powerful personality, and the people had been united solidly behind him since his ascension to the throne. Young, but possessing unusual strength of character and an infallible common sense, he had always been there to advise them and they had always listened. The rumors of his disappearance had shaken the people badly.

But neither Breen Elessedil nor Jon Lin had time to worry about anything but finding the missing King. After skirting Gnome patrols and the main body of the Northland army while they searched, the haggard survivors of the decimated Elven patrols had returned briefly to the tiny outland village of Koos, where they had obtained fresh horses and supplies. Now they were on their way back to pick up the search once more.

Jon Lin Sandor believed he knew where Eventine would be found, if he were still alive. The giant Northland army had moved south toward the Kingdom of Callahorn almost a week earlier, and it would pass no farther until the famed Border Legion had been destroyed. It was probable that if Eventine were a prisoner, as both Breen and he now believed must be the case, then they would find him with the commanders of Brona's invasion force as a hostage of great bargaining value. With Eventine Elessedil defeated, cities whose leaders were lesser men would be more willing to consider surrender.

In any event, the Warlock Lord recognized the importance of Eventine to the Elven people. He was the most revered and beloved leader the Elves had known since Jerle Shannara, and they would do almost anything to have him back safely. Dead, he would serve no purpose to the Spirit King, and his execution might so enrage the Elves that they would reunite in their common desire to destroy him. But alive, Eventine was of immeasurable worth, for the Elven people would not risk injury to their favorite son. Jon Lin Sandor and Breen Elessedil harbored no false illusions that Eventine would be safely returned to them, even if the army did not intervene in the Southland invasion. They were acting on their own initiative, gambling that they could find their friend and brother before his usefulness was ended— before the Southland fell.

"That's enough. Mount up!"

Jon Lin's impatient voice cut through the momentary stillness with biting sharpness, and the lounging riders leaped to their feet hurriedly in response. He stared a final time at the distant blackness, then turned and vaulted easily onto his waiting mount, gathering the reins in one swift motion. Breen was already at his side and seconds later the small body of horsemen was moving down the valley corridor at a fast trot. It was a gray morning, the air tinged with the pungent smell of last night's rain, still lingering on the plainlands. The tall grass was wet and yielding beneath the sharp hooves of the passing horses, muffling their impact. Far to the south a trace of deep blue sky could be seen beyond the clouds. It was a cool day, and the Elves rode comfortably in the moderate temperatures.

They reached the end of the valley quickly, pulling their eager mounts to a slow trot as they entered the eastern corridor of the pass. The riders talked among themselves, though in low tones, for the borders of the Northland lay just beyond the pass gateway. The line of horsemen wound snakelike through the high ridges framing the eastern entryway, and moments later emerged onto the vast expanse of the Plains of Streleheim. Jon Lin glanced almost casually across the emptiness that stretched out before him, and then abruptly reined in his horse.

"Breen—a horseman!"

Instantly the other was at his side and together they peered at the distant rider moving rapidly toward them. The Elves stared curiously, unable to make out the features of the advancing horseman in the hazy light. For one brief instant, Breen Elessedil was convinced it was his brother returning, but a moment later his hopes faded as he realized the man was too small to be Eventine. He was certainly no horseman. As he came up to them, he was hanging on to both the reins and the saddle horn for dear life, his broad face flushed and sweating from the effort. He was no Elf; he was a Southlander.

He brought his mount to a jolting halt in front of the Elven band, pausing to catch his breath before speaking. He studied the amused faces confronting him and his face turned a shade redder.

"I met a man a few days earlier," the stranger began. Then he hesitated to be certain he had their attention. "He asked me to seek out the right arm of the Elven King."

The looks of amusement faded instantly as the Elven riders leaned forward.

"I am Jon Lin Sandor," the patrol commander acknowledged quietly.

The exhausted rider sighed gratefully and nodded.

"I'm Flick Ohmsford, and I've come all the way from Callahorn to find you." With no little effort he dismounted and rubbed his aching backside. "If you'll give me a few minutes' rest, I'll take you to Eventine."

Shea marched in silence between two of his giant Troll captors, unable to shake the feeling that Keltset had betrayed them. The ambush had been cleverly sprung, but they might at least have attempted to fight their way clear. Instead, on Keltset's unexpected command, they had offered no resistance, allowing themselves to be willingly disarmed. Shea had hoped that Keltset might know one of the Trolls in the raiding party or that, being of the same race, he could reason with them and secure their release. But the giant Troll had not even tried to communicate with his captors, docilely permitting them to bind his hands without the slightest struggle. Panamon Creel and Shea had their weapons removed and their hands tied, and the three captives were marched northward into the barren flatlands. The little Valeman still had possession of the Elfstones, but they were useless against the Trolls.

He studied the broad back of Panamon, who was walking directly in front of him, wondering what the irascible thief's thoughts must be. The man had been so astonished at his companion's quick surrender that he had not spoken one word since. Obviously he could not bring himself to believe that he had so misjudged the silent giant, whose life he had saved and whose friendship he had valued. The Troll's behavior was a complete mystery to them both; but, whereas Shea was merely confused, Panamon Creel was deeply hurt. Whatever else there was between them, Keltset had been his friend—the one friend he felt he could depend on. The hardened adventurer's disbelief would quickly turn to hatred, and Shea had always known that whatever the circumstances, Panamon Creel was a dangerous man to make an enemy.

It was impossible to determine where they were being taken. The Northland night was a moonless black, and Shea was forced to turn his concentration to the task of finding his footing as the party wound its way northward through scattered boulders and high ridges strewn with loose earth and rock. The Troll tongue was completely foreign to the Valeman. Since Panamon had lapsed into brooding silence, Shea could learn nothing. If the Trolls had reason to suspect who he was, then they would be taken to the Warlock Lord. The fact that they had not bothered with the Elfstones might be an indication that his captors had seized them merely as intruders without realizing what had brought them to the Northland. The possibility offered little comfort; the Trolls would find him out quickly enough. He wondered suddenly what had become of the fleeing Orl Fane. His tracks had ended where they had been seized, so the Gnome must also be a prisoner. But where had they taken him? And what had become of the Sword of Shannara?

They marched for hours in the impenetrable darkness. Shea quickly lost all track of time, and finally became so exhausted that he collapsed and was carried like a sack of grain over the broad shoulder of one of his captors for the remainder of the journey. He awoke briefly to the flickering light of low-burning wood fires as the party entered an unfamiliar encampment, then felt himself lowered to the earth and led through the opening of a large tent. Inside his hands were checked to be certain the bonds were secure and his feet were bound. Moments later he was left alone. Panamon and Keltset had been taken elsewhere.

Briefly, he struggled with the leather thongs that held his hands and feet, but they would not loosen and finally he gave it up. He could feel himself drifting into sleep, the weariness from the long march flooding through his aching body. He tried to fight it, forcing himself to conceive a plan of escape. The harder he tried, the more difficult it became to think of anything, and everything in his tired mind grew steadily more hazy. He was asleep in five minutes.

It seemed only moments later that he was awakened by rough hands shaking him out of the deep slumber into which he had fallen. He rose dazedly as a heavyset Troll spoke something unintelligible to him and pointed to a plate of food before passing out of the tent into the sunlight beyond. Shea squinted in the darkness of the tent, absently noting the familiar grayness of the Northland morning that signaled the beginning of another day. Realizing with mild astonishment that the leather bonds had been removed, he briskly rubbed his wrists and ankles to restore the circulation and then ate quickly the meal prepared for him.

There appeared to be a great deal of excitement outside his tent, and the shouts and cries of Trolls moving hurriedly about the encampment filled the morning air. The Valeman finished his meal and had just determined to risk a glance through the closed flaps of the tent entrance, when they were abruptly whipped aside. A burly Troll guard stepped inside and motioned for Shea to come with him. With one hand tightly clenching his tunic front, where he could feel the reassuring bulk of the Elfstones, the Valeman reluctantly followed.

An escort of Trolls led the small Southlander through a large encampment consisting of various-sized tents and stone huts constructed on a wide bluff surrounded by a series of low ridges. Glancing at the distant horizon, he could tell that they were high above the barren plainlands they had crossed the previous night. The camp appeared deserted, and the voices Shea had heard earlier had faded entirely. The fires of the night before had died into ashes, and the tents and huts were all empty. A sudden chill struck the frightened captive, and it occurred to him that he was probably being led to his own execution. There was no sign of either Panamon or Keltset. Allanon, Flick, Menion Leah, and all the others were somewhere in the Southland, unaware of his predicament. He was alone, and he was going to die. He was so paralyzed with fear that he could not even attempt to flee. He moved woodenly between his captors as they wound their way through the silent camp. A low ridge, marking the boundary of the encampment, loomed directly ahead of them, and then they were past the huts and tents and standing in a broad, open clearing. Shea stared in disbelief.

Dozens of Trolls were seated in a wide semicircle facing the ridge, their heads turned toward him momentarily as he entered the clearing. At the base of the ridge sat three Trolls of varying sizes and, though Shea could not be certain, probably of varying ages as well, each holding a brightly colored staff with a black pennant. Panamon Creel had been seated within the wide circle to one side. He had a peculiarly pensive look that did not alter as he caught sight of Shea. The attention of everyone was focused on the massive form of Keltset standing motionless in the center of the expectant Trolls, his arms folded as he faced the three staff bearers. He did not turn as Shea was led into the circle and seated next to the thoughtful Panamon. There was a long moment of complete silence. It was the strangest spectacle Shea had ever witnessed. Then one of the three Trolls seated at the apex of the circle rose ceremoniously and tapped his staff lightly to the earth. The assemblage rose as one, turned sharply to face eastward, and spoke in unison several short lines in their own tongue. Then quietly they sat down again.

"Can you imagine? They were praying."

They were the first words Panamon had spoken, and Shea started in surprise. He glanced quickly at the thief, but the big man was looking at Keltset. Another of the three Trolls presiding over the strange assembly rose and spoke briefly to the attentive audience, gesturing several times toward Panamon and Shea. The little Valeman turned expectantly to his companion.

"This is a trial, Shea," the thief declared in a strangely dispassionate tone. "Not for you or me, however. We're to be taken to the Skull Mountain beyond the Knife Edge, the Kingdom of the Warlock Lord, where we'll be held for . . . whatever. I don't think they know who we are yet. It is the command of the Spirit Lord that all outlanders be brought to him, and we're being treated no differently. There's hope still."

"But a trial . . . ?" Shea began doubtfully.

"For Keltset. He has demanded the right to be tried by his own people rather than be turned over to Brona. It's an ancient custom—the request cannot be refused. He was found with us when his people were at war with our race. Any Troll found with a Man is presumed a traitor. There are no exceptions."

Shea glanced involuntarily at Keltset. The massive Troll was seated with rocklike solidity in the center of the waiting assemblage as the voice of the presiding Troll continued to drone on. They had been mistaken, the Valeman thought gratefully. Keltset had not betrayed them; he had not given them away after all. But why had he allowed them to be taken captive so easily when he knew his own life would be forfeit as well?

"What will they do to him if they decide he is a traitor?" he asked impulsively.

A slight smile appeared on the tall man's lips.

"I know what you must be thinking." There was a touch of irony in the mocking voice. "He is risking everything on this trial. If they find him guilty, he will be immediately thrown over the nearest cliff."

He paused meaningfully and for the first time looked directly at the Valeman.

"I don't understand it either."

They lapsed into silence once more as the speaker finished his lengthy statement and sat down. After a moment, a single Troll came to stand before the three presiding Trolls, whom Shea now realized must be judges, and made a brief statement. He was followed by several others, each of whom spoke briefly, responding to questions put to them by the judges. Shea could understand nothing of what was taking place, but supposed that the Trolls were members of the raiding party that had captured them the previous night. The examination seemed to drag on forever, and still Keltset had not moved a muscle.

Shea studied the impassive giant, unable to understand why he had chosen to allow matters to go this way. Both Shea and Panamon had known for some time that Keltset was no ordinary outcast, driven from his home and his people because he was unable to speak. Nor was he simply the thief and adventurer that Panamon had tried to make him. There was intelligence in those strangely gentle eyes. There was an unspoken knowledge of the Sword of Shannara, the Warlock Lord, and even Shea that had never been revealed. There was a past hidden deep within the giant's heart. He was Allanon all over again, Shea thought suddenly. Somehow both held the key to the secret of the power of the Sword of Shannara. It was a strange revelation, and the Valeman shook his head questioningly, doubtful of his own reasoning. But there was no more time to think.

The witnesses had finished, and the three judges had now called upon the accused to rise and defend himself. There was an impossibly long, agonizing moment of unbroken silence as the judges, the assembled Trolls, Panamon Creel, and Shea all waited expectantly for Keltset to rise. Still the giant Rock Troll sat motionless as if caught in an unbreakable trance. Shea was seized with an almost uncontrollable urge to shout wildly, if only to break the unbearable silence, but the sound caught in his throat. The seconds crawled by. Then without warning, Keltset rose.

He drew his massive frame erect, abruptly taking on the appearance of a creature who was somehow more than mortal. There was pride in his bearing as he faced the waiting tribunal, his eyes fixed on the three judges. Without shifting his gaze even slightly, he reached under the broad leather belt that bound his waist and drew forth a large black metal pendant and chain. For a moment he held it in his hands before the eyes of the judges, who leaned forward in obvious surprise. Shea caught a quick glimpse of a cross centered in a circle, and then the giant raised the chain ceremoniously above his head and settled it slowly about his great neck.

"By the gods that gave us life . . . I don't believe it!" Pana-mon gasped in startled disbelief.

The judges, too, rose in astonishment. As Keltset turned slowly about the circle of wondering Trolls, shouts of excitement broke from their mouths and they were on their feet instantly, gesturing wildly at the impassive giant in their midst. Shea stared with the rest of them, completely befuddled.

"Panamon, what's happening?!" he cried finally.

The intense roar of the aroused assemblage nearly drowned out his words, and Panamon Creel was suddenly on his feet, too, one broad hand clapping down on Shea's slim shoulder.

"I don't believe it," the thief repeated with unrestrained joy. "All these months I've never even suspected it. That's what he's been hiding from us all along, my young Valeman! That's why he allowed us to be taken without a fight. But there must be more still . . ."

"Will you tell me what's happening?" Shea demanded heatedly.

"The pendant, Shea—the cross and circle!" the other shouted wildly. "It's the Black Irix, the highest award, the greatest honor the Troll people can give to one of their own! If you see three given in your lifetime, it's unusual. To receive one, you must be the living image of everything the Troll nation cherishes and strives to attain. You must be the closest thing to a god that a mortal being can approach. Somewhere in his past, Keltset has earned this honor—and we never guessed!"

"But what about the fact that he was found with us . . . ?" The little Valeman got only part of the query out.

"Anyone who wears the Irix would never betray his own

people," Panamon cut in sharply. "The honor carries with it an unbreakable trust. The wearer would never breach the laws of his people—he's presumed incapable of even contemplating such a thing. They believe that violation of such a trust would mean an eternity of punishment too horrible to imagine. No Troll would consider it."

Shea stared dazedly back at Keltset as the shouting continued unchecked. The great Troll was again facing his judges while the three vainly attempted to restore order to the unheeding assembly. It took several minutes more before the noise abated enough for anyone to be heard. The Trolls reseated themselves, anxiously waiting for Keltset to speak. There was a brief pause as a Troll interpreter appeared at the side of the silent defendant, then Keltset began to communicate in sign language. His eyes on Keltset's massive hands, the interpreter translated the explanation to the judges in the Troll language. There was a brief exchange with one of the judges, none of which Shea was able to understand, but fortunately Panamon had already begun his own translation, whispering quietly to his anxious friend.

"He told them that he comes from Norbane, one of the larger Troll cities in the far northern Charnal Mountains. His family name is Mallicos—it belongs to a very old and honored family. But they were all killed, supposedly by Dwarfs who had attempted to loot their family home. That judge on the left was asking Keltset how he had escaped; they had thought him dead as well. It must have been a pretty grisly affair for even this distant village to hear about it. But then— wait till you hear this, Shea! Keltset says the emissaries of the Warlock Lord destroyed his family! The Skull Bearers came to Norbane almost a year ago, seizing control of the government and ordering the Troll armies to accept their command. They managed to convince most of the city that Brona had come back from the dead, that he had survived for thousands of years and could not be killed by mortal hands. The Mallicos family was one of the ruling families in Norbane, and they refused to submit, demanding that the city stand firm against the Warlock Lord. Keltset's word carried a lot of weight because he wore the Black Irix. The Warlock Lord had the entire Mallicos family decimated except for Keltset, whom he brought to his fortress in the Knife Edge. The story of the Dwarf looters was a deception to inflame the Troll citizenry to join in the Southland invasion.

"But Keltset managed to escape before they got him to the prisons, wandering southward until I found him. The Warlock Lord had ordered that his voice be burned out to prevent his communication with any living being, but he learned sign language. He waited for his chance to return to the Northland. . . ."

One of the judges suddenly interrupted and Panamon paused momentarily.

"The judge asked why he returned now. Our big friend says he learned of Brona's fear of the power of the Sword of Shannara and the legend that a son of the Elven house would appear to take up the Sword . . ."

Panamon trailed off abruptly as the interpreter turned back to Keltset. For the first time the giant Troll faced toward Shea, the strangely gentle eyes fixed intently on the little Valeman. An involuntary chill shook Shea. Then his massive companion gestured briefly to the waiting judges. Panamon hesitated, then spoke softly.

"He says they must go with him to the Skull Kingdom, and that once inside the fortress, you, Shea, will destroy the Warlock Lord!"

SIX

PALANCE BUCKHANNAH DIED at dawn. Death came quietly, almost unexpectedly, as the first faint golden rays of sunlight crept searchingly into the darkness of the eastern horizon. He died without regaining consciousness. When Balinor was told, he merely nodded his head in acknowledgment and turned away. His friends stayed with him momentarily until Hendel silently motioned for them all to leave. In the hallway beyond the death room, they gathered quietly and spoke in hushed voices. Balinor was the last of the Buckhannahs. If he died in the coming battle, the family name would disappear from the earth. Only history would remember.

In the same hour, the assault on Tyrsis began. It, too, came quietly, born with the dying of the night. As the waiting soldiers of the entrenched Border Legion peered into the gray plains below the great city walls, the light from the slowly rising sun revealed the mammoth Northland army spread out all the way to the distant Mermidon, the carefully drawn formations giving a checkerboard appearance to the deep green of the grasslands. One moment the vast army stood silent, motionless on the plains below the city, shadows etched out of the darkness by dawn into figures of flesh and blood, iron and stone, and in the next they began to advance on the Tyrsian defenders. The silence broke sharply with the sudden booming of Gnome war drums, the deep, throbbing beat ringing ominously against the stone walls of Tyrsis.

The Northlanders came slowly, steadily to the battle, the crashing of the drums matched by the thudding of booted feet marching in ragged time, metal clinking sharply against metal as weapons and armor braced for the assault. They came voicelessly, thousands and thousands of them, armored figures faceless in the deep morning gloom. Great hulking rampways made of timbers bound in iron creaked ponderously as they were pulled and pushed on metal-rimmed wheels through the half-light, mobile pathways to the heights of the fortified bluff.

The seconds ticked away as the massive attack force moved to within a hundred yards of the waiting Legion, and still the crashing drums maintained their unhurried pace. The rim of the sun became sharply visible in the east and the waning night faded entirely in the western horizon. The drums abruptly ceased, and the sprawling army came to a sudden halt. For an instant there was a deep, unbroken silence that hung in frightened hesitation on the morning air. Then a deafening roar rose from the throats of the Northlanders; with a great surge, the massive juggernaut charged, wave upon wave rushing to grapple with the men of the Border Legion.

From beneath the closed gates of the towering Outer Wall, Balinor stared out at the awesome Northland assault, his broad face coolly impassive. His voice was calm and steady as he spoke briefly to his runners, sending one scurrying to find Acton and Fandwick on the left flank, the other to Messaline and Ginnisson on the right. His eyes returned instantly to the terrifying spectacle below the bulwarks as the wild charge drew closer. Behind the hastily constructed defenses, the Legion archers and spearmen waited patiently for his command. Balinor knew they could break even this massive charge from their superior defensive position, but they must first destroy the five broad rampways that were rolling slowly toward the base of the bluff. He had correctly anticipated that such devices would be used to scale the plateau and its low bulwarks, just as the enemy had foreseen that he would destroy the city rampway. The vanguard of the Northland rush was within fifty feet of the bluff, and still the new King of Callahorn watched and waited.

Then abruptly the ground opened beneath the feet of the charging enemy and great holes appeared as the attackers fell screaming into the ring of camouflaged pits concealed all along the base of the plateau. Two of the monstrous rolling rampways tumbled unchecked into the wide openings, the wheels snapping loose and the timbers shattering in splinters. The first wave of the mighty rush hesitated and from atop the low bulwarks the Legion archers rose on Balinor's long-awaited signal, to fire point-blank into the ranks of the suddenly confused enemy. The dead and wounded alike fell helplessly on the plainlands and were quickly trampled under as the second wave of the sustained charge pushed through, struggling to reach the entrenched Legion.

Three of the heavy rampways had avoided the concealed pits and continued to roll unhindered toward the low bulwarks. The Legion archers quickly loosed a flurry of burning arrows onto the vulnerable wooden backs of the ramps, but dozens of nimble yellow bodies were immediately seen to scramble atop the flaming timbers to smother the fires. The Gnome archers were also in position by this time, and for several minutes a concentrated barrage of arrows cut through the ranks of both sides. The completely exposed Gnomes crawling about on the rampways were cut to pieces. Everywhere men fell screaming in pain as the deadly missiles found their human targets. The wounded men of the Border Legion were sheltered in part from further injury by the low bulwarks and could be treated for their wounds. But the fallen Northlanders lay helpless and unprotected on the open field, and hundreds were killed before they could be removed to safety.

The three remaining rampways were still rolling toward the base of the fortified bluff, though one was now burning fiercely, great clouds of billowing smoke obscuring the vision of everyone passing within a hundred yards. When the two remaining ramps were within twenty yards of the bulwarks, Balinor signaled for his final defense. Huge caldrons of oil were lifted to the rim of the Southland defenses and the contents splashed down onto the grassland below, directly in the path of the rolling rampways. Before the charging Northlanders had time to veer in either direction, torches were dropped in the midst of the spreading oil and the entire area disappeared in a mass of flames and heavy black smoke.

The sustained enemy assault broke apart as the oncoming waves of attackers hesitated in fright at the wall of flames confronting them. The foremost ranks of the enemy had been burned alive; only a few managed to flee successfully from the terrible carnage at the base of the Legion defenses. The wind was blowing the dark smoke laterally across the open plains to the west, and for several moments the center and left flank of the two great armies were visually cut off from each other and from the wounded and dying who lay helplessly in the midst of the choking fumes.

Instantly Balinor saw his chance. A sharp counterthrust now might break the assault completely and rout the Northland army. Leaping to his feet, he signaled to Janus Senpre atop the Outer Wall, who had been left in command of the city garrison. Immediately the massive ironbound gates swung ponderously outward, and the mounted regiment of the Border Legion, armed with short swords and long, hooked pikes, their leopard colors flying brightly, galloped onto the bluff, wheeling sharply left to follow the open pathway along the city wall. Within moments they had reached the left flank of the Legion defensive line where Acton and Fandwick had command of the entrenched bordermen. A portable rampway was hastily lowered from the bluff rim onto the smoke-clouded plains below, and the Legion riders, led by Acton, thundered downward and swung left in a wide circle.

Balinor's instructions called for the famed regiment to cut around the wall of smoke and launch a sustained charge on the enemy's right flank. As the Northlanders turned to meet this counterattack, Balinor would bring a regiment of foot soldiers to strike at the exposed Northland front, driving the enemy back toward the Mermidon. If the counterthrust should falter, both commands were immediately to swing back into the covering smoke and return up the waiting rampways. It was a daring gamble. The Northlanders outnumbered the Legion soldiers at least twenty to one, and if the Tyrsians should be cut off, they would be completely decimated.

Small commands of Legion foot soldiers had already descended the mobile rampway on the left flank and staged a short counterattack into the enemy ranks as a defensive measure to protect the mounted regimen's only link with the besieged city. For the moment, the enemy seemed to have disappeared entirely on the left flank, totally obscured by the smoke which was blowing in blinding clouds from the burning rampways at the center of the defensive line.

On the right defensive flank, the fighting was ferocious. Only a light, drifting haze of smoke and dust obscured the vision of the two armies at this point, and the Northland assault continued unchecked. The entrenched Legion archers had decimated the first wave of attackers, but the second wave had reached the base of the bluff and was attempting to gain the fortified heights with the aid of rough-hewn scaling ladders. Lines of Gnome archers fired hundreds of arrows into the low bulwarks in an attempt to keep the defenders pinned down long enough to allow the exposed climbers to scramble over the Tyrsian defenses. The Legion archers returned the fire while their comrades used iron-tipped pikes from the rim of the defenses to push away the enemy assault.

It was a long, bloody fight during which neither side rested. At one point, a particularly fierce band of rangy Rock Trolls breached the Legion defenses and rushed onto the open bluff. A fierce battle raged for a short time as the bulky Legion commander Ginnisson, his florid face as red as his long hair, rallied his soldiers to resist the great Trolls; in bloody hand-to-hand combat, the Legionnaires killed the small band of attackers and closed the breach.

At the summit of the high Outer Wall, four old friends stood in silence with Janus Senpre and watched the terrible spectacle unfolding below them. Hendel, Menion Leah, Durin, and Dayel had all been left inside the city, their assignment to observe the progress of the battle and to aid Balinor in coordinating the movements of the Legion. The rolling smoke clouds totally obscured the giant borderman's vision of the movements of his mounted regiment, and only those atop the towering city walls could advise him of its progress so that he could launch his own assault from the center of the defensive line at the proper moment. The King relied particularly on Hendel's judgment, for the taciturn Dwarf had been fighting nearly thirty years in the Anar border wars.

Now the grizzled hunter, the Southlander, and the Elven brothers stared anxiously at the panorama spread out on the plains beneath them. On the right defensive flank, the fighting was the heaviest, as the determined Northlanders continued to batter the entrenched Legion, struggling to scale the face of the bluff. The Border Legion was holding on, but it was taking everything it had to beat back the ferocious assault. The plains immediately below the city gates at the center of the bulwarks were obscured by the burning oil and wooden rampways, which had crumbled entirely into masses of flaming timbers. At the fringes of the smoke, the disorganized Northlanders were vainly attempting to draw up their confused battle lines to renew the shattered charge. On the left, the Legion horsemen had broken out of the cover of the rolling black smoke and were encountering their first signs of resistance.

A large squad of Gnome cavalry had been stationed on the right attack flank as a defensive measure against exactly the kind of maneuver that was under way. However, the Northlanders had anticipated some advance warning of any flanking assault and were caught completely by surprise. The poorly trained Gnome riders were quickly scattered by the Border Legion and the attack on the Northland army's exposed flank began in earnest. Fanning wide to the north, the fabled regiment lowered its hooked pikes and formed a wall three columns deep, charging into the center of the astonished enemy. Acton led his soldiers in a precision rush that cut deeply into the exposed flank and nearly routed the extreme right of the Northland army. As the little group atop the Outer Wall watched expectantly, the enemy instantly readjusted its lines to the right of center to meet this new attack; as they did so, Hendel immediately signaled down to Balinor. A second rampway was lowered from the center of the defensive lines, and the tall figure of Messaline was seen to appear at the head of a second regiment of Legion soldiers, who descended on foot onto the smoke-clouded grasslands. A rear guard remained posted at the foot of the mobile ramp as the second regiment disappeared into the dark haze. Balinor closed his defensive lines and hurriedly joined his friends atop the great wall to observe the outcome of his counterthrust.

It had been perfectly executed. Just as the surprised right flank of the massive Northland army wheeled to face the oncoming charge of the Border Legion's mounted regiment, the foot soldiers commanded by Messaline attacked from out of the smoke at the center of the defensive line. In a tightly drawn phalanx, with spears bristling through a wall of locked shields, the highly trained Legion advanced into the midst of the unprepared and confused enemy. Like cattle, the Northlanders were herded backward, scores dropping, dying and wounded every few paces. The horsemen of Acton continued to press in from the left. The entire right wing of the enemy line began to collapse, and the cries of terror grew so shrill that even the fierce assault on the right defensive flank wavered momentarily as the bewildered Northlanders stared westward in a vain effort to discover what had happened. From the summit of the Outer Wall, Menion Leah stared in amazement.

"It's unbelievable. The Legion is actually driving them back. They're beaten!"

"Not yet," breathed Hendel softly. "The real test comes in a moment."

The highlander's eyes returned to the battle. The Northlanders were still falling back before the onslaught of the attacking Legion, but there was fresh activity taking place behind the lines of the retreating enemy. The army of the Warlock Lord would not be defeated so easily; what it lacked in training, it made up for in size. Already a vast command of mounted Gnome horsemen was racing around the rear of the driven foot soldiers, called up to meet the attack of the Legion riders. The Gnomes drew up immediately north of Acton's advancing horsemen; supported by several lines of archers and slingers, they rushed to the attack. From the rear center of the enemy army, a vast body of tall figures sheathed entirely in armor had drawn into a tight, boxlike formation and had begun to advance through its own wilting army toward the Legion foot soldiers. For a moment, the men atop the Outer Wall stared speculatively, then started in astonishment as the armored warriors suddenly began to cut their way with pikes and swords through the retreating men of their own army. It was the most savage act Menion had ever witnessed.

"Rock Trolls!" Balinor exclaimed heatedly. "They'll slaughter Messaline and his whole command. Signal retreat, Janus."

Obediently, his newest commander hoisted a large red pennant on a nearby staff. Menion Leah stared curiously at the silent borderman. It seemed that the battle had been nearly won, and still he had called for a retreat. He caught the King's eye, and the borderman smiled grimly at the unspoken question in the highlander's eyes.

"Rock Trolls are trained to fight from birth—it's their way of life. In hand-to-hand combat, they are better fighters than the men of the Border Legion. They are better trained and much stronger physically. We have nothing to gain in pressing the attack. We've already hurt them badly, and we still hold the bluff. If we plan to defeat them, we must chip away at their strength a piece at a time."

Menion nodded in understanding. With a brief wave, Balinor left the battlements to return to his command below. His primary concern at the moment was protecting the path of retreat for his two regiments, and that meant a successful defense of the portable ramps, the soldiers' only link with the city. The highlander watched the broad figure disappear from view, then turned back to the wall. The carnage on the plains below was frightful. The bodies of slain and wounded men lay scattered all the way from the bluff face to the rear lines of the Northland army. It was the worst slaughter that any of the little group had ever witnessed, and they watched speechlessly as the terrible struggle continued.

In the distance, the Legion foot soldiers under Messaline's command had begun an orderly retreat back toward the city defenses, but the giant Rock Trolls had almost succeeded in forcing their way through the milling front ranks of their own army and were preparing to pursue the hated Tyrsians. While the foot soldiers were withdrawing without opposition, the mounted regiment had encountered unexpected resistance from the charging Gnome horsemen. The two forces were engaged in a fierce battle to the left of the advancing Trolls. Acton was apparently either unable or unwilling to break away from the persistent attackers, and his riders were being subjected to a withering cross fire from the double line of Gnome archers positioned directly to his north. A large mixed body of Gnome and Troll swordsmen had worked their way around behind the charging horsemen, and now Acton's command was boxed in on three sides.

Hendel began to mutter angrily to himself. For the first time, Menion became concerned. Even Janus Senpre was pacing the walkway nervously. Their worst fears were realized a moment later. The pursuing body of Trolls, fresh for the wearing chase, had rushed forward so rapidly that the retreating men of Tyrsis, tired and worn from their counterattack, had been unable to gain the safety of the bluff. Almost a hundred yards from the waiting rampway, they turned to fight. The billowing smoke from the scattered fires rolled like a black wall in front of the low bulwarks, completely obscuring Balinor's vision as he waited before the city gates, but the unexpected turn of events was clearly visible to the horrified men watching from atop the towering city wall.

"I've got to warn Balinor!" Hendel exclaimed abruptly, leaping down from his position on the parapets. "That whole command will be cut to pieces!"

Janus Senpre left with him, but Menion and the Elven brothers continued to stare helplessly, unable to tear themselves away as the giant Rock Trolls bore down on Messaline's weary men. The Legion soldiers had drawn together with shields locked and spears extended, the shafts braced against the hard earth for the rush. The Trolls, too, had gone into a phalanx formation, somewhat wider than it was long, their intention clearly to close in on the Southlanders from three sides and break their defense by sheer strength. Menion glanced hastily over the wall, but Balinor had not moved, still unaware that an entire regiment of the famed Border Legion was on the verge of annihilation. Even as the highlander shifted his glance back to the plainlands, he saw Hendel and Janus reach the tall borderman's side, gesturing wildly. It would not be in time, Menion shouted inwardly. They were going to be too late.

But suddenly a strange thing happened. Acton's entire mounted command, momentarily forgotten by the viewers on the city wall, unexpectedly broke away from the attacking Gnome horsemen with an abrupt surge and came together in perfect formation, swinging in a sharp arc directly east behind the pursuing Rock Trolls. At a full gallop, the superb horsemen cut through the Gnome riders who barred their way. Oblivious to the hail of arrows showered down from the enraged Gnome archers, they raced directly toward the Troll ranks. Pikes lowered, the regiment struck the rear lines of the Troll phalanx in a raking movement, continuing its sweep eastward across the plains. The giant warriors were caught by surprise and dozens crumpled to the ground as the pikes cut into them.

But these were the finest fighting men in the world, and they recovered instantly, closing their ranks and turning to meet this new threat. As Acton's horsemen swung westward once more, racing back at breakneck speed, raking across the rear of the Troll phalanx a second time, the Northlanders struck back viciously with hurled pikes and maces. Over a dozen riders fell lifelessly from their mounts, and an equal number slumped wounded in their saddles as the regiment charged eastward and then cut sharply south for the safety of Tyrsis.

Acton had accomplished his purpose; the timely diversion

had permitted Messaline's besieged regiment to make a sudden break for the concealing smoke. It was a brilliantly executed maneuver, and atop the Outer Wall those watching shouted with unrestrained admiration.

Though pursued by the foremost ranks of the infuriated Trolls, the Legion foot soldiers had escaped into the concealing smoke, and most, with the aid of Balinor at the head of a relief squad, gained the safety of the waiting ramp. A sharp battle was fought at the foot of the bluff as the regiment struggled to withdraw the lowered bridge before the enemy could seize it. Finally, it was simply cast loose from the bulwarks and dropped onto the plain below, where it lay intact only moments before the Tyrsians set it ablaze and destroyed it.

On the left defensive flank, the embattled rear guard fought bravely to hold the other rampway, as Acton's command raced still another time within range of the maddened Gnome archers and still more died. It was a running battle all the way, and at one point the horsemen had to charge directly through the center of a thin line of swordsmen that rushed down to cut off their escape. But at last the harried riders reached the haven of the bluff, galloping up the rampway almost without slowing and swinging toward the opened gates of the city, where they were greeted by crowds of cheering soldiers and citizens. As the last of the returning cavalry gained the heights, the rear guard hastily withdrew behind their defenses and the rampway was hauled to safety.

It was midday by this time, and the heat of the noon sun settled like a humid blanket over the men of both armies. In sullen reluctance, the Northland army withdrew from the battle to regroup, dragging with it hundreds of dead and wounded. The smoke from the burning oil hung in an unmoving haze over the strangely silent grasslands as the morning wind faded quietly away. The ground before the bluff face was littered with the charred bodies of the dead, and small fires still burned persistently as the great timbers of the shattered rampways turned slowly to ashes. A foul stench began to rise from the terrible battlefield, and scavengers that flew and crawled appeared with shrill, eager cries to feast. Across the battered land, the armies watched each other with undisguised hatred, weary and racked with pain, but eager to resume the killing that had been thrust upon them. For several long hours, the once green land lay empty beneath the cloudless blue sky as its scarred surface baked and dried in the heat of the summer sun. It began to appear to those who allowed their reason to slip in favor of wishful thinking that the assault had ended—that the destruction was finished. Thoughts turned hopefully from killing and survival to family and loved ones. The shadow of death lifted momentarily.

Then in the late hours of the waning afternoon, the Northland army attacked again. As lines of Gnome archers showered the low bulwarks and the bluff beyond with a seemingly endless barrage of arrows, large bands of mixed swordsmen, Gnome and Troll, made sharp rushes at the Southland defenses, trying vainly to discover a weak point. Portable ramps, small scaling ladders, and grappling hooks with knotted ropes—all were tried to force a breach in the Legion lines, but each time the attackers were repelled. It was a wearing, vicious assault designed to tire and discourage the men of Tyrsis. The long day died slowly into dusk, and still the pitched battle wore on. It ended in darkness and tragedy for the Border Legion. As twilight descended on the bloodied land, the weary foes launched a final hail of spears and arrows at one another across the hazy void they could scarcely see through. A stray arrow caught Acton through the throat as the Legion cavalry commander was returning from his command on the left defensive flank, knocking the great fighter from his mount into the reaching arms of his attendants, where he died moments later.

The kingdom of the Warlock Lord was the single most desolate, forbidding piece of country in the known world—a barren, lifeless ring of impassable death traps. The tender, life-giving hand of nature had long since been driven from this thankless domain of darkness, and the wilderness that remained lay wrapped in silence. Its eastern borders were mired in the gloom and fetid stench of the vast Malg Swamp, a dismal, sprawling bog that no living creature had ever successfully traversed. Beneath the shallow waters, on which floated loose patches of colorless weeds that grew and died in the span of a day, the earth had turned to mud and quicksand, and all that came within its grip were sucked quickly from sight. The Malg was said to be bottomless, and while scattered throughout its vast expanse, small bits of solid earth and great, skeletal limbs of dying trees could still be glimpsed, even these were fading one by one. Across the far northern stretches, extending westward from the Malg, was a rambling series of low-backed mountains appropriately named the Razors. There were no passes through these mountains and their wide, sloped backs were craggy, jutting slabs of rock, seemingly pushed upward from the bowels of the earth. An experienced and determined climber might still have found the Razors passable—one or two men had even made the attempt—had it not been for the particularly venomous species of spider that nested in vast numbers throughout the barren mountains. The bleached bones of the dead, scattered in small white patches among the darkened rocks, gave mute testimony to their unavoidable presence.

There was a break in the deadly ring where the Razors tapered off into foothills at the northwest corner of the kingdom, and for over five miles southward the country was easily passable, opening directly into the center of the circle of barriers. Here there was no natural protection against intruders, but this small gateway to the interior of the kingdom was also the obvious approach, and hence the trapdoor to the cage through which the Lord and Master waited for the unwary to step. Eyes and ears responsive only to his command guarded the narrow strip of land carefully. The ring could be locked instantly. Directly below the foothills, a vast, arid wasteland called the Kierlak Desert ran southward for nearly fifty miles. A heavy, poisonous vapor hung invisibly over the sprawling, sand-covered plains, drawn from the waters of the River Lethe, a venomous stream that wound lazily into the fiery emptiness from the south and emptied into a small lake in the interior. Even birds chancing to fly too close to the deadly haze were killed in seconds. Creatures dying in the terrible furnace of sand and poisonous air decayed in a matter of hours and turned to dust, so that nothing remained to show their passing.

But the most formidable barrier of all stretched menacingly across the southern boundary of the forbidden domain, beginning at the southeasterly edges of the Kierlak Desert and running eastward to the marshy borders of the Malg Swamp. The Knife Edge. Like great stone spears driven into the hard earth by some monstrous giant, these mountains towered thousands of feet into the sky. They had the appearance not so much of mountains as a series of awesome peaks jutting in broken lines that blocked the dim horizon like fingers stretching painfully. At their base swirled the toxic waters of the River Lethe, which had its origin in the Malg Swamp and meandered westward at the base of the great rock barrier to disappear into the impregnable vapors of the Kierlak Desert. Only a man driven by an unexplainable madness would have attempted to scale the Knife Edge.

There was a passage through the barrier, a small, winding canyon that opened onto a series of craggy foothills which ran for several thousand yards to the base of a single, ominously solitary mountain just within the southern boundary of the ring. The scarred surface of this mountain was chipped and worn by time and the elements, lending the southern facing a singularly menacing appearance. On even the most casual inspection, one was immediately struck by the frightening similarity the south wall bore to a human skull, stripped of flesh and life, the pate rounded and gleaming above the empty sockets of the eyes, the cheeks sunken, and the jaw a crooked line of bared teeth and bone. This was the home of the Lord and Master. This was the kingdom of Brona, the Warlock Lord. Everywhere it bore the stamp of the Skull, the indelible mark of death.

It was midday, but time seemed strangely suspended, and the vast, wasted fortress lay wrapped in a peculiar stillness. The familiar grayness screened the sun and sky, and the drab brownish terrain of rock and earth lay stripped of mortal life. Yet there was something more in the air this day, cutting through the silence and the emptiness to the flesh and blood of the men in the winding column passing through the single gateway in the massive Knife Edge. It was a pressing sense of urgency that hung poised over the blasted face of the kingdom of the Warlock Lord, as if events to come had rushed through time too quickly and, jammed together in eager anticipation, waited for their moment.

The Trolls shuffled guardedly through the twisting canyon, their comparatively huge frames dwarfed by the towering heights of the peaks so that they appeared little more than ants in the sprawling, ageless rock. They entered the kingdom of the dead the way in which little children enter an unfamiliar dark room, inwardly frightened, hesitant, but nevertheless determined to see what lay beyond. They marched unchallenged, though not unseen. They were expected. Their appearance came as no surprise, and they entered without danger of harm from the minions of the Master. Their impassive faces disguised their true intentions or they would never have passed the southern shores of the River Lethe. For in their midst was the last of a bloodline the Spirit King had thought destroyed, the last son of the Elven house of Shannara.

Shea marched directly behind the broad frame of Keltset, his hands seemingly tied at his back. Panamon Creel followed, his arms similarly bound, the gray eyes dangerous as they stared watchfully at the great rock walls on either side of the winding column. The ruse had worked perfectly. Apparent captives of the Rock Trolls, the two Southlanders had been marched to the shores of the River Lethe, the sluggish, vile stream that flanked the southernmost borders of the Skull Kingdom. The Trolls and their silent charges had boarded a wide-backed raft of rotted wood and rusted iron spikes, whose voiceless captain was a bent, hooded creature who seemed more beast than man, his face shielded in the folds of the musty black cloak, but his hooked, scale-covered hands clearly visible as they fastened tightly on the crooked leverage pole and guided the ancient craft across the tepid, poison waters. The uneasy passengers felt a growing sense of revulsion from the mere presence of their pilot and were openly relieved when, after finally permitting them to disembark on the far shore, he vanished with his ancient barge into the haze that lay across the dark river waters. The lower Northland was now entirely lost to them, the grayness so heavily disseminated through the stale, dry air that nothing beyond the river was visible. In contrast, the soaring, blackened cliffs of the Knife Edge loomed starkly before them, the great fingers of rock brushing the mist aside in the halflight of the northern midday. The party passed wordlessly through the corridor that split the vast heights, winding deeper into the forbidden domain of the Warlock Lord.

The Warlock Lord. Somehow Shea felt that he had known from the very beginning, from the day Allanon had told him of his remarkable ancestry, that it would happen this way—that circumstances would demand he face this awesome creature who was trying so desperately to destroy him. Time and events merged into a single instant, a flash of jumbled memories of the long days spent in flight, running to stay alive, running toward this frightening confrontation. Now the moment was drawing near, and he would face it virtually alone in the most savage land in the known world, his oldest, most trusted friends scattered, his only companions a band of Rock Trolls, an outcast thief and a vengeful, enigmatic giant. The latter had persuaded the tribunal to place under his command a detachment of Troll warriors, not so much because they believed that the insignificant Valeman accompanying him somehow possessed the ability to destroy the immortal Brona as because their massive kinsman was the holder of the honored Black Irix.

The three judges had also revealed the fate of Orl Fane. The Trolls had seized the little fugitive about an hour before his determined pursuers had been taken captive, and he had been marched under guard to the main encampment. The Maturen tribunal had quickly concluded that the Gnome was completely mad. He had babbled insanely to them of secrets and treasures, his wizened yellow face contorted in a hideous fixed grin. At times he had appeared to be talking to the air about him, brushing violently at his bare arms and legs as if living things had fastened there. His sole link with reality seemed to be the ancient sword that was his only possession, the sword he clung to so violently that his captors could not pry it free. They allowed him to keep the worthless piece of metal, binding his clenched yellow hands to its rusted sheath. Within the hour he was taken north to the dungeons of the Warlock Lord.

The canyon wound wickedly through the towering peaks of the Knife Edge, at times dwindling from a broad trailway to little more than a split in the rocks. The burly Trolls scrambled through the twisting passage without resting. A few had been there before, and they led the others at a steady, tiring pace. Speed was essential. If they delayed too long, the Spirit King would hear that Orl Fane and the ancient weapon he refused to release, even for the briefest moment, were safely shut away in the Warlock Lord's own dungeons.

Shea shuddered at the possibility. It might already have happened—they could be walking straight to their own execution. Each time before on the long journey from Culhaven, the Warlock Lord had seemed to know every move they had made; each time he had been waiting for them. It was madness—this terrible risk! And even if they did succeed, even if Shea finally held the Sword of Shannara within his grasp . . . why, what then? Shea laughed inwardly. Could he face the Warlock Lord without Allanon beside him, without any idea what would trigger the hidden power of the legendary talisman? No one would even know he had the Sword.

The Valeman had no idea what the others intended, but he had already determined that if by some miracle he could get his hands on the elusive weapon, he was going to run for his life. Everyone else could do as he wished. He was certain that Panamon Creel would have approved of the plan, but the two had scarcely exchanged ten words since the journey to the Skull Kingdom had begun. Shea sensed that for the first time in Panamon's life, a life composed primarily of narrow escapes and hair-raising escapades, the scarlet-clad thief was frightened. But he had gone with Keltset and Shea—gone because they were his only friends, gone because his pride would let him do no less. His most basic instinct was to survive at any cost, but he would not permit himself to be shamed even to stay alive.

Keltset's reasons for this dangerous undertaking were less apparent. Shea thought he understood why the giant Troll had quietly insisted that they must retrieve the Sword of Shannara, and it was much more than personal vengeance for the slaughter of his family. There was something about Keltset that reminded Shea of Balinor—a quiet confidence that lent strength to those less certain. Shea had felt it when Keltset indicated that they must go after Orl Fane and the Sword. Those gentle, intelligent eyes told the Valeman that he believed in him, and while Shea could not explain it in rational terms, he knew he had to go with his giant friend. If he turned away now, after the long weeks spent searching for the Sword of Shannara, he would be betraying both his friends and himself.

The cliff walls on either side fell away abruptly, and the canyon opened into a sloping valley that seemed like a wide depression in the rugged interior of the Skull Kingdom, its surface barren and dry, the earth broken by a scattering of rocky hillocks and dry riverbeds. The party halted silently, every pair of eyes involuntarily drawn to the solitary mountain in the bowl of the little valley, the southern face staring sightlessly at them from two huge, empty sockets that resembled the eyes of a skull. The blasted face waited in timeless anticipation for the coming of the Master. Standing at the mouth of the draw, Shea felt the hair on the back of his neck rise and a sudden chill surge through his small frame.

From out of the rocks to either side, a number of misshapen, lumbering creatures shuffled, their great bodies as drab as the dying land, their faces nearly featureless. Once they might have been human, but they were no longer so. They stood upright on two legs and two arms swung aimlessly at their sides, but the resemblance ended there. Their skin was the texture of chalky putty, almost rubbery in appearance, and they moved in the manner of mindless beings. Like apparitions out of some frightening nightmare, the strange creatures came all around the Trolls, staring blankly into their barklike faces as if to be certain of what manner of creatures had come to them. Keltset turned slightly and motioned to Panamon Creel.

"The Trolls call them Mutens," the adventurer whispered quietly. "Stand easy—remember that you are supposed to be a prisoner. Stay calm."

One of the misshapen beings spoke in rasping tones to the lead Trolls, gesturing briefly at the two bound men.

There was a short exchange, and then one of the Trolls said something over his shoulder to Keltset, who immediately motioned for Shea and Panamon to follow him. The trio detached themselves from the main group. Accompanied by two other Trolls, they silently followed one of the lumbering Mutens as he turned and moved rather unsteadily toward the inner cliff wall to their left.

Shea glanced back once and observed the Trolls scattering idly to either side of the canyon entrance, seemingly waiting for their companions to return. The remaining Mutens had not moved. Looking ahead once more, the Valeman saw that the cliff face was split by a long fissure that ran several hundred feet up and that this gap was a passage to something beyond. The little group moved into the rock wall, their eyes trying to adjust to the sudden darkness. There was a pause as their guide took a torch from a wall rack and lit it, handing it absently to one of the Trolls before proceeding. Apparently his own eyes were accustomed to the inky darkness, for he continued to lead them.

The party passed into a dank, foul-smelling cavern that branched out into several fathomless passageways. From somewhere far away, Shea thought he detected the faint, chilling sound of screams ringing over and over as echoes against the rock walls. Panamon cursed harshly in the flickering torchlight, his broad face streaked with sweat. The silent, heedless Muten shuffled ahead into one of the passages, and the faint light from the fissure opening faded into blackness.

The lingering echo of booted feet on rock was the only sound as the men moved down the darkened corridor, their eyes wandering briefly to the windowless iron doors bolted into the face of the rock on both sides of the passageway. The screams still rang faintly in their ears, but they seemed more distant now. There were no human sounds from the cells they were passing. Finally the guide halted before one of the heavy doors, gesturing briefly and speaking in the same guttural tones to the Trolls. He turned to continue down the passage and had taken his first step when the foremost Troll brought his great iron mace crashing down on the creature's bulky head. The Muten dropped lifelessly to the cave floor. Keltset moved to loosen the ropes binding Shea and Panamon as the two remaining Trolls stood watchfully before the cell door. When his friends were freed, the massive Northlander moved catlike to the iron door and slid the latches clear of their loops. Grasping the bars, he pulled on the ancient door. With a sharp grating sound, the heavy portal swung open.

"Now we shall see," breathed Panamon harshly. Taking the light from Keltset, he stepped cautiously into the tiny room, his two companions close behind.

Orl Fane sat hunched against the far wall, his scrawny legs shackled in chains that were bolted into the rock flooring, his clothing torn and dirtied almost beyond recognition. He was clearly not the same creature they had captured several days earlier on the Plains of Streleheim. He stared at the three faces with mindless disregard, his thin, yellow face fixed in a hideous grin as he babbled meaninglessly to himself. His eyes were strangely dilated in the bright torchlight, and he glanced all about as he talked, behaving as if there were others in the little cell, creatures invisible to all eyes but his own.

The two men and the giant Troll took in his condition at a glance, their eyes traveling instantly to the bony hands that still clutched possessively the battered leather and metal scabbard that sheathed the elusive object of their long pursuit. The ancient hilt flickered back dully in the torchlight, giving them a shadowy image of the raised hand holding the burning torch. They had found it. They had found the Sword of Shannara!

For a moment no one moved as the maddened Gnome clutched the Sword closer to his emaciated frame, his eyes showing a momentary flicker of recognition as he caught sight of the sharp pike glinting at the stumped end of Panamon's slowly raising arm. The adventurer stepped forward menacingly and bent close to the Gnome's thin face.

"I've come for you, Gnome," he said harshly.

Orl Fane seemed to undergo a sudden transformation at the sound of Panamon Creel's voice, and a frightened shriek escaped his lips as he struggled to move farther back.

"Give me the Sword, you treacherous rat!" the thief demanded.

Without waiting for a response, he seized the weapon, trying to wrest it from the now thoroughly terrified Gnome's astonishingly strong grip. But even with death staring him directly in the eye, Orl Fane would not give up his precious possession. His voice rose to a scream, and in sudden fury, Panamon brought the heavy iron binding on his piked hand down across the little fellow's unprotected skull. The Gnome crumpled unconscious to the cold floor.

"All those days we chased this miserable creature!" Panamon cried. He stopped abruptly and lowered his voice to a harsh whisper. "I thought I would at least have the pleasure of watching him die, but . . . it's no longer worth it."

In disgust, he reached for the hilt of the Sword, intent on drawing it from its binding, but Keltset stepped forward and placed a restraining hand on his shoulder. Still angered, the thief stared back coldly as the Rock Troll motioned silently toward the watching Shea, then both stepped back.

The Sword of Shannara was Shea's birthright, but he hesitated. He had come so far, been through so much, all for this moment—and now he found himself afraid. He felt cold inside as he looked at the ancient weapon. For an instant, he considered refusing, knowing that a part of him could not accept the awesome responsibility that he was being asked to assume—a responsibility that had been forced on him. He recalled in a flash the terrible power of the three Elfstones. What then of the power of the Sword of Shannara? In his mind he pictured the faces of Flick and Menion and the others who had fought so hard to gain possession of the Sword for him. If he turned away now, he would have betrayed the trust they had extended him. In effect, he would be telling them that everything they had gone through for him had been pointless. He saw again the dark, enigmatic face of Allanon chastising him for his foolish ideals, his refusal to see men for what they were. He would have to answer to him as well, and Allanon would not be pleased. . . .

Woodenly he moved to the fallen Orl Fane and bent over him, his fingers closing firmly around the cold metal hilt of the weapon, feeling the raised image of the burning torch in his sweating palm. He paused. Then slowly he drew forth the Sword of Shannara.

SEVEN

𝒯 HE SECOND DAY of the battle for Tyrsis bore witness to the same wholesale slaughter of the men of the Northland army as the first. The giant invasion force attacked at dawn, marching toward the face of the bluff in precision formation to the deep booming of the Gnome war drums, pausing in silence within a hundred yards; then, with an earshattering yell, the army rushed headlong into the terrible struggle to gain the heights. With the same utter disregard for their own lives, the attackers threw themselves in wave after wave against the outer defenses of the entrenched Border Legion. They came without the aid of the monstrous rampways, which there had been no time to rebuild, relying instead on thousands of small scaling ladders and grappling irons. It was a ferocious, merciless, and bitter contest. Hundreds of the Northlanders died in the first few minutes.

With Acton gone, Balinor did not choose to risk the Legion mounted command a second time in counterattacking the massive enemy army. He decided instead to dig in on the bluff face and hold his position as long as possible. Burning oil and the Legion archers shredded the first waves of the assault, but this time the attackers did not break apart and run. They came in an endless, sustained charge, finally eluding both arrows and flames to reach the base of the wide plateau where scaling ladders were thrown against the bluff. Swarms of screaming Northlanders struggled upward and the fighting was reduced to basic hand-to-hand combat.

For nearly eight hours the valiant defenders of Tyrsis repelled an enemy twenty times its size. Scaling ladders and grappling hooks were methodically shattered and cut apart, Northlanders were pushed away as quickly as they gained the summit, and momentary holes in the defense lines were closed before a breach could be opened. The acts of bravery performed by individual members of the famed Legion were too numerous to recount. They fought against impossible odds without rest, without relief, knowing all the while that no quarter would be given them by the enemy, should they fail. For eight hours the enraged Northland army struggled to break through the Legion bulwarks without success. But finally a breach was opened on the defensive left flank. With a ragged shout of victory, the enemy rushed onto the bluff.

After the death of Acton, the aged Fandwick had been left in sole command of this section of the defensive lines. Calling on his diminished reserves, the Legion commander moved to block the Northland rush. An intense, fierce battle raged in the open breach for long minutes as the determined attackers battled to hold and enlarge the newly gained opening. Dozens died on both sides, including the valiant Fandwick.

Balinor rushed more reserves from the center of the line in an effort to close the breach, and he finally succeeded. But moments later a second and then a third hole opened in the left defensive flank, and the whole command began to waiver and break apart. The King of Callahorn realized his army could no longer hold the outer defenses, and passed the word to his remaining commanders to begin an orderly re-treat into the city. Rallying the crumbling left flank, the giant borderman drew in his outermost defenses while holding the enemy at bay, and quickly moved the entire command into the city.

It was a bitter moment for the Southlanders, who now rushed to defend the great Outer Wall. But the Northland army did not advance to the attack. Instead, they began tear-ing down the defensive bulwarks and moving them inward on the bluff face, where they constructed their own defensive position, just out of range of the Legion archers. The weary soldiers of the Border Legion watched silently from atop the city walls as the sunlit afternoon turned slowly to dusk above the busy invaders. The Northland camp was moved forward to the plains below the city and the army began to light its watch fires as darkness closed in around them.

In the final moments of daylight, the enemy revealed a portion of its plan to scale the walls of Tyrsis. Great, sloping rampways from the plains to the bluff were hurriedly set in place, supported by stone and timber over the remains of the shattered walkways. Then from out of the twilight, three massive siege towers rolled into view, each one easily the height of the Outer Wall. The towers were moved to the rear of the enemy encampment within plain view of the city and anchored for the night. It was clearly a piece of psychological warfare designed to unnerve the besieged Border Legion.

From above the gates to the city, Balinor watched impas-sively with his Legion commanders and his companions from Culhaven. He toyed briefly with the idea of a night as-sault against the encamped Northlanders for the express purpose of burning the siege towers, but quickly discarded it. They would expect him to try something like that, and the city gates would undoubtedly be under careful watch the entire night. Besides, it would be no problem for the Legion to set fire to these towers as easily as they had fired the rampways, once they were moved to the attack.

Balinor shook his head and frowned. There was something very wrong about the whole Northland attack concept but he couldn't put his finger on it. Surely they must be aware that the siege towers would never enable them to breach the city's Outer Wall. They had to have something else in mind. He wondered for the hundredth time whether the Elven army would reach the beleaguered city in time. He could not believe that Eventine would fail them. It was dark now and, after ordering a double watch on all sectors of the wall, he invited the men with him to share dinner.

Concealed in a grove of trees on the summit of a low ridge several miles west of Tyrsis, a small band of horsemen surveyed the carnage of the terrible battle below them as evening settled in. They watched silently as the huge siege towers were wheeled into position at the rear of the Northland army for the morning assault on the fortress city.

"We should get a message to them," Jon Lin Sandor whispered quietly. "Balinor will want to know that our army is on its way."

Flick glanced expectantly at the bandaged figure of Eventine. The strange eyes seemed to burn as he studied the besieged city.

"I trust the army is on its way," the Elven King muttered almost inaudibly. "Breen has been gone almost three days. If he has not returned by tomorrow, I'll go myself."

His friend placed an understanding hand on the King's good shoulder.

"You are in no condition to travel, Eventine. Your brother will not fail you. Balinor is a seasoned fighter and the walls of Tyrsis have never been breached by an invader in the lifetime of the city. The Legion can defend long enough."

There was a long moment of silence. Flick looked back at the darkened city and wondered if his friends were all right. Menion must be inside those walls, too. The highlander could not know what had befallen Flick, nor what had happened to Eventine. Nor for that matter what had become of the unpredictable Allanon, who for no apparent reason at all had disappeared shortly after the Valeman's return with the Elven search party. While the Druid had been purposely vague about a great many things since his appearance in Shady Vale, he had never gone off without an explanation. Perhaps he had spoken with Eventine. . . .

"The city is encircled and guarded." Eventine's voice broke out of the growing darkness. "It would be extremely difficult to get past their lines even long enough to get a message to Balinor. But you're right, Jon Lin—he should know we have not forgotten him."

"We don't have a large enough force to break through to Tyrsis or even to strike the rear guard of the Northlanders," his friend declared thoughtfully. "But . . ."

He looked quickly at the dark bulk of the siege towers standing deserted on the plains below.

"A small gesture," finished the King meaningfully.

It was not yet midnight when Balinor was hurriedly summoned to the watchtower above the gates to the city. Moments later he stood speechless on the ramparts in the company of Hendel, Menion, Durin, and Dayel and stared down upon the chaos spreading through the half-wakened enemy camp. To the rear of the sprawling encampment, the centermost of the three giant siege towers was a burning pyre that lit the grasslands for miles. Frantic Northlanders rushed wildly over the timbers of the adjoining towers, desperately trying to prevent the flames from spreading. It was obvious that the invader had been taken completely by surprise. Balinor looked at the others and smiled wryly. Help was not so distant after all.

The morning of the third day dawned with a sullen stillness that hung shroudlike over the land of Callahorn and the armies of the North and South. Gone was the mighty crashing of the Gnome drums, the muffled thudding of booted feet marching to the battle, and the thunderous yells of attack. The sun rose fiery red in the distant east, the dark hue spreading across the fading night like blood. A deep haze clouded the dew-covered face of the land. There was a complete absence of movement, of sound. On the walls of Tyrsis, the soldiers of the Border Legion waited nervously, their eyes peering blankly into the gloom for signs of the enemy.

Balinor was in command of the center section of the Outer Wall. Ginnisson held the right and Messaline the left. Janus Senpre again commanded the city garrison and the reserves. Menion, Hendel, and the Elven brothers stood silently at Balino's side and shivered in the cold of early morning. They had rested poorly, but they felt unusually alert and strangely calm. They had quietly accepted their situation during the past forty-eight hours. They had seen men die by the thousands, and their own lives seemed almost insignificant compared to the terrible carnage that had engulfed this ancient land—yet very precious at the same time. The grasslands beneath the city were torn and rutted, the earth discolored with blood and littered with death. There was nothing to look forward to but more of the same, and still more, until one army or the other was destroyed. Forgotten for all the defenders of Tyrsis was the moral purpose behind the word survival; war had become a mechanical reflex that served as its own excuse for the acts men performed.

The bloodred of the morning sun grew sharper, and now the shapes of men and horses came into focus as the Northland army was rediscovered, a maze of carefully drawn formations spread all across the expanse of yesterday's battlefield from the bluff defenses to beyond the charred timbers of two fallen siege towers. They did not move; they did not speak. They simply waited. Hendel recognized what was happening and whispered hurriedly to Balinor. Swiftly, the Legion Commander sent runners along the walls to his subordinates, warning them of what was expected, cautioning them to keep their soldiers calm and in place.

Menion was about to ask what was happening when suddenly there was movement on the bluff immediately below the city gates. A single armored warrior walked slowly out of the gloom, tall, erect, to stand before the giant wall. In one hand he carried a long staff with a single red pennant. With slow, deliberate movements he planted the pole in the earth, then stepped back ceremoniously, turned and strode back into his lines. Again there was a moment of complete silence. The long, low, wailing cry of a distant horn sounded mournfully across the plains—once, twice, a third time. Then silence.

"The death watch." Hendel broke the stillness with a hushed whisper. "It means we're to be given no quarter. They intend to kill us all."

The air was rent violently by the sudden crashing of

Gnome war drums, and everyone began moving at once. With a rush, thousands of Gnome arrows filled the sky, sweeping downward to the ramparts of the city walls. Spears, pikes, and maces flew upward from charging Northlanders. Out of the haze of the plains below appeared the bulk of the one remaining siege tower, groaning and creaking with its own ponderous weight as hundreds of the enemy pulled and pushed the towering monster up the newly constructed rampway toward the Outer Wall. From within the city, Legion archers fired down upon the darting forms of their attackers as the balance of the men of the Border Legion hugged the stone of the defenses and waited for Balinor's order.

The giant borderman waited until the massive siege tower was within twenty-five yards of the wall. Already the enemy was attempting to scale the great barrier with grappling hooks and ladders, and the rough stone was dotted with clinging figures vainly scrambling toward the summit. Abruptly the cauldrons of oil poured downward from the ramparts, splashing over man and machine alike to saturate the bluff face immediately below. Burning torches followed, and instantly the entire front of the Northland assault force was engulfed in flames. The siege tower and the men around it simply disappeared as the black smoke billowed skyward, blotting out for the Legion defenders the carnage below them, but not the shrieks of terror and agony. The attackers attempting to scale the Outer Wall were trapped. A few managed to reach the ramparts where they were quickly dispatched, but most simply lost their hold or were overcome by the heavy smoke and dropped screaming into the fire.

Within minutes the assault was broken and the entire Northland army had again completely disappeared from view. The men on the ramparts peered watchfully into the swirling smoke, vainly trying to discover what form the next assault would take. Balinor looked at his companions and shook his head doubtfully.

"That was utter foolishness. They must have known what would happen—yet they came ahead anyway. Are they mad?"

"Perhaps they did it to confuse us . . ." muttered Hendel quietly. "Like this smoke screen we so obligingly provided them with."

"All that dying just to get a smoke screen?" Menion exclaimed incredulously.

"If so, then they have something very definite in mind—something they are certain cannot fail," declared Balinor. "Keep an eye on things here. I'm going down to the gates."

He turned away abruptly and disappeared down the winding stone stairway almost at a run. The others watched him go without comment and turned back to the wall. In front of them, thick clouds of the heavy black smoke still rose skyward as the oil on the plains continued to burn. The cries of death had ceased and there was a strange silence.

"What are they up to?" Menion voiced the question at last.

For a moment there was no response at all.

"I wish we had been able to catch Stenmin," Durin muttered at last. "I haven't felt safe even behind these walls with that madman running loose somewhere in the city."

"We almost had him," Dayel interjected quickly. "We followed him into that room, but he seemed to disappear into thin air. There must have been a secret passage."

Durin nodded in agreement and the conversation dropped off again. Menion stared into the smoke and thought about Shirl waiting for him at the palace, about

Shea, Flick, his father, and his homeland—all in a rush of images that flooded his wandering mind. How was it all going to end for them?

"Shades!" Hendel jerked him around so sharply that he was momentarily startled. "I've been a fool. It was right in front of me all the time. A secret passage! In the basement of the palace, beneath the wine cellar, in the dungeons sealed off all these years—a passageway that leads through the mountains to the plain beyond. The old King spoke of it once to me, years and years ago. Stenmin must know of it!"

"A way into the city!" exclaimed Menion. "They'll catch us with our backs to them." He paused sharply. "Hendel! Shirl's back there!"

"We don't have much time." Hendel was already starting down the steps. "Menion, come with me. Dayel, find Janus Senpre and tell him to get help to us at the palace immediately. Durin, find Balinor and warn him. Hurry now, and pray we're not too late."

They were down the worn stairs in a rush, scattering across the barracks ground as if possessed. Hendel and Menion broke into a dead run, pushing their way heedlessly through clusters of soldiers toward the gates to the Tyrsian Way. Too slow, Menion's harried brain screamed at him! He nearly jerked Hendel off his feet in an effort to turn him toward a small group of saddled reserve mounts tethered to their right. Knocking an interfering attendant aside without pausing, the duo leaped into the saddles of the two nearest mounts and wheeled them toward the city. At a gallop, the horses tore through the open gateway, past the flustered guards, past swarms of reserves posted just inside the gates; with the path cleared, they raced at breakneck speed for the palace.

Everything that followed seemed to come in a rush that negated time and space. People and buildings flashed by them in a blur as the two horsemen galloped over the ancient stones of the Tyrsian Way. Precious moments were lost and then the wide arc of the Bridge of Sendic loomed in the distance, spanning the People's Park to the palace of the Buckhannahs. A train of baggage carts scattered wildly at the foot of the bridge as the two riders tore past them without slowing, racing their mounts across the stone arch toward the open gates of the monarchial home. Dashing into the garden-ringed courtyard, Hendel and Menion drew their sweating horses up sharply and vaulted to the ground.

Everything was silent. Nothing seemed amiss. A single attendant strolled almost leisurely out of the shadows of a great willow to take the reins from the heated riders, his eyes reflecting only mild curiosity. Hendel gave the man a sharp glance and dismissed him, beckoning Menion after him as he moved hurriedly toward the front doors. Still nothing. Maybe they were in time. Maybe they were even mistaken . . .

The hallways of the ancestral manor loomed empty and silent as the two searchers paused once more in the foyer, casting quick glances at open doorways and deep alcoves, drawn tapestries and curtained windows. Menion turned to find Shirl, but his companion stopped him with a word. The red-haired daughter of kings would have to wait. Slowly now, on cat's feet, the little man led the anxious highlander down the opposite passageway toward the cellar door. At the bend in the corridor they hesitated, then flattening themselves against the polished woodwork, peered cautiously around the corner.

The massive, ironbound door to the now-familiar wine cellar stood ajar. In the open entryway, three armed men kept watch over the vacant hall. All bore the insignia of the falcon. Menion and Hendel drew back silently. For the first time, the Prince of Leah realized he was unarmed. He had left the sword of Leah hanging from the saddle pommel of his horse. Quickly he scanned the hall behind him, his eyes coming to rest at last on a set of crossed pikes fastened to the far wall. A pike was hardly the weapon he needed, but he had no other choice. Noiselessly, he retrieved one unwieldy lance and rejoined Hendel. A long look passed between them. They would have to be quick. If the cellar door were to be closed and fastened from within before they could reach it, they would have lost their chance at Stenmin and the passageway. In any event, they were only two. How many more of the enemy awaited them below?

They didn't stop to consider it further. In a sudden rush, they were out of hiding and down the hallway. The three guards barely had time to look around before their attackers were upon them. Menion shoved his lance through the man nearest the doorway and was on top of the second a moment later. The final guard dropped soundlessly before Hendel's great mace. It was over almost before it had started and the two fighters were through the cellar entryway, charging down the worn stone steps to meet the most deadly battle of their lives.

The ancient wine cellar was ablaze with torchlight. The small fires seemed to burn from every wall, cutting through the musty darkness like hazy sunlight in early morning. In the center of the vast chamber, the great stone trapdoor that led to the forgotten dungeons below was thrown open, and from out of the darkness of the pit came the distant sounds of metal striking stone. The cellar was swarming with armed men and they came at the two intruders from all directions.

Hendel and Menion met the rush with a ferocious counterassault that carried them into the very midst of their assailants. The highlander had retrieved a sword from one of the fallen guards at the top of the stairway. Standing back to back with Hendel, he began to cut away the number of his attackers. From the corner of his eye, he saw a familiar scarlet-robed figure emerging from the black pit of the dungeon; at the sight of the hated Stenmin, the Prince of Leah felt a savage rage well up inside. With renewed fury, he charged into the enemy guards, trying to cut through their ranks and reach the man who had betrayed them. An unmistakable look of fear crossed the mystic's lean features as he shrank from the terrible battle.

Back to back, the Dwarf and the highlander fought as if they had gone mad. Men lay dead and dying all about them. Both were wounded in a dozen places, but they didn't feel the pain. Twice Menion had slipped on the bloodied floor and gone down, and each time Hendel had driven off the attackers while the highlander scrambled back to his feet. Only five of the enemy were still standing, but Hendel and Menion Leah were nearly finished. They fought like mechanical creatures now, their bodies soaked in blood and sweat, their limbs leaden and nerveless. As if suddenly regaining his wits, the terrified Stenmin raced to the edge of the pit and began screaming for help. The Prince of Leah responded instantly. With a final burst of strength, he crashed into two of his attackers, knocking both sprawling. A third rushed to stop him, but the charging highlander put his sword into the man up to the hilt and left it there. Grasping a fallen lance, he pounced upon the cringing mystic and stunned him with a sweeping blow from the great weapon. As the lean frame crumpled to the stone floor, Menion Leah gripped the edges of the heavy trapdoor and heaved upward with the last of his fading strength.

It was as if the stone had been chained in open position to the cellar floor. It did not move. From far below, the sounds of metal on stone ceased, replaced by the thudding of booted feet as men raced toward the trapdoor. Only seconds remained. If they reached the stairs, Menion was a dead man. Bracing himself, the wounded man again threw all of his weight into lifting the massive piece of stone, and this time it rose. Groaning with the terrible strain, the highlander raised upward against the great trapdoor until at last it came over and fell with a great booming thud into place in the ancient floor. With numb, sweating hands he bound the chain through the sealing rings and fastened it with an iron bar. The passageway was closed. If the Northland army sought entrance here, they would have to cut their way through several feet of stone and iron.

"Menion."

The sound of his name broke the sudden silence in a cracked whisper. The highlander had fallen to his hands and knees, but his groping hand found a discarded sword and he raised his battered face. Across a floor littered with a tangled mass of fallen enemy guards, their twisted bodies either lifeless or in their final death throes, the eyes of the Prince of Leah found his friend. The Dwarf stood with his back to the wall near the bottom of the cellar stairway, the great mace still gripped tightly in one hand. There were dead bodies all about him. He had killed them all. No one had escaped. The hardened eyes met Menion's for just an instant, and it was as if they were again meeting for the first time in the lowlands beyond the Black Oaks. He was the old Hendel—taciturn, grim-faced, ever resourceful. Then the mace slipped from his hand, his eyes glazed over; with a long sigh, his body slid slowly, lifelessly to the death that had finally claimed him.

Hendel! The name raced through Menion's stunned, disbelieving mind as he struggled numbly to his feet and stood swaying unsteadily in the flickering shadows. Tears welled into his reddened eyes and ran in dark streams down his battered face. With leaden steps he picked his way over the lifeless bodies of the enemy dead, gasping now in unrestrained fury and helplessness. He was only dimly aware of Stenmin regaining consciousness somewhere behind him. He reached the Dwarf's side and knelt beside him, gently cradling the limp form next to his breast. How many times had Hendel saved his life? How many times had he saved them all, only to . . . ? He couldn't finish the thought. He could only cry. Everything seemed to break inside of him at once.

Stenmin raised himself slowly to one knee and stared blankly about the cellar at the mass of tangled corpses. His men all dead, the stone trapdoor closed and chained, and . . . Fear surged up inside his pain-wracked body. One of the intruders was still alive—the highlander! He hated that man, hated him so badly he fleetingly considered trying to kill him, but then the fear returned even stronger than before and abruptly his thoughts turned to escape. Escape so that he could live! There was only one way out—up the stairs past the kneeling man and through the open cellar door. Already he was on his feet, moving noiselessly through the carnage, half walking, half slinking toward the unguarded steps.

The highlander's back was turned to him, still holding the body of the Dwarf. Sweat beads broke out on Stenmin's forehead and the thin lips curled menacingly—yet it was fear that kept him moving. Only a few more steps. He would be free again. The city was doomed; all of them would die—all of his enemies. But he would survive. He had to fight down the sudden impulse to laugh aloud. One hand touched the stone of the ancient stairway, one foot followed; the highlander was only feet away, still unsuspecting, the outer cellar door was ajar and unguarded. Freedom! Just steps . . .

Then Menion turned. A shriek of terror escaped the mystic's lips as his eyes viewed the terrible look on the face of the Prince of Leah. Stenmin clawed his way frantically toward the open doorway, stumbling blindly in the long red robes.

He was only halfway up the steps when Menion caught him.

At the walls of Tyrsis, the impossible was happening. Upon descending from the parapets of the Outer Wall, Balinor had moved quickly to the massive city gates. The Legion guardsmen stationed before the great iron portals had snapped quickly to attention. Everything appeared to be as it should. The series of inner lock bolts, controlled mechanically from the tower gatehouse, had been run firmly into place in the crease where the gates swung outward. The cumbersome iron bar that served as an additional safeguard lay snugly in its fittings across the width of both gates. Balinor stared fixedly at the great wall, a nagging doubt persisting. Something was going to happen; he could feel it. The gates were the key to the city, the one weak link in the otherwise impenetrable stone wall that bound Tyrsis. Siege towers, grappling hooks, scaling ladders—all these were futile attempts to breach that great wall, and the Warlock Lord had to know it. The gates were the key.

His eyes drifted skyward to the tower gatehouse, a squat, windowless stone enclosure which housed the mechanism

that controlled the inner locks. Two Legion soldiers stood
attentively at the single door. A picked squad of men had
been given the responsibility of protecting that crucial
mechanism, men selected by Balinor and commanded by
Captain Sheelon. On both sides of the small housing, the
men of the Border Legion defended the battlements. It
seemed impossible that the Northlanders expected to seize
the gatehouse. Still . . .

Already the tall borderman had moved to the foot of the
narrow stairway that led to the gatehouse and had begun to
climb the worn stone blocks. Sudden cries from the wall di-
verted his attention momentarily, and he paused as the air
sounded with the deep humming of a thousand bowstrings,
and a rush of arrows swept the ramparts of the Outer Wall.
Hurriedly Balinor gained the battlements and in three short
strides reached the wall. He peered carefully down at the face
of the bluff, littered with bodies and debris and dotted with
small oil fires that burned hazily in the morning mist. The
Northlanders had temporarily abandoned any direct assault.
Instead, lines of archers five men deep were raking the defenders on the ramparts with a concentrated barrage.

The reason for this new tactic was immediately obvious.
At the rim of the bluff, a detachment of heavily armored
Rock Trolls pushed forward a ponderous, mobile battering
ram, shielded from the top and sides by a broad canopy of
sheet iron. While the Border Legion was pinned down by
heavy fire from the archers, the giant Trolls would move the
great ram into place before the city gates and force an entry.

The plan appeared at first glance both preposterous and
unworkable. Yet if the gatehouse fell to the enemy, the inner
lock bolts could be released and only the long, iron crossbar
would hold the gates closed. The bar alone would not be

enough to stand against the massive battering ram. Balinor ran toward the small gatehouse. The guards came silently to attention. He gave them a passing glance, his hand reaching anxiously for the door handle. Sheelon was nowhere in sight. The door swung inward, and he was a step into the closed room when he realized he had never seen either of the sentries.

The giant borderman reacted instinctively, sidestepping the noiseless rush of the guard behind him, seizing the outstretched lance that barely grazed his back and wrenching it free from the would-be assassin. His back to the wall, the King had only a moment to survey the dimly lighted room. The bodies of Sheelon and his men lay to one side, twisted in death, their stiffened corpses stripped naked of armor and clothing. From out of the shadows at the rear of the housing a group of faceless attackers rushed the borderman, daggers raised for the kill. Balinor threw the heavy lance crossways into their midst and broke for the open doorway. But the second sentry, who had remained just outside, saw him coming and quickly pulled the door shut from the other side. The trapped King had no time to force his way free. There was barely enough time to draw the great broadsword before his assailants were upon him. They bore him roughly to the floor, daggers chipping and glancing off the protective coat of chain mail that had saved his life so many times. With a mighty surge, Balinor shook himself free and regained his footing. In the faint light of the shuttered room, his attackers were only shadows, but his eyes were adjusting, and he cut at them as they moved toward him. Two of the dark forms screamed and dropped lifelessly as the great blade cut through them, but their companions had already broken past the sweeping sword and closed with the King.

For a second time, Balinor was wrestled down, but again he twisted free and the battle surged back across the little room. The din of the attack outside completely obscured the sounds of battle from within the stone housing; the border-man knew that unless he managed to get the door open, no one would come to his aid. He placed his back to the wall once more and swung the broadsword sharply as the shad-owed enemies resumed the assault. Three were dead and sev-eral were wounded, but those who remained in the battle were beginning to wear him down with their repeated rushes. He had to get free quickly. Then an audible grinding of levers and gears filled the gatehouse, and he realized in horror that someone was releasing the inner lock bolts of the front gates. With a wild charge, he broke for the lock mech-anism, but the determined attackers barred his path, and he was forced into a circling movement away from his objective. A moment later there was a sharp grating of metal on metal, followed by a series of hammering blows. They were jam-ming the release levers! In complete disregard for his own safety, the infuriated Balinor threw himself on the remaining enemies.

Then the gatehouse door burst open and the body of the traitorous sentry was thrust violently through the entryway. Gray daylight flooded the darkened room and the lean figure of Durin appeared from out of nowhere at the side of his friend. In grim silence they cut away at the few enemy at-tackers who remained, forcing them away from the jammed machinery, away from the open doorway and escape, and into the far corner of the small housing. There, locked to-gether in ferocious hand-to-hand combat, they destroyed them. Without a second glance at the dead men, the blood-ied King rushed back to the damaged lock mechanism, his face lined in fury as he surveyed the twisted mass of metal levers and gears. Angrily he threw his weight against the main release. It would not move. Durin turned pale as he realized what had happened.

"We don't have enough time!" Balinor exploded heatedly, wrenching violently at the jammed levers.

A great booming crash resounded through the stone housing, vibrating through the walls and shaking the two men ominously.

"The gates!" Durin exclaimed in dismay.

A second crash rocked the gatehouse, and a third. The rushing of booted feet sounded on the ramparts outside and a moment later Messaline's dark face appeared in the open doorway. He started to speak, but Balinor was already issuing commands and moving toward the battlements.

"Get this room cleared away and have our machinists try to free those gears. The gate locks are released and jammed!" Messaline looked as if he had received a mortal blow. "Fortify the gates with timbers and put your best regiment in phalanx formation fifty paces back and to either side. The Northlanders are not to break through. Put two lines of archers on the Inner Wall to bottle up the gate entrance. Reserves and the garrison command will defend the Inner Wall. All others will stay where they are at the Outer Wall. We will hold it as long as we can. If it falls, the Legion will retreat to the secondary defense and hold. If we lose that, we will regroup at the Bridge of Sendic. That will be the last line of defense. Anything else?"

Quickly Durin explained where Hendel had gone. Balinor shook his head wearily.

"We have been betrayed at every turn. Hendel will have to do what he can without our help for the moment. If the palace falls and they break through from the rear, we are finished anyway. Messaline, you'll hold the right flank of the phalanx, Ginnisson will take the left, and I'll be in the center. The enemy is not to break through! Pray that Eventine arrives before our strength fails us."

Messaline disappeared outside in a crouching run. The shattering thrusts of the massive battering ram continued to shake the great wall as Balinor and Durin faced each other across the little room. Already the gray light of day was growing dimmer as the shadow of the Warlock Lord continued to roll ominously closer to the doomed city. The giant borderman reached out slowly and gripped the slim hand of his Elven friend.

"Good-bye, my friend. This is the end for us. Time has just about run out."

"Eventine would not willingly fail us . . ." the Elf began earnestly.

"I know, I know," Balinor replied. "Nor would Allanon. He has not found the Sword or the heir of Shannara. His time has run out as well."

There was a brief silence between them, broken by the shouts of the men on the walls and the crashing of the ram against the gates of Tyrsis. Balinor wiped the blood away from a deep cut over one eye.

"Find your brother, Durin. But before you leave the Outer Wall, have the last of the oil poured onto that ram and fired. If we can't stop them altogether, we'll at least make it a hot place for them to work."

He smiled grimly and slipped quietly out of the gatehouse. Durin stared blankly after him, wondering what perverse fate had brought them to this unjust end. Balinor was the most remarkable man the Elf had ever met. Yet he had lost everything—his family, his city, his home, and now his life was to be taken from him as well. What kind of world permitted such terrible injustice, where good men were stripped of everything and soulless creatures of malice and hatred survived to glory in their pointless death? Once he had been so sure they would not fail, that somehow they would find a way to destroy the hated Warlock Lord and save the four lands. But that dream was ended.

Durin looked up dazedly as several burly Legion machinists entered the gatehouse to begin their hopeless work on the jammed lock mechanism. Quickly, the lean Elf moved out onto the ramparts. It was time to find Dayel.

The struggle to hold the Outer Wall was incredibly vicious. Despite the devastating barrage concentrated against the men of the Border Legion by the lines of Gnome archers below the bluff, the valiant defenders managed to cut away at the Trolls that manned the great battering ram before the weakened gates. The remaining cauldrons of oil were moved to the fortifications above the ram and poured on the enemy machine and its handlers as they worked. Torches followed, and instantly the entire area was consumed in a mass of flames and rolling black smoke. Metal melted and smoldered and the Trolls were burned alive after the first few minutes of the terrible heat, their armor becoming a furnace they could not escape. But new enemy soldiers quickly filled the breach and the mighty ram continued to break against the city gates in crashing, booming blows that first bent, then split the crossbar and the timbers that held the tall portals secure.

The gray sky turned black from the oily smoke that rose above the burning grasslands to cloak the city walls and their defenders in a deep, murky haze. The smell of burnt flesh choked the nose and lungs of the Legion soldiers as the charred, blackened bodies of the Troll attackers lay in heaps before the Outer Wall. Desperately the two opponents strove to break each other's strength, but the stalemate continued. For a short time, it seemed that the day might end without any further change in the fortunes of either army.

But at last the great crossbar snapped in two, the supporting timbers sagged and splintered, and the giant battering ram forced a breach in the gates of Tyrsis. In a rush, the first Northlanders poured into the parade grounds and were dropped instantly by Legion archers positioned atop the Inner Wall. Drawn up in a three-sided box opening toward the Outer Wall gates, the Legion phalanx braced for the enemy rush, spears bristling through locked shields. The ram pushed forward and the gates opened farther still, and then the foremost ranks of the Northland invasion force surged through the gap and threw themselves against the spears of the Border Legion. The Legion defenses wavered slightly, but held, thrusting the attackers backward, where they milled in confusion as they were cut to pieces by the archers on the walls both above and behind them. In seconds the parade ground was blanketed with Northland dead and wounded, and the breach in the gates had momentarily been bottled up so thoroughly that the great invasion forces could not advance farther.

Durin had positioned himself next to the gatehouse on the Outer Wall, and from there he watched the Northland assault break apart on the Legion phalanx. He had discovered that his brother had gone with Janus Senpre to the palace, and reluctantly he decided to remain with Balinor for as long as possible. The enemy was attempting to regain its momentum now; on the plains below, Maturens directed the great Rock Troll commands toward the breach in the gates of the besieged city. The Northland army was calling on the backbone of its strength in a determined effort to crush the Southlanders once and for all. The Outer Wall was under attack again from all angles, as hordes of Gnomes and lesser Trolls rushed forward with ladders, ropes, and grappling hooks. The thinned ranks of the Legion defenders who remained on the battlements fought desperately to prevent a breakthrough, but their men were dying and the numbers of the Northland army seemed limitless. The battle was turning into a telling war of attrition that the men of Tyrsis could not hope to win.

Then, into the growing blackness of the sky north of the besieged city, two winged figures rose and hovered menacingly, and Durin felt his blood turn cold. Skull Bearers! Were they so certain of victory that they dared reveal themselves in daylight? The Elf felt his heart sink. He had done all he could here; it was time to join his brother. Whatever fate awaited them, they would at least face it together.

Nimbly, he turned and moved along the wall in a crouching run until he was just behind the left flank of the Legion phalanx. A steep causeway led downward to the barracks grounds that lay between the walls of the city, several hundred feet behind the Legion rear lines. A deafening roar erupted from the men engaged in battle on the walls. As Durin neared the base of the rampway, he saw the tall, armored forms of the great Rock Trolls pouring through the breach in the gates of the Outer Wall. He paused involuntarily, sensing that the next few minutes would be crucial ones for the Border Legion.

The phalanx tightened its formation and braced for the assault as the massive Trolls drew up their ranks and moved slowly toward the center of the defensive line, where Balinor held command. Ten feet separated the combatants when, to everyone's surprise, the entire Troll regiment wheeled abruptly to the left and charged directly into the Legion flank. There was a crunching sound as the two forces joined and a terrific clash of metal as spear met mace and shield struck armor. For a moment the Legion phalanx held firmly and the foremost of the giant Trolls were killed and thrown down. But the superior strength and sheer weight of the Northlanders pressed back against the smaller men of the Border Legion until at last the right end of the phalanx began to break apart.

The commanding figure of Ginnisson moved quickly into the gap, his red hair flying as he fought to hold the line. The Trolls were driven back step by step as Balinor closed on the right and Messaline from the rear. It was the most ferocious man-to-man combat Durin had been witness to in this terrible conflict, and he watched in awe as the great Rock Trolls held off the men of the Border Legion and once again pressed forward. An instant later the breach in the phalanx was forced and Ginnisson disappeared from view entirely as a rush of massive attackers overwhelmed him and raced toward the barracks and the Inner Wall.

Durin was directly in their path. There might have been time to gain the safety of the walls, but the Elf was already on one knee, the ash bow armed and drawn back. The first Troll fell at fifty paces, the second ten closer, the third at twenty-five. Legion soldiers from the wall rushed to the attack, and archers from the lesser heights of the Inner Wall tried desperately to halt the Troll offensive. Everything in front of the Elf was confusion as Troll and Legionnaire surged toward him, locked together in desperate hand-to-hand combat.

Still the massive Northlanders continued to come at him, and Durin fired the last of his arrows into their midst.

He threw down the bow, and for the first time thought about escape. But there was no time left, and he barely managed to seize a discarded sword before the surging mass of fighters was upon him. He struggled wildly to keep his balance as he was forced back against the barracks wall. A giant Rock Troll loomed directly over him, a black mass of bark-like skin and armor, and the Elf twisted desperately to one side as a huge mace swung downward. He felt a blinding pain in his left shoulder, followed by a strange numbness. Grimly he fought to stay conscious, his pain abruptly returning in a flood that wracked his lean frame. But he was already falling. His face lay against the earth as he breathed in shallow gasps. A terrible heaviness pushed down on him as he felt the tide of the battle move beyond him. He tried to see, but the effort of looking was too great and he slipped quietly into unconsciousness, through which pain still seemed to penetrate in great bursts.

Menion Leah bent his blood-streaked face over the body of Hendel and carefully raised the inert form in his arms. With studied, mechanical steps, he threaded his way through the bodies of their fallen enemies to reach the stairs and climbed slowly toward the open doorway, stepping carefully, but without looking, over the headless lump tangled in a loose mass of reddened robes that sprawled grotesquely across the center of the ancient stairway. Dazedly, the highlander passed through the cellar entryway and moved down the vacant palace hall, gripping the lifeless form of the Dwarf close to him. He walked aimlessly, his eyes shockingly blank, his face stricken with a terrible stunned look that screamed in silent agony for release. He reached the palace foyer and there halted as the sound of running feet echoed hollowly from the eastern corridor. Gently he laid his burden on the polished floor and stood quietly as the slim, titian-haired girl slowed in front of him, sudden tears streaming down her beautiful face.

"Oh, Menion," she whispered faintly. "What have they done?"

His eyes flickered and his mouth moved dumbly as he fought for the words that would not come. Quickly Shirl reached for him, the slim arms coming tightly around his stooped frame, her face close to his own. A moment later she felt his strong arms come around her shoulders and the terrible agony trapped deep within him broke soundlessly and flooded over her to disappear in her silence and warmth.

On the ramparts of the Inner Wall, Balinor completed a final check of the Legion defenses and paused wearily above the heavily barricaded gates. The Northlanders were already massing for a final rush. Just moments earlier, the impregnable Outer Wall had fallen and the courageous soldiers of the Border Legion had been forced back to the second line of defense. Balinor stared grimly at the enemy swarming over the heights of the towering wall and gripped the hilt of his great broadsword until his knuckles turned white beneath the chain mail. His cloak and tunic had been shredded in the terrible combat to hold the breach in the gates of the Outer Wall against the Troll assault. Balinor had held together the center of the Legion phalanx, but both wings had collapsed. Ginnisson had been killed, Messaline was severely wounded, and hundreds of Southlanders had died holding the Outer Wall until all hope was gone. Even Durin had disappeared in the fighting. Now the King of Callahorn stood alone.

He gestured sharply to the men bracing the timbers that supported the gates below, the chain mail on his arm glinting brightly in the graying light, showing where a dozen blows had chipped and nicked the protective metal. For a moment he allowed his courage to give way entirely to despair. They had failed him—all of them. Eventine and the Elven army. Allanon. The whole Southland. Tyrsis was on the brink of complete annihilation and with it the land of Callahorn, and still no one came to their aid. The Legion had fought alone to save them all—the final defense for the Southland. What purpose had it served? He caught himself quickly, roughly pushing down the doubts and despondency. There was no time to indulge himself. There were too many lives to be saved, and he was the one they depended upon.

The Northland army was drawing up its lines along the base of the Outer Wall, the familiar scaling ladders, ropes, and grappling irons held ready for the assault. Already scattered bands of the massive Rock Trolls had scaled the Inner Wall during the battle on the parade grounds and broken into the city proper. He wondered briefly what had become of the reliable Hendel and Menion Leah. Apparently they had secured the palace and prevented any rear assault, or the city would have already fallen. Now they would have to hold in the event isolated groups of the enemy breached the Inner Wall and broke for the palace.

Bits of soot from the rolling clouds of oil smoke stung his eyes, and he rubbed them until they watered freely. Everything seemed masked in a heavy gray haze as he glanced quickly at the wall fortifications. The Legion had been placed in an impossible defensive position against an enemy so vast that the loss of hundreds from their ranks was insignificant. He thought of Hendel's words after the deaths of his father and brother. The last Buckhannah. The name would die with him, die as Tyrsis and her people died. The familiar roar rose in thunderous echoes from the throats of the Northlanders, and they charged recklessly for the Legion's walled defense. The long scar on the giant borderman's cheek turned a deeper shade of purple, and he brought the broadsword up menacingly.

At almost the same moment, the first scattered remnants of the Troll advance force came together at the foot of the Bridge of Sendic and hesitated. A line of determined Legion soldiers spanned the center of the wide stone arch, barring all passage to the home of the Buckhannahs. Janus Senpre stood foremost, flanked on one side by Menion Leah, his battered frame erect as he gripped the sword of Leah with both hands, and on the other by Dayel, his youthful face drawn, but resolute. Behind the Rock Trolls, the air was thick with rolling smoke as fresh fires rose from the buildings of the city. Frightened cries sounded above the clamor of battle at the Inner Wall. In the distance, darting figures were seen scurrying across the deserted Tyrsian Way for the safety of their homes. Silently the forces faced one another, the number of Trolls growing quickly as others appeared to swell their ranks. They studied the Southlanders with the blank, experienced look of professional soldiers, confident in the knowledge that they were the best-trained fighting unit in the world. The defenders on the bridge numbered less than fifty.

The afternoon sky had gone suddenly black, and an eerie stillness settled over the two armies. From somewhere in the burning city, Menion caught the faint, clear cry of a small child. Several feet to his left, Dayel felt the cold north wind fade with a low, sighing whisper. Before them, the giant Trolls moved carefully into formation, the great maces held loosely; then as a unit, they lumbered forward. At the center of the bridge, the city's last line of defense braced for the Northland rush.

On the ridge west of the city, Flick Ohmsford and the little band of Elven horsemen watched helplessly as the destruction of Tyrsis mounted. Flanked by Eventine and Jon Lin Sandor, the Valeman felt the last trace of hope fade as the hordes of the mammoth Northland army poured unchecked through the breached gates of the Outer Wall. Clouds of dark smoke rose now from within Tyrsis, and the last remnants of the proud Border Legion had been driven from her walls. The city's defenses had been broken. He stared in horror as the grotesque figures of the Skull Bearers hovered in full view above the advancing enemy, black wings spread wide against the darkening noon sky. The worst that Allanon had foreseen had come to pass. The Warlock Lord had won.

Then a sharp cry sounded from a rider to his left, and Eventine's flushed countenance surged into view as he spurred his mount forward, crowding the Valeman aside in his eagerness. Across the wide expanse of the empty grassland, still many miles to the west, a faint, dark line grew against the grayness of the horizon. A low rumble of pounding hooves broke out of the distance to blend with the clamor and fury of the battle behind them.

The dark line grew quickly in size and became horsemen, thousands strong, banners and lances flashing color and iron. Strident and clear, the booming wail of a war horn sounded their arrival. Cheers rose from the little band of

Elves as the massive body of horsemen began to blanket the plains, sweeping at breakneck speed toward Tyrsis. Forewarned of their approach, the rear guard of the Northland army had already closed ranks and turned to face the advancing tide. It was the Elven army come at last—for the defenders of Tyrsis, for the beleaguered nations of three lands, for everything mankind had fought so hard to preserve through the ages. Come perhaps too late!

EIGHT

I N A SINGLE SMOOTH, silent motion, Shea slid the ancient blade free from its battered sheath. The metal gleamed in the faint torchlight with a deep bluish tint, the iron surface flawless as if the legendary Sword had never been carried in battle. It was unexpectedly light, a slim, balanced blade of exceptional workmanship, the handle carefully engraved with the now familiar crest of a raised hand holding forth a burning torch. Shea held the weapon guardedly, glancing quickly at Panamon Creel and Keltset, seeking their reassurance, afraid suddenly of what was going to happen. His grim-faced companions remained motionless, their expressions blank and impassive. He gripped the Sword tightly with both hands, bringing the blade around sharply until it pointed skyward. His palms were sweating freely, and he felt his body grow cold in the cell's darkness. There was a faint stirring to one side, and a feeble moan broke from the lips of Orl Fane. Moments passed, and Shea was conscious of the raised impression of the crest pressing into the palms of his clenched hands. Still nothing happened.

... In the gray half-light of the empty chamber at the peak of Skull Mountain, the dark waters of the stone basin

191

were quiet and smooth. The power that was the Warlock Lord lay dormant. . . .

Abruptly the Sword of Shannara grew warm in Shea's hands, and a strange, pulsating wave of heat coursed from the dark iron into the palms of the astonished Valeman and then disappeared. Startled, he took a quick step backward and lowered the blade slightly. An instant later, the sudden warmth was replaced by a sharp tingling sensation that surged out of the weapon into his body. Though there was no pain, the abruptness of the sensation caused him to wince reflexively, and he felt his muscles tighten. Instinctively, he sought to release the talisman; to his shock, he found that he could not let go. Something touched deeply into him to forbid it, and his hands locked securely around the ancient handle.

The tingling sensation rushed through him, and now he was conscious of a return flow of energy that pulled at his life force, carrying it down through the cold metal of the Sword itself, until the weapon became a part of him. The gilt paint that coated the carved pommel began to strip away beneath the Valeman's hands, and the handle turned to polished silver, laced with reddish streaks of light that seemed to burn and twist in the bright metal like living things. Shea felt the first stirrings of something coming awake, something that was a part of him, yet foreign to everything he knew himself to be. It pulled at him, subtly but firmly, drawing him down deeper inside himself.

Several steps away, Panamon Creel and Keltset watched with growing concern as the little Valeman seemed to slip into a trance, his eyelids drooping heavily, his breathing slowing, his form turning statuelike in the dim torchlight of the cell. He held the Sword of Shannara before him in both hands, its blade raised and pointed skyward, the polished silver handle gleaming brightly. For an instant, Panamon considered taking hold of the Valeman and shaking him awake, but something restrained the thief. From out of the shadows, Orl Fane began crawling across the smooth stones toward his precious sword. Panamon hesitated a moment and then nudged him back roughly with his boot.

Shea felt himself being drawn inward, borne like a cork caught in an undertow. Everything around him began to fade from view. The walls, ceiling, and floor of the stone cell disappeared first, then the cringing whimpering figure of Orl Fane; finally even the granite forms of Panamon and Keltset vanished. The strange current seemed to wrap around him completely, and he found that he could not resist it. Slowly he was pulled into the innermost recesses of his being, until all was blackness.

. . . A momentary shudder rippled the still basin waters in the cavern depths at the crown of the solitary death's head, and the frightened, crawling beings that served the Master scampered from their places of concealment in the stone walls. The Warlock Lord stirred warily from his broken sleep. . . .

In the vortex of emotion and basic self that comprised the centermost region of his being, the bearer of the Sword of Shannara came face-to-face with himself. For a moment, there was a chaos of uncertain impressions; then the current seemed to reverse itself, carrying him off in a new direction entirely. Pictures and impressions loomed up before him. Thrust suddenly before his eyes, the world that was his birthplace and life source, from past to present, lay open and revealed to him, stripped bare of his carefully nurtured illusions, and he saw the reality of existence in all its starkness.

No soft dreams colored its view of life, no wishful fantasies clothed the harshness of its self-shaped choices, no self-conceived visions of hope softened the rawness of its judgments. Amid its sprawling vastness, he saw himself displayed for the pitiful, insignificant spark of momentary life that he represented.

Shea's mind seemed to explode within him, and he was paralyzed by what he saw. He struggled wildly for his grasp of the vision of self that had always sustained him, for what had been his hold on sanity, fighting to shield himself from the awesome view of his inner nakedness and the weakness of the thing he was compelled to recognize as himself.

Then the force of the current seemed to diminish slightly. Shea forced his eyes open, avoiding for an instant the inner vision. Before him was the upright Sword, ablaze with a blinding white light that surged downward from the blade to the pommel. Beyond it, he could see Panamon and Kelt-set, standing motionless, their gaze fixed on him. Then the eyes of the giant Troll shifted slightly, centering on the Sword. There was a strange understanding and urgency in the gesture, and as Shea looked back to the Sword of Shannara, its light seemed to pulsate feverishly. There was a sense of impatience about its movement as it strained to advance from the blade into his body and was somehow thwarted in its efforts.

For a moment more, the Valeman struggled against this advance, then his eyes again closed and the inner vision returned. The first shock of revelation was past him now, and he made an effort to understand what was happening. He concentrated on the images of Shea Ohmsford, immersing himself completely in the thoughts, emotions, judgments, and motivations that made up this character that was both alien and familiar.

The images cleared with frightening sharpness, and abruptly he saw another side to himself, a side he had never been able to recognize—or perhaps had simply refused to accept. It revealed itself in an endless line of events, all caricatures of the memories he had believed in so strongly. Here was an accounting of every hurt he had caused to others, every petty jealousy he had felt, his deep-seated prejudices, his deliberate half-truths, his self-pity, his fears—all that was dark and hidden within himself. Here was the Shea Ohmsford who had fled the Vale, not to save and protect family and friends, but in fear of his own life, seeking any excuse for his panic—the Shea Ohmsford who had selfishly allowed Flick to share his nightmare and thereby ease the pain of it. Here was the Valeman who had sneered at and belittled the moral code of Panamon Creel, while at the same time allowing the thief to risk his own life to save Shea's. And here . . .

The images went on endlessly. Shea Ohmsford recoiled in horror from what he was seeing. He could not accept it. He could never accept it!

Yet drawing from some inner well of strength and understanding, his mind opened receptively to the images, expanding outward to embrace them, persuading him, or perhaps forcing him, to admit the reality of what he had been shown. He could not sensibly deny this other side of his character; like the limited image of the person he had always believed himself to be, this was only a part of the real Shea Ohmsford—but it was indeed a part, however difficult he found it to accept.

But he had to accept it. It was the truth.

. . . Filled with white-hot rage, the Warlock Lord came fully awake. . . .

Truth? Shea opened his eyes again to stare at the Sword of Shannara, gleaming whitely from blade to handle. A warm, pulsating feeling spread rapidly through him, bringing no new vision of self, but only a deep, inner awareness.

Abruptly, he realized that he knew the secret of the Sword. The Sword of Shannara possessed the power to reveal Truth—to force the man who held it to recognize the truth about himself; perhaps even to reveal the truth about others who might come in contact with it. For an instant, he could not bring himself to believe any of it. He hesitated in his analysis, trying desperately to follow up on this unexpected revelation—to find something more because there simply had to be more. But there was nothing else to discover. That was all there was to the Sword's vaunted magic. Beyond that, it was no more than what it appeared to be—a finely crafted weapon from another age.

The knowledge of what this meant ripped through his mind and left him stunned. No wonder Allanon had never revealed the secret of the Sword. What kind of weapon was this against the incredible power of the Warlock Lord? What possible defense could it offer against a being that could crush the life out of him with little more than a thought? With chilling certainty, Shea knew that he had been betrayed. The Sword's legendary power was a lie! He felt himself begin to panic, and he closed his eyes tightly against the chill he was feeling. The blackness about him began to churn violently until he grew dizzy with its sweep and seemed to lose consciousness altogether.

. . . In the bleak, gray emptiness of his mountain refuge, the Warlock Lord watched and listened. Slowly his rage began to subside, and the misty darkness within the hood nodded in satisfaction. The Valeman he had thought destroyed had survived. In spite of everything, he had found the Sword. But the man was pitifully weak, lacking the knowledge necessary to understand the talisman. He was already overcome with fear, and he would be vulnerable. Swiftly, noiselessly, the Master glided from the cavernous chamber. . . .

The tall figure of Allanon paused hesitantly at the crest of a barren, windswept hill, his dark eyes invisible beneath the heavy brow as they studied the stark, solitary line of mountains that rose hauntingly against the gray northern horizon. They seemed to stare back at him, their cavernous faces scarred and worn, reflecting the soul of the land that had spawned them so many years ago. A deep silence hovered expectantly over the whole of the vast wilderness that was the Northland. Even the high mountain winds had died into stillness. The Druid wrapped his black robes about him and breathed sharply. There could be no mistake; his extended mind sweep would not lie to him about this. That which he had worked so hard to achieve had finally come to pass. In the deep recesses of the Knife Edge, still far distant from where the mystic stood, Shea Ohmsford had drawn forth the Sword of Shannara.

Yet it was all wrong! Even though the Valeman might be able to withstand and accept the truth about himself and perhaps recognize the secret of the Sword, he was still not prepared to use the talisman properly against the Warlock Lord. There would be no time for him to grow into the necessary confidence while he was alone and unaided, deprived of the knowledge that only Allanon could give him. He would be filled with self-doubt and torn by fear, easy prey for Brona. Even now, the Druid could sense the awakening of the enemy. The Dark Lord was beginning the descent from his mountain refuge, fully confident that the bearer of the Sword was blind to the full power of the talisman. His attack would come quickly and savagely, and Shea would be destroyed before he could learn to survive.

Only brief minutes remained before the confrontation, and Allanon knew that he could never arrive in time to help. He had realized at last that Shea and the Sword of Shannara had somehow both gone northward. Leaving the others in Callahorn, he had rushed to the Valeman's aid. But matters had developed too quickly. Now there was only one chance for him to be of any use to Shea—if, indeed, there was any real chance at all—and he was still too far away. Clutching his robes about his spare frame, the Druid moved swiftly down the hillside, scattering the dusty surface in small clouds as he went, his features tight with determination.

Panamon Creel started forward as Shea crumpled to one knee, but Keltset's massive arm reached in front of him. The Troll was facing back toward the entrance to the caverns, listening. Panamon could hear nothing, but a sudden sensation of fear and growing horror reached down inside him, halting his motion toward the Valeman. Keltset's eyes turned, as if marking the progress of someone passing through the corridor beyond the cell, and Panamon felt his fear deepen.

Then a shadow fell over everything. The torchlight that outlined the tiny cavern room dimmed sharply. Standing at the doorway of the cell was a tall form shrouded in black robes. Instinctively, Panamon Creel knew that this was the Warlock Lord. Where a face should have been, beneath the closely drawn hood, there was nothing but darkness and a deep, green mist that moved sluggishly about twin sparks of reddish fire. The sparks turned first toward Panamon and Keltset, freezing them instantly into motionless statues, sending all the fears and terrors they had ever known rushing through their paralyzed forms. The thief struggled to cry a warning to the little Valeman, but he found that he could not speak, and he watched helplessly as the faceless cowl shifted slowly toward Shea.

The Valeman felt himself drift back into consciousness in the shadowed dampness of the little cell. Everything seemed strangely distant to him, though there was a vague warning signal sounding somewhere in the back of his clouded mind. But he responded sluggishly, and for a time there was only the musty smell of stale air and rock and the faint flickering of a single torch. Through a haze, he saw the motionless forms of Panamon and Keltset no more than five feet from him, fear mirrored in their hard features. Orl Fane crouched at the rear of the cell, twisted into a small yellow ball that whimpered and mumbled incoherently. Before him, the blade of the Sword of Shannara gleamed brightly.

Then instantly, the secret of the Sword came back to him—and with it, the helplessness of his situation. He started to lift his head, but his eyes seemed locked in front of him. Sudden fear and despair washed over him like a river of ice, and he felt himself drowning in it. He began to sweat coldly and his hands were shaking. A single thought screamed in his mind: Escape! Flee, before the fearsome creature whose forbidden kingdom he had dared invade should discover his presence and destroy him! The purpose for which he had risked everything no longer mattered; all that remained in his mind was the compelling need to flee.

He staggered erect. Every fiber of his being screamed at him to break and dash for the doorway, to throw down the Sword and run. But he could not do it. Something inside him refused to release the Sword. Desperately he fought to control his fear, his hands closing tightly about the handle of the Sword, gripping the metal until the knuckles turned white with pain. It was all that he had left, all that stood between himself and complete panic. He clung to it in desperation, his sanity held together by a talisman he knew to be useless.

MORTAL CREATURE, I AM HERE!

The words were a chilling echo in the deep silence. Shea's eyes fought to look toward the doorway. At first he found only shadows; then the shadows tightened slowly, gathering together to form the cloaked figure of the Warlock Lord. It hovered menacingly at the chamber door, an impenetrable, dark, formless robe. From within the recesses of the cowl, the green mists swirled and the sparks of flame that were its eyes flashed and grew.

MORTAL CREATURE, I AM HERE. BOW DOWN BEFORE ME!

Shea turned white with fear. Something huge and black struck at his mind, and he balanced precariously on the thin edge of total panic. A bottomless chasm seemed to open before him. It would take only one small shove . . . He forced himself to concentrate on the Sword and his own desperate need to stay alive. A crimson haze slipped over his mind, bringing with it the voices of countless doomed creatures that cried for mercy without hope. Crawling, twisted things were clinging to his arms and legs, pulling at him, drawing him downward into the chasm. His courage turned to water.

He was so small, so vulnerable. How could he resist a being as awesome as the Warlock Lord?

At the far side of the cell, Panamon Creel watched the black-robed figure draw nearer to Shea. The Warlock Lord seemed to be a thing of no substance, a faceless cowl, an empty robe. But he was obviously too much for Shea to handle alone, Sword or not. With a quick warning nod to Keltset, Panamon fought back against the sense of panic ripping at him and attacked, the piked arm coming up in a wicked sweep. Almost casually, the dark figure turned to him, now no longer seemingly empty, but filled with awesome power. An arm gestured, and the thief felt something ironlike grip his throat and hurl him back against the wall. He struggled once more to break free, but he was held fast and Keltset with him. Helplessly, they watched the Warlock Lord turn back toward the Valeman.

The struggle was almost over for Shea. He still held the Sword protectively before him, but the last of his resistance was breaking down before the assault of the Dark Lord. He could no longer think rationally. He was powerless against the emotions tearing him apart. From out of the darkness of the hood, a terrible command wrenched at him.

LAY DOWN THE SWORD, MORTAL CREATURE!

Desperately, Shea fought against the urge to obey. Everything became hazy and he struggled to breathe. Far back in his mind, a familiar voice seemed to be calling his name. He tried to answer, screaming inside himself for help. Then the voice of the Warlock Lord ripped at him again.

LAY DOWN THE SWORD!

The blade dipped slightly. Shea felt his mind begin to grow numb, and the darkness moved closer to him. The Sword was of no use to him. Why not discard it and be done?

He was nothing to this awesome being. He was only a frail, insignificant mortal.

The Sword dipped farther. Orl Fane suddenly screamed in mindless terror and fell sobbing on the floor of the darkened cell. Panamon had gone white. Keltset's massive form seemed pressed into the cell wall. The tip of the Sword of Shannara hovered just inches from the stone floor, wavering slowly.

Then the voice in Shea's mind called out to him again. From out of nowhere, the words reached him in a whisper so faint that he could barely distinguish it.

"Shea! Have courage. Trust the Sword."

Allanon!

The Druid's voice pierced the fear and doubt that tightened about the Valeman. But it was so distant—so distant . . .

"Believe in the Sword, Shea. All else is illusion. . . ."

Allanon's words disappeared in a scream of rage from the Warlock Lord as the creature shut the hated Druid's voice from the Valeman's mind. But awareness came too late for Brona. Allanon had thrown a lifeline, and Shea clung to it, pulling himself back from the edge of defeat. The fear and doubt drew back. The Sword came up slightly.

The Warlock Lord seemed to move backward a step, and the faceless cowl turned slightly in the direction of Orl Fane. Instantly the whimpering Gnome came erect with the jerking motion of a wooden puppet. No longer his own master, the pawn of the Dark Lord surged forward, the gnarled yellow hands grasping desperately for the Sword. His fingers closed about the exposed blade and wrenched futilely at it. Then abruptly Orl Fane screamed as if in agony, jerking his hands free of the talisman. His features twisted as he dropped to the floor, and his hands groped at his eyes, covering them as if to shut out some horrible vision.

Again the Warlock Lord gestured. The trembling form struggled to its feet, and the Gnome flung himself back into the battle, shrieking his dismay. Again he seized the flashing blade. Again he screamed in anguish and dropped to his knees, releasing the talisman a second time, his eyes streaming with tears.

Shea stared down at the crumpled form. He understood what was happening. Orl Fane had seen the truth about himself, just as Shea had done upon first touching the Sword. But for the Gnome, the truth was unbearable. Yet there was something strange in all this. Why had not Brona himself attempted to wrest the Sword away? It should have been a simple effort; instead, the Warlock Lord had first tried illusion to force Shea to release the Sword, then had used the already maddened Orl Fane as his cat's-paw. Master of so much power, Brona yet seemed unable to grasp the Sword away. It should have been a simple effort; he groped for the answer, so close now—then there was the first small glimmer of understanding.

Orl Fane was on his feet once more, still hopelessly obedient to the commands of the Warlock Lord. He came at Shea in maddened desperation, his gnarled fingers groping wildly at the air before him. The Valeman tried to avoid the rush, but Orl Fane was beyond reason, his mind gone, his soul no longer his own. With a shriek of fear and frustration, he threw himself against the Sword. For an instant, the wiry form convulsed about the bright metal as the Gnome held himself wrapped about the one thing that still mattered to him in this world. For an instant, it was his at last. Then he died.

Stunned, Shea backed away, pulling the weapon free from the lifeless body. Instantly, the Warlock Lord renewed his assault, thrusting viciously at the Valeman's mind in an effort to crush all resistance. Brutal and direct, he employed no clever twists of doubt, no insinuation of uncertainty, no tricks of self-deception. There was only fear, overwhelming and devastating, hurled with the force of a sledgehammer blow. Visions swam through Shea's mind—the awesome power of the Warlock Lord pictured in a thousand horrible ways, all directed toward his extermination. He felt himself reduced down to the smallest, least significant living thing that crawled upon the earth; in another second, it seemed, the Warlock Lord would grind the helpless human into dust.

But Shea's courage held. He had almost succumbed to madness once, and this time he had to stand firm, to believe in himself and in Allanon. Both hands gripped the Sword as he forced himself to take one small step forward into the constricting haze, into the wall of fear assailing him. He tried to believe that it was only illusion, that the fear and growing panic he felt were not his own. The wall gave slightly, and he fought harder against it. He remembered the death of Orl Fane and built upon his memory a mental picture of all the others who must die should he fail them now. He remembered the whispered words of Allanon. And he concentrated on what he believed to be the Warlock Lord's own weakness, revealed in his strange refusal to grasp the Sword. Shea forced himself to believe that the real secret of the talisman's power was a simple law that affected even a creature as awesome as Brona.

The haze thinned suddenly and the wall of fear splintered. Shea stood again before the Warlock Lord, and the red sparks flashed wildly now in the dim green mists beneath the cowl. The cloaked arms came up quickly as if to ward off some pressing danger, and the dark figure shrank from him. From the dimness of the far wall, Panamon Creel and Keltset suddenly broke free and came rushing forward, weapons drawn. Shea felt the last traces of the Warlock Lord's resistance to his advance break apart and fade. Then the Sword of Shannara came down.

An eerie, soundless shriek of terror ripped from the convulsed shroud and a long, skeletal arm jerked wildly upward. The Valeman pressed the gleaming blade hard against the writhing form, forcing it back against the nearest wall. There would be no escape, he swore softly. There would be an end to the monstrous evil of this creature. Before him, the dark robes shuddered in response as the hooked fingers clawed painfully at the damp cell air. The Warlock Lord began to crumble, and he screamed his hatred of the thing destroying him. Behind his scream, the echo of a thousand other voices cried out for a vengeance that had been too long denied them.

Shea felt the horror of the creature rush through the Sword into his mind, but with it came strength from those other voices, and he did not relent. The touch of the Sword carried with it a truth that could not be denied by all the illusion and deceit of the Warlock Lord. It was a truth he could not admit, could not accept, could not abide—yet a truth against which he had no defense. For the Warlock Lord, the truth was death.

Brona's mortal existence was only an illusion. Long ago, whatever means he had employed to extend his mortal life had failed him, and his body had died. Yet his obsessive conviction that he could not perish kept a part of him alive, and he sustained himself through the very sorcery that had driven him to madness. Denying his own death, he held his lifeless body together to achieve the immortality that had escaped him. A creature existing as a part of two worlds, his power seemed awesome. But now the Sword was forcing him to behold himself as he really was—a decayed, lifeless shell sustained only by a misconceived belief in his own reality—a sham, a fantasy created by force of will alone, as ephemeral as the physical being he had made himself appear. He was a lie that had existed and grown in the fears and doubts of mortal men, a lie that he had created to hide the truth. But now the lie was exposed.

Shea Ohmsford had been able to accept the weakness and frailty that were a part of his human nature, as it was a part of all men. But the Warlock Lord could never accept what the Sword revealed, because the truth was that the creature he had supposed himself to be had ceased to exist almost a thousand years before. All that remained of Brona was the lie; and now that, too, was taken from him by the power of the Sword.

He cried out a final time, a whimper of protest that echoed mournfully through the cell, blending with a rising shout of triumph from a chorus of other wraithlike cries. Then all sound ceased. The outstretched arm began to wither and turn to dust, falling from his shuddering form like ash as his body broke apart beneath the robes. The tiny glints of red glimmered once in the thinning green mist and disappeared. The cloak crumpled and sank emptily, falling to the floor in a pile, with the hooded cowl gradually collapsing, until only a worn tangle of cloth remained.

An instant later, Shea began to sway unsteadily. Too many emotions had chased themselves through his nerves and too much tension over too long a time were demanding their price from his overstrained body. The floor seemed to tilt beneath his feet, and he was falling slowly, slowly into darkness.

In the city of Tyrsis, the long, terrible struggle between earth-born mortal and spirit creature peaked with shocking suddenness. From deep within its rock-encrusted heart, the earth began to rumble, the tremors rippling to the scarred surface in steady, menacing shudders. On the low hills east of Tyrsis, the small band of Elven riders fought roughly to control their frightened mounts, and a haggard Flick Ohmsford stared in bewilderment as the land about him began to shake with the strange vibrations. Atop the Inner Wall, the giant, indestructible figure of Balinor repelled assault after assault as the Northland army sought vainly to breach the Southland defense, and for several minutes the tremors went entirely unnoticed in the ferocity of the battle. And on the Bridge of Sendic, the advancing Trolls halted and glanced uneasily about as the rumbling continued to build. Menion Leah started as long cracks appeared in the ancient stone, and the bridge defenders stood poised to run. The deep vibrations grew rapidly, building with frightening power into a titanic avalanche of booming shudders that swept through the earth and rock. The wind broke over the land with ferocious thrusts that bore down upon and scattered the Elven army still racing to relieve Tyrsis. From Culhaven in the Anar to the farthest reaches of the vast Westland, the great wind roared. Massive forest trees splintered and snapped, and ragged sections of mountains were torn free and crumbled into dust as the blistering force of wind and earthquake gripped the four lands. The sky had deepened into a solid black—cloudless, sunless, and empty, as if the heavens had been obliterated with the single stroke of a massive brush. Huge, jagged streaks of red lightning cut through the darkness, spanning the sky from horizon to horizon in an impossible web of electrical energy. It was the end of the world. It was the end of all life. The holocaust promised since the beginning of the spoken word had finally arrived.

But a moment later it was over, dying instantly into complete and utter stillness. The silence hung shroudlike and complete, until from out of the impenetrable blackness the sound of wailing cries rose dismally, turning quickly into screams of anguish. In the city of Tyrsis, the battle was forgotten. Northlander and Southlander watched in horror as the Skull Bearers drifted skyward like formless wraiths, writhing in unspeakable agony, their hooked limbs twisting as they screamed. They hovered momentarily in full view of the men below, who blanched in horror but could not turn away. Then the winged forms began to disintegrate, their dark bodies breaking slowly into ashes and drifting earthward. Seconds later nothing remained but the vast, empty blackness, which began to move in a huge, rushing sweep that carried it northward, pulling in its borders as if they were the ends of a blanket. To the south first, and then the east and west, blue sky shot into view and the sun swept across the lands with dazzling brightness. In awe, mortal men watched the impossible darkness fold into a single black cloud far to the north, hover motionlessly above the horizon, and then sink downward into the earth and disappear forever.

Time drifted away as Shea floated senselessly in a vast, black, empty void.

"I don't think he made it."

A voice reached into his mind from somewhere far, far away. His hands and face felt the sudden chill of smooth stone against his heated skin.

"Wait a minute, his eyes are blinking. I think he's coming around!"

Panamon Creel. Shea's eyes opened and he found himself lying on the floor in the little cell, yellowish torchlight flickering through the darkness in a hazy glow. He was himself again. One hand still clenched the Sword of Shannara, but the power of the talisman had left him, and the strange bond that had briefly joined them together was gone. He stumbled awkwardly to his hands and knees, but a deep, ominous rumbling shook the cavern and he pitched forward. Strong hands reached out to grab him as he fell.

"Easy now, slow down a minute." Panamon's rough voice sounded almost in his ear. "Let me take a look at you. Here now, look at me." He practically jerked the little Valeman about and their eyes locked. There was just a trace of fear in the thief's hard stare, and then he was smiling. "He's all right, Keltset. Now let's get out of here."

He brought Shea to his feet and started moving toward the open doorway. The massive form of Keltset lumbered several feet ahead. Shea took a few uncertain steps and halted. Something held him back.

"I'm all right," he muttered almost inaudibly.

Then abruptly everything came back to him—the power of the Sword coursing through his body to link them together, his inner visions of the truth about himself, the frightening battle against the Warlock Lord, the death of Orl Fane . . . He screamed and faltered.

Panamon Creel reached down impulsively with his good arm and held the little Valeman close.

"Easy, easy, it's all over, Shea. You've done it—you've won. The Warlock Lord is destroyed. But this whole mountain is shaking apart. We've got to get out of here before the whole place comes down around our ears!"

The low rumbling had grown steadily louder, and chunks of rock were being dislodged from the cavern walls and ceiling and falling in small showers of dust and gravel. Cracks were appearing along the ancient stone as the heavy shaking continued to mount. Shea looked at Panamon and nodded.

"You'll be all right." The scarlet-clad thief rose quickly. "I'm going to get you out of this. That's a promise."

Swiftly the three men moved into the dark passageway leading from the chamber. The craggy tunnel twisted and wound through the heart of the Knife Edge, the rough walls split by jagged seams and fissures. More breaks quickly appeared as the rumbling grew stronger and the walls began to crack and fall apart. The mountain shook as if the earth were threatening to open and swallow it whole, quaking with the force of the thunderous reverberations that echoed brokenly from the core of the earth. They passed through countless small passageways and connecting chambers, moving steadily, yet unable to find an exit to safety. Several times one or more went down under a cascade of rock and dust, but each time they worked themselves free. Huge chunks of rock fell crashing before them to block the tunnel passage, but the powerful Keltset heaved the boulders aside, and the small party continued quickly on. Shea began to lose all sense of what was happening to them, a strange weariness settling into his body, pressing remorselessly down and sapping the little stamina that remained. When he thought he could no longer continue, Panamon was at his side to support him, the strong arm alternately lifting him over and shoving him through the stone rubble.

They had reached a particularly narrow section of the passageway that angled sharply to the right when a violent, wrenching quake shook the dying mountain. The entire ceiling of the corridor cracked with a grating snap and began to settle slowly downward. Panamon yelled frantically and pulled Shea down in front of him, trying to protect the Valeman with his own body. Instantly Keltset was there, the giant frame bracing as the great shoulders hunched upward against the tons of breaking rock. Dust rose in blinding clouds and for a moment everything was obscured from view. Then Panamon Creel was pulling the Valeman to his feet, hastening him past the straining form of the Rock Troll. Shea glanced up once as he crawled and scrambled through the broken stone, and the gentle eyes met his own. The ceiling dropped several inches farther, and the massive human support threw all the awesome strength of a Rock Troll against it, the barklike body rigid with the tremendous strain. Shea hesitated, but Panamon's powerful grip closed over his shoulder, pulling him ahead, thrusting him beyond the tunnel angle into a wider corridor. They collapsed in a pile of loose rock and dust, gasping for air. They had just a glimpse of Keltset, his great frame still braced against the crumbling stone. Panamon made a sudden move to start back into the passage, but a deep rumble tore through the core of the mountain; with a groan of sliding, shifting rock, the tunnel behind them came apart and collapsed entirely. Tons of stone crashed downward and the way back disappeared altogether. Shea screamed and threw himself against the wall of rock, but Panamon pulled him back roughly, pushing the piked hand into his face.

"He's dead! We can't help him now."

The haggard face of the Valeman stared back in shock.

"Get moving—get out of here!" The thief was livid with rage. "Do you want him to have died for nothing? Move!"

He yanked Shea violently to his feet and thrust him toward the open section of the tunnel. The deep rumbling continued to vibrate through the mountain, and a series of sharp, wrenching quakes nearly threw the two men to the cavern floor as they stumbled ahead. Shea was running blindly now, his eyes clouded with dust and tears. It was becoming difficult to see clearly, and he blinked and squinted in an effort to clear his fading vision. Panamon's labored breathing was close in his ear, and he felt the iron stub of the piked hand shoving against his back, urging him to run faster. Shards of rock splintered from the passage walls and ceiling and rained down on his unprotected body, cutting and bruising it, tearing the forest clothing into tattered strips that hung from the thin, sweating form. In his hands he clutched the gleaming Sword, useless to him now except as proof that what had happened to him was more than an imagined madness.

Abruptly the tunnel dissolved in the gray light of the Northland sky, and they were free of the mountain. Before them, the scattered bodies of Troll and Muten lay broken in death. Without slowing, the two men raced for the mouth of the winding pass that split the monstrous Knife Edge. The hardened earth was quaking violently, long jagged cracks appearing from the base of Skull Mountain and snaking crookedly toward the ring of natural hazards that bound the forbidden land. A sudden, grating crash, louder than any that had preceded it, brought the two runners about. In speechless awe, they watched the gaunt face of the skull begin to sag and break apart. Everything seemed to shatter at once, and the mark of the Warlock Lord disappeared as tons of rock cascaded downward and Skull Mountain ceased to exist. A thick cloud of yellow dust surged skyward and a heavy booming sound burst from the bowels of the earth and echoed through the vast emptiness of the Northland. Violent winds swept over the remains of the dying mountain and the rumbling in the earth began to build once more. In horror Shea saw the monstrous Knife Edge begin to shake with the force of this new convulsion. The entire kingdom was disintegrating!

Already Panamon was running brokenly for the pass, pulling a dazed Shea with him. But the Valeman needed no urging this time and quickly picked up the pace on his own, his form flying through the tangle of dead bodies. From some final reservoir of courage and determination, he summoned the last of his strength, and a surprised Panamon Creel suddenly found himself running to keep up. By the time they reached the mouth of the mountain pass, pieces of the towering Knife Edge were beginning to break apart and fall, snapping free with piercing cracks as the booming quakes continued to shake the land. Massive boulders fell with crushing force into the winding canyon, and a heavy avalanche of loose stone slid steadily from the heights of the ancient peaks, building in force as the seconds slipped by. Through the center of this holocaust the two Southlanders dodged and twisted—the tattered half Elf, brandishing his ancient Sword, and the one-handed thief. The force of the wind broke over their backs, thrusting them faster through the hail of stone and dust. Twists and turns in the rock walls came and disappeared, and they knew they were closing on the far end of the canyon and the open foothills beyond. Shea was suddenly aware that his eyesight was blurring once more and he stumbled uncertainly, his free hand rubbing angrily to clear his vision.

Suddenly the entire west wall of the canyon seemed to break apart and come crashing down on both men, burying them in a choking rush of broken rock and dirt. Something sharp struck his exposed head, and for a moment Shea slipped into blackness. He lay partially covered by the mass of rubble, his groping mind trying to shake itself awake. Then Panamon was digging him free, the strong arm lifting him clear of the shattered stone and holding him upright. Through a gray haze, Shea saw blood on the big man's face. Slowly Shea rose to his feet, leaning heavily on the Sword of Shannara for support.

Panamon remained on his knees. His piked hand pointed to the pass behind them. Shea glanced anxiously past him. To his dismay, he caught sight of a misshapen, lumbering creature slowly bearing down on them from out of the rising clouds of dust. A Muten! The formless, plastic face was turned toward them and the monster shuffled steadily forward. Panamon looked up at Shea and smiled grimly.

"He's been with us all the way from the other end. I thought we might lose him in the rocks, but he's persistent."

He rose slowly and drew free the long broadsword.

"Get going, Shea. I'll catch up shortly."

The startled Valeman shook his head speechlessly. He must have misunderstood.

"We can outrun him," he burst out finally. "We've almost

reached the end of the pass anyway. We can fight him there—together!"

Panamon shook his head and smiled sadly.

"Not this time, I'm afraid. I've done something to my leg. I can't run anymore." He shook his head as Shea opened his mouth to speak. "I don't want to hear it, Shea. Now run—and keep running!"

Tears were streaming down the Valeman's face as he stared at the man.

"I can't do that!"

A sudden rumble shook the Knife Edge, throwing Panamon and Shea to their knees again. Boulders crashed down the crumbling mountainside as the heavy convulsions continued to build from deep within the earth. The Muten lumbered mindlessly toward them, unaffected by the tremors. Panamon climbed shakenly to his feet, pulling Shea after him.

"The whole pass is coming down," he stated quietly. "We don't have time to argue. I can take care of myself—just as I did long before I met you or Keltset. Now I want you to run—get clear of this pass!"

He put one hand on the Valeman's slim shoulder and gently shoved him away. Shea took several steps backward and hesitated, bringing the Sword of Shannara up almost threateningly. Panamon Creel's broad face showed a flicker of surprise, and then the familiar devilish grin appeared and the eyes turned to fire.

"We'll meet again, Shea Ohmsford. You watch for me."

He waved the piked hand once in farewell, and turned to meet the advancing Muten. Shea stared after him momentarily. His fading eyesight must be fooling him—for an instant it seemed that the scarlet thief was not limping, after all. Then the heavy tremors rippled through the mountain pass still another time, and the Valeman broke for the safety of the foothills. Slipping and stumbling through the loose rock and earth, dodging the cascade of stone and debris that tumbled from the heights of the Knife Edge into the narrow canyon, he ran on alone.

NINE

᷒HE AFTERNOON was almost gone. Sunlight slipped in
long, hazy streamers through the drifting white clouds, settling with warm touches over the barren, empty Northland
terrain. Here and there the light fell providently on small
patches of green—the first signs of a permanent life that one
day soon would flourish in this earth that had lain parched
and desolate for so many years. In the distance, the blunted
tips of the shattered Knife Edge broke starkly against the
northern horizon, and from the devastated valley beyond,
the dust still hung suspended above the ruins of the Skull
Kingdom.

Shea seemed to appear out of nowhere, wandering aimlessly through the tangle of ravines and ridges that carved
out the foothills immediately below the Knife Edge. Half-
blind and completely exhausted, the tattered figure was
barely recognizable. He came toward Allanon without seeing
him, both hands gripping tightly the silver-handled sword.
For just an instant, the Druid stared speechlessly at the
strange spectacle of the stumbling, ragged swordsman. Then
with a sharp cry of relief, he rushed forward to gather in the
thin, battered frame of Shea Ohmsford, and held him close.

.   .   .

The Valeman was asleep for a long time, and when he came awake again, it was night. He was lying in the shelter of a rock-encrusted overhang that opened into a deep, wide-bottomed ravine. A small wood fire crackled peacefully, lending added warmth to the cloak that was wrapped tightly about him. His troubled vision had begun to clear, and he found himself staring up into a bright, starlit night sky that stretched canopylike from ridge top to ridge top above him. He smiled in spite of himself. He could imagine himself in Shady Vale once again. A moment later Allanon's dark shadow moved into the dim firelight.

"Are you feeling better?" the Druid asked in greeting and seated himself. There was something strange about Allanon. He seemed more human, less forbidding, and there was an unusual warmth in his voice.

Shea nodded. "How did you find me?"

"You found me. Don't you remember anything?"

"No, none of it—nothing after . . ." Shea paused hesitantly. "Was there anybody . . . did you see anybody else?"

Allanon studied his anxious expression for a moment, as if debating his answer, then shook his dark face.

"You were alone."

Shea felt something catch in his throat, and he lay back in the warmth of the blankets, swallowing hard. So Panamon, too, was gone. Somehow, he had not expected it to end like this.

"Are you all right?" the Druid's deep voice reached out to him in the darkness. "Would you like to eat something now? I think it would be good for you if you did."

"Yes." Shea pushed himself up into a sitting position, the cloak still wrapped protectively about him. By the fire, Allanon was pouring soup into a small bowl. The aroma reached out to him invitingly, and he breathed it in. Then suddenly he thought of the Sword of Shannara and looked for it in the darkness. He saw it almost immediately, lying next to him, the bright metal gleaming faintly. As an afterthought, he felt through the pockets of his tunic for the Elfstones. He could not find them. Panicked, he began searching desperately through his clothing for the little pouch, but the result was the same. It was gone. A sinking sensation gripped him, and he lay back weakly for a moment. Perhaps Allanon . . .

"Allanon, I can't find the Elfstones," he said quickly. "Did you . . . ?"

The Druid moved over to his side and handed him the steaming bowl of soup and a small wooden spoon. His face was an impenetrable black shadow.

"No, Shea. You must have lost them when you fled the Knife Edge." He saw the crestfallen look on the other's face and reached over to pat the slim shoulder reassuringly. "There's no point in worrying about them now. The stones have served their purpose. I want you to eat something and go back to sleep—you need to rest."

Mechanically, Shea sipped at the soup, unable to forget quite so easily the loss of the Elfstones. They had been with him from the beginning, protecting him every step of the way. Several times, they had saved his life. How could he have been so careless? He thought back for a moment, trying vainly to remember where he might have lost them, but it was useless. It could have happened anytime.

"I'm sorry about the Elfstones," he apologized quietly, feeling that he had to say something more.

Allanon shrugged and smiled faintly. He seemed weary and somehow older as he seated himself beside the Valeman.

"Maybe they'll turn up later."

Shea finished the bowl in silence, and Allanon refilled it without being asked. The warm liquid relaxed the still-weary Valeman, and a numbing drowsiness began to seep slowly through his body. He was falling asleep again. It would have been so easy to give in to the feeling, but he could not. There were still too many things bothering him, too many unanswered questions. He wanted those answers now from the one man who could give them to him. He deserved that much after everything he had been through.

He struggled to a sitting position, aware that Allanon was watching him closely from out of the darkness beyond the little fire. In the distance, the sharp cry of a night bird broke through the deep silence. Shea paused in spite of himself. Life was coming back to the Northland—after so long. He placed the bowl of soup on the ground next to him and turned to Allanon.

"Can we talk awhile?"

The Druid nodded silently.

"Why didn't you tell me the truth about the Sword?" the Valeman asked softly. "Why didn't you?"

"I told you all that you needed to know." Allanon's dark face was impassive. "The Sword itself told you the rest."

Shea stared at him incredulously.

"It was necessary for you to learn the secret of the Sword of Shannara for yourself," the Druid continued gently. "It was not something that I could explain to you—it was something that you had to experience. You had to learn to accept the truth about yourself first before the Sword could be of any use to you as a talisman against the Warlock Lord. It was a process in which I could not involve myself directly."

"Well, could you not at least have told me why the Sword would destroy Brona?" Shea persisted.

"And what would that have done to you, Shea?"

The Valeman frowned. "I don't understand."

"If I had told you everything that it was in my power to tell you about the Sword—remembering now that you would not have the benefit of hindsight, as you do now, to enlighten you—would that have helped you in practical terms? Would you have been able to continue your search for the Sword? Would you have been able to draw the Sword against Brona, knowing that it would do no more than reveal to him the truth about himself? Would you have even believed me when I said that such a simple thing would destroy a monster with the power of the Warlock Lord?"

He hunched down closer to Shea in the dim firelight.

"Or would you have given up on yourself and the quest then and there? How much truth could you have withstood?"

"I don't know," Shea answered doubtfully.

"Then I will tell you something I could not tell you before. Jerle Shannara, five hundred years earlier, knew all these things—and still he failed."

"But I thought . . ."

"That he was successful?" Allanon finished the thought. "Yet if he had been successful, would not the Warlock Lord have been destroyed? No, Shea, Jerle Shannara did not succeed. Bremen confided in the Elven King the secret of the Sword because he, too, thought that knowing how the talisman would be used might better prepare the bearer for a confrontation with Brona. It did not. Even though he had been forewarned that he would be exposed to the truth about himself, Jerle Shannara was not prepared for what he discovered. Indeed, there was probably no way that he could have adequately prepared himself beforehand. We build too many walls to be completely honest with ourselves. And I don't think that he ever really believed Bremen's warning about what would happen when he finally held the Sword. Jerle Shannara was a warrior king, and his natural instinct was to rely on the Sword as a physical weapon, even though he had been told that it would not help him in that way. When he confronted the Warlock Lord and the talisman began to work on him exactly as Bremen had warned, he panicked. His physical strength, his fighting prowess, his battle experience—all of it useless to him. It was just too much for him to accept. As a result, the Warlock Lord managed to escape him."

Shea looked unconvinced.

"It might have been different with me."

But the Druid did not seem to hear him.

"I would have been with you when you found the Sword of Shannara, and when the secret of the talisman revealed itself to you, I would have explained then its significance as a weapon against the Warlock Lord. But then I lost you in the Dragon's Teeth, and it was only later that I realized you had found the Sword and gone northward without me. I came after you, but even so, I was almost too late. I could sense your panic when you discovered the secret of the Sword, and I knew the Warlock Lord could sense it as well. But I was still too far away to reach you in time. I tried to call out to you— to project my voice into your mind. There wasn't time enough to tell you what to do; the Warlock Lord prevented that. A few words, that was all."

He paused, almost as if he had gone into a trance, his dark gaze fixed on the air between them.

"But you discovered the answer on your own, Shea—and you survived."

The Valeman looked away, reminded suddenly that, although he was alive, it seemed that everyone who had gone with him into the kingdom of the Skull was dead.

"It might have been different," he repeated woodenly.

Allanon said nothing. At his feet, the small fire was dying slowly into reddish embers as the night closed about them. Shea picked up the bowl of soup and finished it quickly, feeling the drowsiness slip through him once more. He was nodding when Allanon stirred unexpectedly in the darkness and moved next to him.

"You believe me wrong in not telling you the secret of the Sword?" he murmured softly. It was more a statement of fact than a question. "Perhaps you are right. Perhaps it would have been better for everyone if I had revealed it all to you from the first."

Shea looked up at him. The lean face was a mask of dark hollows and angular lines that seemed the wrappings of some perpetual enigma.

"No, you were right," the Valeman replied slowly. "I'm not sure I could have handled the truth."

Allanon's head tilted slightly to one side, as if considering the possibility.

"I should have had more faith in you, Shea. But I was afraid." He paused as a trace of doubt clouded the Valeman's face. "You don't believe me, but it's true. To you, to the others as well, I have always been something more than human. It was necessary, or you would never have accepted your role as I gave it to you. But a Druid is still a human being, Shea. And you have forgotten something. Before he became the Warlock Lord, Brona was a Druid. Thus to some extent, at least, the Druids must bear responsibility for what he became. We permitted him to become the Warlock Lord. Our learning gave him the opportunity; our subsequent isolation from the rest of the world allowed him to evolve. The entire human race might have been enslaved or destroyed, and the guilt would have been ours. Twice the Druids had the opportunity to destroy him—and twice they failed to do so. I was the last of my people, and if I were to fail as well, then there would be no one left to protect the races against this monstrous evil. Yes, I was afraid. One small mistake and I might have left Brona free forever."

The Druid's voice dropped to a whisper and he looked down for an instant.

"There is one more thing you should know. Bremen was more to me than simply my ancestor. He was my father."

"Your father!" Shea came fully awake for an instant. "But tha's not poss . . ."

He trailed off, unable to finish. Allanon smiled faintly.

"There must have been times when you guessed that I was older than any normal man could be, surely. The Druids discovered the secret of longevity following the First War of the Races. But there is a price—a price that Brona refused to pay. There are many demands and disciplines required, Shea. It is no great gift. And for our waking time, we pile up a debt that must be paid by a special kind of sleep that restores us from our aging. There are many steps to true longevity, and some are not pleasant. Not one is easy. Brona searched for a way different from that of the Druids, a way that would not carry the same price, the same sacrifices; in the end, he found only illusion."

The Druid seemed to retreat into himself for a long moment, then continued.

"Bremen was my father. He had a chance to end the menace of the Warlock Lord, but he made too many mistakes and Brona escaped him. His escape was my father's responsibility—and if the Warlock Lord had succeeded in his plans, my father would have earned the blame. I lived with the fear of that happening until it was an obsession. I swore not to make the mistakes he had made. I'm afraid, Shea, that I never really had much faith in you. I feared you were too weak to do what had to be done, and I hid the truth to serve my own ends. In many ways, I was unfair to you. But you were my last chance to redeem my father, to purge my own sense of guilt for what he had done, and to erase forever the responsibility of the Druids for the creation of Brona."

He hesitated and looked directly into Shea's eyes. "I was wrong, Valeman. You were a better man than I gave you credit for being."

Shea smiled and shook his head slowly.

"No, Allanon. You were the one who so often spoke to me of hindsight. Now heed your own words, historian."

In the darkness across from him, the Druid returned the smile wistfully.

"I wish ... I wish we had more time, Shea Ohmsford. Time to learn to know each other better. But I have a debt that must be paid ... all too soon ..."

He trailed off almost sadly, the lean face lowering into shadow. The puzzled Valeman waited a moment, thinking that he would say something more. He did not.

"In the morning, then." Shea stretched wearily and burrowed deep into the cloak, warm and relaxed by the soup and the fire. "We've a long journey back to the Southland."

Allanon did not reply immediately.

"Your friends are close now, looking for you," he responded finally. "When they find you, will you relate to them all that I have told you?"

Shea barely heard him, his thoughts drifting to Shady Vale and the hope of going home again.

"You can do the job better than I," he murmured sleepily.

There was another long moment of silence. At last he heard Allanon moving in the darkness beyond, and when the tall man spoke again, his voice sounded strangely distant.

"I may not be able to, Shea. I'm very tired—I've exhausted myself physically. For a time now, I must . . . sleep."

"Tomorrow," Shea mumbled. "Good night."

The Druid's voice came back a whisper.

"Good-bye, my young friend. Good-bye, Shea."

But the Valeman was already sleeping.

Shea awoke with a start, the morning sunlight streaming down on him. His eyes snapped open at the sound of horses' hooves and booted feet, and he found himself surrounded by a cluster of lean, rangy figures clothed in forest green. Instinctively his hand dropped to the Sword of Shannara, and he struggled to a sitting position, squinting sharply to see their faces. They were Elves. A tall, hard-featured Elf detached himself from the group and bent down to him. Deep, penetrating green eyes locked into his own, and a firm hand came up to rest reassuringly on his shoulder.

"You're among friends, Shea Ohmsford. We are Eventine's men."

Shea climbed slowly to his feet, still grasping the Sword guardedly.

"Allanon . . . ?" he asked, looking about for the Druid.

The tall man hesitated for a moment, then shook his head.

"There is no one else here. Only you."

Stunned, Shea moved past him and pushed his way through the ring of horsemen, his eyes quickly searching the length of the wide ravine. Gray rock and dust stared back at him, an empty, deserted passage that twisted and disappeared from sight. Except for the Elven riders and himself, there was no one else. Then something the Druid had said came back to him—and he knew then that Allanon was really gone.

"Sleeping . . ." he heard himself whisper.

Woodenly, he turned back to the waiting Elves, then hesitated as tears streamed down his haggard face. But Allanon would come back to them when he was needed, he told himself angrily. Just as he had always done before. He brushed away the tears, and glanced momentarily into the bright blueness of the Northland sky. For just an instant, he seemed to hear the Druid's voice calling to him from far, far away. A faint smile crossed his lips.

"Good-bye, Allanon," he answered softly.

TEN

S O IT ENDED. Little more than ten days later, those who still remained of the little band that had journeyed forth from Culhaven so many weeks ago bade farewell to one another for the last time. It was a bright, clear day filled with sunshine and summer's freshness. From out of the west, a gentle breeze ruffled the emerald green carpet of the Tyrsian grasslands, and in the distance, the sluggish roar of the Mermidon floated softly through the early-morning stillness. They stood together by the roadway leading out from the walled city—Durin and Dayel, the former without the use of his left arm, which was splinted and wrapped. Dayel had found him among the wounded, and now he was healing rapidly. Balinor Buckhannah in chain mail and royal blue riding cloak, a still-pale Shea Ohmsford, the faithful Flick, and Menion Leah. They spoke in quiet tones for a time, smiling bravely, trying to appear amiable and relaxed without much success, glancing from time to time at the tethered horses that grazed contentedly behind them. At last there was an awkward silence, and hands were extended and taken, and mumbled promises to visit soon were quietly exchanged. It was a painful good-bye, and behind the smiles and the handshakes, there was sadness.

Then they rode away, each to his own home. Durin and Dayel traveled west to Beleal, where Dayel would finally be reunited with his beloved Lynliss. The Ohmsfords turned south to Shady Vale and, as Flick had repeatedly announced to his brother, a well-deserved rest. As far as Flick was concerned, their traveling days were over. Menion Leah went with them to the Vale, determined to see to it personally that nothing further befell Shea. From there, he would return for a time to the highlands to be with his father, who would be missing him by now. But very soon, he knew he must come back again to the border country and to the red-haired daughter of kings who would be waiting.

Standing silently by the empty roadway, Balinor watched after his friends until they were no more than small shadows in the distant green of the flatlands. Then slowly he mounted his waiting horse and rode back into Tyrsis.

The Sword of Shannara remained in Callahorn. It had been Shea's firm decision to leave the talisman with the border people. No one had given more to preserve the freedom of the four lands. No one had a better right to be entrusted with its care and preservation. And so the legendary Sword was implanted blade downward in a block of red marble and placed in a vault in the center of the gardens of the People's Park in Tyrsis, sheltered by the wide, protective span of the Bridge of Sendic, there to remain for all time. Carved upon the stone facing of the vault was the inscription:

Herein lies the heart and soul of the nations.
Their right to be free men,
Their desire to live in peace,
Their courage to seek out truth.
Herein lies the Sword of Shannara.

. . .

Weeks later, Shea perched wearily on one of the tall wooden stools in the inn kitchen and studied blankly the plate of food on the counter in front of him. At his elbow, Flick was already starting on his second helping. It was early in the evening, and the Ohmsford brothers had spent the entire day repairing the veranda roof. The summer sun had been hot and the work had been tedious; yet, although he was tired and vaguely disgruntled, Shea found himself unable to locate his appetite. He was still picking at his food when his father appeared in the hall doorway, mumbling blackly to himself. Curzad Ohmsford came up to them without a word and tapped Shea on the shoulder.

"How much longer is this nonsense going to continue?" he demanded.

Shea looked up in surprise.

"I don't know what you mean," he answered truthfully, glancing at Flick, who shrugged blankly.

"Not eating much either, I see." His father spied the dinner plate. "How do you expect to get your strength back if you don't eat properly?"

He paused for a moment, and then seemed to recall that he had gotten off the subject entirely.

"Strangers, that's what I mean. Now I suppose you'll be off again. I thought that was all done with."

Shea stared at him.

"I'm not going anywhere. What in the world are you talking about?"

Curzad Ohmsford seated himself heavily on a vacant stool and eyed his foster son closely, apparently resigned to the fact that he was not going to get a straight answer without a little unnecessary effort.

"Shea, we have never lied to each other, have we? When you came back from your visit with the Prince of Leah, I never pressed you about what went on while you were there, even though you left in the middle of the night without a word to anyone, even though you came back looking like your own ghost and very carefully avoided telling me exactly how you got that way. Now answer me," he continued quickly when Shea tried to object. "I never once asked you to tell me anything, did I?"

Shea shook his head silently. His father nodded in satisfaction.

"No, because I happen to believe that a man's business is mostly his own affair. But I cannot forget that the last time you disappeared from the Vale was right after that other stranger appeared asking for you."

"Other stranger!" the brothers exclaimed together.

Instantly all the old memories came back to them—Allanon's mysterious appearance, Balinor's warning, the Skull Bearers, the running, the fear . . . Shea slid down from his stool slowly.

"There's someone here . . . looking for me?"

His father nodded, his broad face clouding darkly as he caught the look of concern mirrored in his son's furtive glance at the doorway.

"A stranger, like before. He got in several minutes ago, looking for you. He's waiting out in the lobby. But I don't see . . ."

"Shea, what can we do?" Flick interrupted hurriedly. "We don't even have the Elfstones to protect us anymore."

"I . . . I don't know," his brother mumbled, desperately trying to think through his confusion. "We could slip out the back way . . ."

"Now wait a minute!" Curzad Ohmsford had heard enough. He gripped their shoulders tightly and turned them about to face him, staring at them in disbelief.

"I did not raise my sons to run away from trouble." He studied their worried faces a moment and shook his head. "You must learn to face your problems, not run from them. Why, here you are in your own home, among family and friends who will stand by you, and you talk about running away."

He released them and stepped back a pace.

"Now we'll all go out there together and face this man. He looks a hard sort, but he seemed friendly enough when we talked. Besides, I don't think a one-handed man is any kind of a match physically for three whole men—even with that pike."

Shea started abruptly.

"One-handed . . . ?"

"He looks like he traveled a long way to get here." The elder Ohmsford did not seem to have heard him. "He's carrying a little leather pouch that he claims belongs to you. I offered to take it, but he wouldn't give it to me. Said he wouldn't give it to anyone but you."

Now suddenly Flick understood.

"It must be something important," his father declared. "He told me you dropped it on your way home. Now how could that happen?"

Curzad Ohmsford had to wait awhile longer for his answer. In a rush, his sons were past him, through the kitchen door, and halfway down the hallway to the lobby of the inn.